"Do you ~~think~~ we're hopeless?"

"Ummm." Lisa pursed her lips thoughtfully in order to suppress a smile. "No, 'hopeless' is a pretty extreme word for us, I think."

"But rather?"

"I'd say we're two people who have always had very definite ideas about how childless career women and solo fathers live their lives. And even when some of those ideas don't fit, we have a hard time letting go of them."

Rob hooked his fingers over the frame of the bedroom door. "What are we going to do about that?" His crystal blue eyes were twinkling, but the question was posed seriously.

Lisa needed no invitation to slip her arms around his torso, displayed so invitingly in the doorway. "Dump all our preconceived notions, for starters."

ABOUT THE AUTHOR

Laurel Pace can't remember a period in her life when she wasn't writing. Her "big break" came when she was called to write copy, in an emergency, for an advertising agency, where she was employed. This, Laurel's first American Romance, was inspired by the Carolina Raptor Center—a special place dedicated to the rehabilitation of wounded birds of prey. Davidson, North Carolina, is home for Laurel and her husband, Douglas.

On Wings of Love
Laurel Pace

Harlequin Books

TORONTO • NEW YORK • LONDON
AMSTERDAM • PARIS • SYDNEY • HAMBURG
STOCKHOLM • ATHENS • TOKYO • MILAN

With special thanks to Dr. Richard Brown
and the staff of the Carolina Raptor Center

Published March 1987

First printing January 1987

ISBN 0-373-16192-1

Chapter One

A light breeze rustled the slats of the venetian blinds, stirring the untidy piles of paper littering the desk. Not looking up from the green plastic box of file cards that she was examining, Lisa Porter swept a loose strand of tawny hair away from her brow, then groped with one hand in a half-opened drawer until she touched something solid and heavy. Still studying the cards, she settled an unopened can of diet soda on the fluttering papers and edged the drawer shut with her knee.

Ralph. Her dark eyes lingered on the smudged typed label. Withdrawing Ralph's card, Lisa leaned back, letting the ancient desk chair swivel aimlessly from side to side. A frown darkened her honey-tanned face for a moment as she scanned the various entries scribbled on the card. Ralph had been with them for two months now, and it was time for him to start making some progress. Of course, when she considered his initial condition, he had made remarkable strides toward recovery. After being force-fed during his first few days at the center, he had advanced to a light diet of cooked chicken. Lisa's generous mouth curved in satisfaction as she noted the quantities of minced mouse meat he was now devouring. His antibiotic dosage had been reduced, too. She tapped the card with her finger. Ralph had come a long way since the park ranger had brought him to the center in the wake of a forest fire. For a screech owl suffering from third-degree burns, he was proving a spunky little patient. *But when is he ever going to grow feathers?* she thought.

Making a mental note to phone one of the veterinarians who volunteered his services to the Wildlife Rehabilitation Center, she stuffed Ralph's card into the bulging plastic box. In her line of work she often had to be content with small gains made over a long period of time, but, like everyone at the center, she always cherished the hope that the birds and wild animals they treated would someday be fit enough to return to their natural habitat. And to do that, Ralph would definitely need feathers.

The telephone's brisk buzz interrupted her thoughts, causing Lisa to wheel the chair around and propel herself awkwardly across the narrow room. She grimaced as the wastebasket corner clipped her knee. Scooting aside a tattered loose-leaf binder, she grabbed the receiver on the third ring.

"Piedmont Wildlife Rehabilitation," she announced, her bright tone belying the tension that inevitably gripped her every time she picked up the center's phone. At seven o'clock on a Sunday evening someone would be calling for only one reason: to report a sick or injured animal.

"Lisa?" a man's deep voice responded. "Lisa, this is Neil Clark at the clinic."

"What can we do for you, Neil?" Lisa smiled in recognition of the friendly young veterinarian who often worked the weekend shift at Charlotte's emergency animal hospital.

"I have a hawk, Lisa, a red-tailed, and it's been shot."

"How badly is it hurt?" Lisa bit her lip and gripped the receiver a little tighter.

"That's hard to say," Neil hedged. "The bullet sliced through the left wing. I've set the fracture and pumped a dose of ampicillin into him, but as far as a prognosis is concerned, well, that's your department. I'm grateful that the Bird Lady is on duty at the center today, though."

Lisa pulled a face at Neil's playful nickname for her. Although she was a trained ornithologist, she never felt she quite lived up to the young vet's conviction that she worked miracles with her feathered patients. "Shall I send someone to pick him up? I think Roger is on call this evening."

"Don't need to," Neil interposed. "The folks who found the bird are still here. They say they'll be glad to deliver the patient to you. I'm sure we still have one of your airline animal carriers around here somewhere," he added quickly, anticipating her concerns.

"Good. Send 'em on, then," Lisa said. "Oh, and thanks, Neil. Again."

"Don't mention it. Bye." The good-natured veterinarian's voice was cut short by an abrupt click on the line.

Lisa sat staring at the phone for a minute, rolling a pencil nub between nervous fingers. She had been through this so many times before that she was surprised her anger still rose with the same intensity. Of all the hazards that filled the center's cages with wildlife, a gunshot wound always seemed the most senseless.

Shaking her head, she threw the pencil at the table where it landed just short of the silent telephone. With a fury that sent the creaking office chair rolling across the room, she pushed herself to her feet and stomped out of the little office.

A mild September breeze cooled her flushed cheeks as she hurried along the path leading to a long blue-and-white trailer. Even in such a tense situation, the aura of the surrounding forest always managed to soothe her. By the time she had assembled a new cage in the trailer's intensive-care ward and checked her emergency supplies, Lisa was feeling much calmer.

She was sitting on the trailer steps, watching the sunset drain through the trees, when the low drone of a motor sounded from the drive. Soon two pinpricks of light pierced the dusk, and a dark blue Mercedes sedan slowly emerged from between the pines. When the driver hesitated, Lisa waved and pointed to the row of railroad ties that delineated the small parking lot.

The left front window of the Mercedes glided noiselessly down, admitting an angular, tanned face through the opening. "Is it all right if we leave the car here?"

"Yes, that's fine," Lisa assured him. She felt her pulse quicken at the sight of the startlingly handsome face, but she quickly told herself she was only reacting in her usual fashion to the nerve-racking arrival of a new patient. "Dr. Clark said he had a carrier for you to transport the hawk in." She cast an uncertain look at the man climbing out of the car.

Concern clouded the brilliant Aegean blue of the man's eyes, but he nodded reassuringly. "We have him right here in the back seat. He hardly seemed to stir during the drive out here. I guess that's a good sign?" The marine blue eyes appealed to Lisa for a word of encouragement.

"It's always best if the bird doesn't thrash around and compound its injury." Lisa leaned through the rear door the man was holding open for her and gently pulled the animal crate along the leather seat.

"See, Daddy! It *is* Dr. Porter!" Lisa started at the unexpected sound of her name. Looking up, she found a cherub's face beaming admiration at her from the front seat. A little girl not more than six years old was leaning against the leather upholstered seat back, watching Lisa's every move with rapt attention. Thick dark bangs evenly bridged her wide-set eyes that were the same intense shade of blue as those of the man waiting anxiously outside the car.

"How do you know who I am?" Lisa asked with a smile.

"Don't you remember?" The child's dark brows knit in consternation. "You visited my Brownie troop just this April. You and William the owl. You told us all about the good things that hawks and owls do and what we should do if we ever found one that was hurt. Daddy and I did just what you said when we found the hawk today," she added solemnly.

"Oh, yes, now I remember," Lisa fudged. She must have given a score of talks to various clubs and school classes in the past six months; the memory of this particular Scout troop had blurred somewhat. "I think that was one of the first times I took William with me to help give a speech. But he did very well, didn't he?"

"He sure did." The little girl's head bobbed in agreement.

"When the vet at the emergency clinic told us he wanted to refer the case to this center, Karen insisted that she knew all about the work you do here. She kept talking about a wonderful lady and her owl-friend, but I never expected to meet this amazing person today," the little girl's father said, as he reached through the car door and effortlessly lifted the carrier, brushing lightly against Lisa's arm in the process.

"The center has a very good education program," Lisa acknowledged quietly, but something more than modesty prompted her to avoid the blue eyes studying her as she went on. "But it always helps when children pay such close attention." She glanced down at the little girl, who had scrambled out of the car and was now waiting at her father's side.

"I'm sure that's true, but I was really impressed at how much Karen knew about handling injured wild animals when we found the hawk. By the way, I'm Rob Randolph." He offered his hand. The corners of those startling eyes crinkled with good humor as he added, "I suppose you and Karen don't need an introduction."

"Lisa Porter." She felt his proffered hand close over hers and give it a solid shake. When he released her hand she left it hanging in midair for a moment, as if she had forgotten what to do with it. *For heaven's sake, get a hold on yourself, Porter,* she snapped inwardly. *The last thing you need is an attack of giddiness when this injured bird requires all of your attention. Especially when those heart flutters are brought on by a married man with a daughter,* her stern internal guardian added for good measure.

"Where should I take this?" Rob Randolph rested the animal carrier against one knee and waited for her instructions.

"I can get it." Lisa hastened to relieve him of the bulky crate, but Rob clung to the plastic handles as if he were afraid she would collapse under the carrier's insignificant weight. She sensed that he was one of that vanishing breed, the considerate gentleman; it would be pointless to argue with him. "The intensive care unit is in the trailer over here. Watch your step," she cautioned as they left the well-lighted parking area and headed down the path leading to the various animal shelters.

In the short time since the Randolphs' arrival, night had blanketed the center's thickly forested grounds, relieved only by a pale frost of moonlight. Karen, who had raced ahead, halted at Lisa's warning. When the two adults caught up with her, she quickly latched on to the Bird Lady's outstretched hand.

"Do you work here all of the time?" Rob asked, shortening his long strides to match his companions' pace.

Lisa cut a glance up at him. The night had rendered his face a chiseled silhouette next to her shoulder, but even the suggestion of those finely hewed features sent a shiver racing through her. "I do volunteer work whenever there's a bird around that needs me, which is pretty often," she replied with a chuckle that helped relieve some of the unaccustomed tension building within her. "Back in my other life in Charlotte, I'm an assistant professor of biology at the university. Ornithology is my speciality, and, although I like teaching, I have to confess my heart is really out here with these birds." Her tangled ponytail had worked its way down inside the neck of her sweatshirt; when she tossed her head to free it, she narrowly grazed Rob's sturdy shoulder.

Rob shifted the carrier for a better grip. "When I was a kid I once found a baby sparrow that had fallen out of its nest. It was just a tiny, peeping, bald thing, but everyone in the family took turns feeding it with a medicine dropper.

You know, I still feel pleased when I remember the day we watched the little fellow at last fly off on his own.''

"I know that feeling well," Lisa commented. *What a nice man,* she thought to herself. *But we'll just have to leave it at nice.* Rob Randolph was too much the perfect father for her to doubt him any less the perfect husband. Besides, she would never be silly enough to let herself get involved with a married man, even though, at thirty, she had encountered a few of them who seemed devoid of such scruples.

"What's or-tho-no-lo..." Karen chirped, interrupting the unsettling thoughts flooding Lisa's mind.

"Ornithology. It's a fancy word for the study of birds," Lisa explained.

"That's what I'm going to do when I grow up." The small hand tightened its hold on Lisa's with conviction.

"What happened to ballet dancing and flying airplanes? You were pretty fired up to do those things a couple of weeks ago," Rob teased his daughter.

"That was before I knew about ornithology," Karen countered, carefully enunciating the last word to prove the seriousness of her intentions.

Lisa gave the small fingers a light squeeze. "You still have lots of time to make up your mind. When I was your age I believe my greatest ambition was to be a big high school girl who could stay up past eight o'clock." Lisa laughed at the memories evoked by her comical confession. "It took me a few years to realize I enjoyed studying birds more than anything else."

"My mommy said she always knew just what she wanted to be: a champion horsewoman," Karen insisted gravely.

"Really? That sounds very exciting. Is that what your mommy does?" Lisa asked.

"Not now. Now she's in heaven."

Lisa stiffened at this unexpected response. She glanced down at the little girl clinging to her hand, but Karen seemed preoccupied with dragging furrows through the pine needle carpet with the toes of her sneakers. *She's still such a tiny thing,* Lisa thought. *The death of a parent is something she can accept more innocently than we adults.* But what about Rob? She caught a glimpse of his strongly defined face over her shoulder as she fumbled with the latch on the trailer door. The squared jaw was set with practiced control, but he remained silent. Grateful that the distraction of the bird of prey ward was now at hand, she beckoned them to follow her into the trailer.

"This is where we keep the new arrivals," she began, hoping the cheer in her voice didn't sound as questionable as she feared. She held the trailer's rusty door while Rob hoisted the carrier inside.

Karen immediately knelt beside the styrene box and squinted through one of the narrow air holes. "He's looking at me," she told them.

"Careful, sweetheart." Rob lifted the little girl gently to her feet. "He's had a pretty rough time of it, and we don't want to frighten him, do we?"

Karen nodded sadly. "Poor hawk."

"He'll feel a lot better when he's in a nice, comfortable cage," Lisa consoled the little girl. "While I make him at home, I bet you'd like to look through our scrapbook. I think there may even be a picture of William in here." She pulled a green vinyl album from the bookshelves and handed it to the child. Her eyes met Rob Randolph's, and they exchanged smiles as Karen promptly seated herself on the floor and began to leaf through the album.

Rob lifted the carrier and accompanied Lisa down the trailer corridor. "It looks as if Neil has sent along a full medical report," she commented, twisting her head to one side for a better look at the manila envelope taped to the side of the crate. When Rob hoisted the carrier onto an enamel table in the examining room, she reached over his shoulder and plucked the envelope free.

"How serious is it?" Rob asked, watching her frown over the veterinarian's cryptic scrawl.

"This hawk apparently lost quite a bit of blood," she conceded slowly. "But Neil has already tubed him with electrolytes, so that problem should be under control for the time being. And at least he isn't dehydrated. The fewer complications we have to deal with in these cases the better." Her voice had dropped to a low monotone, almost as if she were talking to herself.

When Lisa looked up she was startled by the pained expression hovering on Rob's face. *He's genuinely concerned,* she thought with a renewed wave of empathy for this man who had made such a strong impression on her in a remarkably short time. As she slid an X-ray film out of Neil's envelope and inserted it into a small viewer located on the counter, she tried to offer him a reassuring smile. But bending over the illuminated outline of the hawk's fractured wing, she felt her heart sink.

"Is he going to make it?" Rob asked gently after she had snapped off the viewer lamp.

"I'm pretty sure he's going to live," she told him quietly without meeting his probing gaze. As she pulled on the pair of leather gloves she kept in the examining room to protect her hands from sharp beaks and talons, she cleared her throat. "The question of his flying again is more touch and go. With a fracture so close to the joint, there's always the danger that the joint itself will calcify along with the break." She looked up to see how Rob was taking this disturbing news, but he only nodded.

Carefully lifting the lid of the carrier, Lisa grasped the hawk, sliding her hands down its wings to hold them close to the body, and lifted it onto the table. It was a full-grown male and quite alert, but traces of congealed blood still clung to its reddish brown plumage. The left wing was completely immobilized, thanks to Neil's expert veterinary work; the right one throbbed weakly beneath her firm clasp.

With an efficiency that was by now second nature, Lisa examined the injured hawk. Satisfied that her appraisal corroborated Neil's, she rested the bird briefly on the scale before placing it in a small cage and securing the door. "He hasn't lost very much weight" was her only comment as she attached a blank chart to the clipboard and began to fill it in.

"You say that as if it were the only good news you have to offer." Rob had been watching in silence while Lisa handled the hawk, but now he joined her at the counter.

"We'll just have to wait and see," she hedged. "It's a big advantage, of course, that he didn't lie out in the forest for days before someone found him, thanks to you and Karen." She smiled for the first time since they had entered the antiseptic-scented examining room.

"We had spent the weekend at Bryson City. I wanted to drive us back to Charlotte around noon today, but Karen insisted we take one last walk through the woods. I'm glad I listened to her, or that hawk might not have been so lucky."

"I don't suppose you have any idea who might have shot him?"

"Unfortunately, none." An angry glint flared like a blue flame in his eyes as he continued, "We heard random shots all morning, but as far as the hawk is concerned..." His shoulders lifted in a despairing gesture. "Believe me, as an attorney, I can certainly see the value of prosecuting these cases, but I'm afraid we haven't a shred of evidence on this one."

Lisa's mouth twisted ruefully. "At least you found him before it was too late."

"We couldn't have done him much good on our own. Even the vet told us that rehabilitating a hawk was beyond his expertise. You ought to be really proud of the work you're doing here." A tender expression softened the lean angles of his face as he rested an arm on the counter and faced her.

"I'm just glad I can put my training to good use." Lisa bent over the clipboard and mentally checked the entries she had just made. Here and there, she retraced a notation, more to steady the quiver of excitement stirring through her than to clarify her scribbles. She wasn't used to working under a stranger's scrutiny, she told herself in an attempt to explain away the unfamiliar emotions. But she was too honest to attribute her flutters to professional tension; it required only one furtive sidelong glance to identify the six-foot-tall, blue-eyed stimulus of those sensations.

Fortunately Rob Randolph seemed oblivious to the effect he was having on her. Hands clasped boyishly behind his back, he was leaning forward across the counter, inspecting the photograph of a bald eagle perched on a gloved hand.

"That's Patrick Henry," Lisa offered, pleased that her voice at least sounded as cool and collected as usual.

Rob chuckled. "Do you always name your patients?"

"Although we don't tame those that can be returned to the wild, they all have names while they're with us. It seems more appropriate than referring to them as 'Barred owl, number forty-six,' or whatever."

"Have you decided what you're going to call the hawk?"

Lisa paused, tapping the ballpoint against the clipboard. After a moment's thought she printed bold letters across the top of the chart. "Randolph," she announced. "In honor of his rescuers."

"Karen will be delighted when she hears that." Rob's broad smile assured her that he approved of her choice, too.

When they returned to the anteroom they found Karen still parked in front of the low bookcases. The little girl was practically standing on her head in an effort to read the spines of large volumes stored there, but the moment she spotted the adults she jumped up. "Our hawk is going to get well, isn't he, Dr. Porter?" she demanded.

Lisa squatted to meet the earnest dark gaze straight on. Although she wanted to shield the child from the harshest realities, she knew that building false hopes would be equally cruel. "I'm going to do everything I can to see that your hawk is able to return to his home in the woods. And while he stays with us, he's going to get lots of good food and good care. You know, I bet you can't guess what his name is, can you?''

Karen thought for a long second before shaking her head.

''Randolph.'' Lisa looked up at Rob to catch his reaction. She heard Karen repeat the name ''Randolph'' as if she were trying out its sound, but somehow she couldn't take her eyes off Rob's face. The harsh overhead light illuminated his strong features, throwing the aquiline nose, the sinewy line of his jaw into stark relief. His even, white teeth gleamed when he smiled. That smile, she marveled. There was something about it that warmed her whole being, something that managed to brighten even this messy room with its crooked framed photographs and pervasive bird odor.

Pushing herself to her feet, she dusted the knees of her baggy fatigues and refocused her attention on Karen. ''You'll have to tell all of your friends in the Brownie troop about rescuing Randolph. I know they'll be very proud of you.''

''Daddy helped me lots,'' Karen confessed.

''But you were the expert,'' Rob reminded her.

His lean face broke into a touching smile as he looked down at his little girl, a smile prompted by the tender emotions that Lisa imagined only parents experience. She had been shocked at the revelation that Karen's mother was deceased; a slight pinch of guilt stung her when she recalled her earlier musings on Rob's marital status. When she had first seen the handsome, athletic man and his angelic-looking daughter climb out of their expensive car she would never have guessed that their lives had been touched by such tragedy.

''It's getting late, Karen. I think you and I had better let Dr. Porter get back to her work,'' Rob suggested gently. His long fingers playfully ruffled the child's hair.

''I'm in no hurry tonight,'' Lisa began before catching a pleading look from Rob. Karen was so enthralled by the Wildlife Center, it was easy to imagine the difficulty her father anticipated in pointing her toward home. "But I do need to close up the office pretty soon," she added carefully.

"We can come back," Rob assured Karen as he gently pivoted her toward the door.

"That's right!" Lisa chimed with unnecessary eagerness. "If you're ever interested in seeing the whole complex, we give tours on Saturdays and Sundays."

"Okay. I'm hungry now anyway," Karen agreed with a resigned heave of her little shoulders.

"Would it be all right if I gave you a call, just to see how Randolph is doing?" Rob asked as he held the trailer door open for them. "I know Karen won't give me any peace if we never hear anything about her hawk again," he hastened to add.

"Please feel free to call," Lisa said. *Please,* she added privately. She jammed her hands into her pockets as if she feared they would somehow reveal the strong emotions hiding behind her words.

"I will," Rob said quietly, but he was looking at her in a way that made her grateful for the darkness that masked the heightened color of her face.

Damn it, she was never one to feel flustered, not in front of her first class of students, not even in the face of a critically injured bird, and certainly not because some man she scarcely knew gave her a little attention. But right now, away from her domain among the caged raptors she felt like an overgrown, gawky kid in her sloppy fatigues and faded sweatshirt.

"Hey, Lis!" A resonant baritone intruded on her thoughts, signaling the approach of Pat Taylor, the center's live-in caretaker. "Did you check that little raccoon...oh—," He broke off. Sprinting headlong down the dark path, the husky graduate student had not seen the Randolphs until he had almost collided with Rob. "I didn't realize we still had visitors." He halted awkwardly, hitching his perennially sagging blue jeans up around his waist.

"We were just leaving." Rob patted Karen's back, propelling her in the direction of the parked Mercedes. "Thank you again, Dr. Porter. I hope we didn't take up too much of your time."

No, not at all, Lisa wanted to say, and for a minute a crazy impulse to reach out and take his hand, to do anything to delay his departure, seized her. But just as quickly she recovered her normal professional manner. "I should thank both of you for finding Randolph." She watched as Rob opened the door of the Mercedes and Karen clambered inside. No sooner had the powerful engine hummed to life than the little girl put the window down and thrust her head out.

"Goodbye, Dr. Porter," her childish voice sang from the moonlit drive, and Lisa picked out the dim form of a small hand waving vigorously from the front window. Her eyes strained to follow the car as it glided between the trees; she watched the glowing red taillight bars until they finally disappeared behind a screen of pines.

"Nice people," Pat commented.

"Yeah," Lisa agreed. "Very nice." Pushing the sleeves of her sweatshirt up to her elbows, she slowly turned to follow Pat back to the animal trailers.

As she made the necessary examinations and meted out doses of antibiotics before leaving Pat in charge for the night, Lisa found her mind drifting back to the Randolphs. Or more accurately, back to Rob Randolph. She couldn't remember the last time a man had made such an impression on her; come to think of it, she wasn't sure one ever had.

While her gloved hands gingerly struggled to steady a rambunctious female barred owl on the scale, she mentally diagnosed her preoccupation with Rob. *Deprivation*, she thought severely. *If you would loosen up and make some time to go out more often, you wouldn't overreact to the first good-looking man fortune sends your way.*

Lisa replaced the owl in her cage and clamped the door shut. Penciling information on the bird's chart, she shook her head. No, it wasn't as simple as that; more than Rob Randolph's mesmeric blue eyes and hewed-granite jaw had attracted her. It was something in his voice, something in the way he cared about his little girl and cared about this hawk that had drawn her to him. *A real man who is sensitive, too,* she thought, precisely the sort she never met when she made time to go disco-hopping with her next-door neighbor, Anne Torrence.

When she had completed her rounds Lisa stopped by the office to find Pat already occupied with his studies. "I'm going to call it a day, Pat," she announced, sticking her head into the paper-strewn library.

"Fine, Lis." Pat shifted his heels where they were propped on the edge of a scarred file cabinet and looked up from his biology text long enough to wave. "Have a good evening."

"You, too," Lisa called over her shoulder. Digging in her canvas shoulder bag for her car keys, she skipped down the steps and headed for the parking lot.

Lisa eased behind the steering wheel of the yellow Chevette, pushing aside the stack of papers that seemed to have doubled in size during the six hours since she had last seen them. *Grading,* she thought, allowing herself an audible moan. If there was any doubt as to how she would spend the remainder of her evening, that formidable pile of exams begging to be evaluated settled the question.

A refreshing gust of air whistled through the half-open vent and lifted the strands of sun-streaked hair that had worked loose from her ponytail. As she turned onto the two-lane highway leading back to the Interstate, she speculated on the way in which Rob Randolph probably passed his evenings. What did he like to do? He enjoyed the out-doors, or he would not bother spending a weekend in the mountains. But he couldn't very well go hiking at night. A

man as attractive and obviously well-heeled as he surely
never lacked for female company, she mused.

Craning her neck to adjust the rearview mirror, she
caught a glimpse of the perturbed frown furrowing her face
and quickly repented. Rob, after all, was a single parent, not
an easy task under any circumstances. It was unfair of her
to imagine his leading a playboy's social life when she considered the time that little Karen would certainly require.
Anyway, she felt faintly ridiculous speculating on Rob's
private life at all; she would be lucky if she ever saw him
again. To distract herself from the tedious drive, Lisa flicked
on the radio. After adjusting the easy-listening station to a
soothing level, she began to plan Monday's laboratory exercises in her head.

She was pleased that her mental organization of that task
had progressed quite well by the time she wheeled the
Chevette between the untrimmed privet hedge flanking her
driveway. She hadn't expected to get home so late and had
neglected to turn on the porch light that morning, but fortunately Anne was home. Practically every window on her
side of the duplex blazed as if a party were in progress.

"Sorry I'm running late with supper, Chuck," Lisa
apologized to the large yellow cat that wove his way between her ankles the moment she opened the front door.

Chuck responded with a miffed meow, but deigned to
follow his mistress to the kitchen. As Lisa flicked on the
light she could not help but wince. The place was a disaster,
unfit for woman or cat. An unopened jar of peanut butter,
assorted coffee mugs, three loose-leaf binders and an Afri-
can violet in the terminal stages of root rot were arranged on
the counter in no particular order.

"You might think about cleaning this place up in your
spare time," she hinted to the purring cat who had sprung
onto the counter and by some miracle found a place to seat
himself among the clutter. Chuck greeted her suggestion
with a toothy yawn and waited for her to open a can of cat
food.

"Come and get it," she announced, placing a dish piled with a concoction called "Fisherman's Feast Supreme" in Chuck's corner. Watching the handsome animal pounce on his supper reminded her of the growing hunger pangs in her own stomach.

Lisa opened the cabinet again and searched its contents for something vaguely edible that wouldn't require two hours' simmering. The selection seemed pretty grim until her eyes at last lighted on a can of tuna wedged between the rows of cat food. Someday she would plan real meals that you had to sit down at a table to eat, she promised herself. The image of a family seated around a pleasantly decked dinner table, laughing and chatting as they ate, rose in her mind; although her mental censor quickly deleted any names, the faces of the smiling diners were unmistakably those of the Randolphs.

Fantasizing about someone she had scarcely met was kid stuff, she remonstrated as she plopped the tuna onto a saucer. It even looked like Chuck's food, sitting there in a rigidly molded disk. Lisa gamely mashed the caked fish with a fork, but the results only resembled something she had poked down a convalescing owl's throat earlier that day. Turning to the refrigerator in desperation, she found a handful of cherry tomatoes and some bottled salad dressing that she used to disguise the tuna.

As she nibbled at her supper, Lisa wandered through her dining room. No smiling family sat grouped around the walnut drop-leaf table, eagerly awaiting a home-cooked meal, and she didn't even bother to turn on the light. In the living room she collapsed on the sectional sofa. Leaning across to the tiered end table, she punched on her telephone recorder and settled back to catch up on the day's calls while she ate.

"Hello, honey. You know, when I picked up the phone to call today, I told Lucille I bet I'd end up talking to this darned machine," the first caller complained. Lisa grinned, imagining the amused frown on her father's face when her recorded voice greeted him on the line. "Well, no need to waste any more money on this—" he resigned himself with a sigh that rasped on the tape "—just give your old dad a call when you have time, baby. You know I love you." Lisa could tell the last words were awkward for him to speak into an answering machine, regardless of the many times he had done so before, and she made a mental note to call him soon.

The machine whirred and clicked before replaying the next message. "Lisa, darling," the woman spoke right up. She obviously shared none of Mr. Porter's inhibitions about answering machines. "No need for you to call me back. I just wanted to let you know that I'll be in New York next week. I'll give you a buzz when I get back home. Love ya."

New York, Lisa thought, as she stretched to the coffee table and deposited the empty saucer on a stack of scientific periodicals. To be honest, she had never quite managed to keep up with her mother's travels since that feisty lady had opened a trendy boutique in Miami Beach. Sarah Porter seemed to be in perpetual motion, jetting from one fashion center to another to ferret out the most chic designs for her shop.

"Dr. Porter," a reedy voice filtered from the machine. Addressing her by her title was a dead giveaway that this caller was one of her students. "Uh, this is Jack Mayhew in your intro biology course, and I'm calling about that test on Friday." Lisa squirmed at the reminder of the ungraded exams lying in her car, but she let Jack continue. "I guess I'm not telling you anything you don't already know, but I really blew that one, and I'd like to talk with you about it on Monday. Thanks a lot, Dr. Porter," Jack concluded, in anticipation of her response.

"Hey, Lisa," the next caller boomed, pushing aside poor Jack Mayhew. Lisa instantly recognized the smug masculine voice. She adjusted the volume to a murmur and reached to stroke Chuck, who was inspecting the empty saucer for overlooked flakes of tuna. The last person she wanted to hear from tonight was Jerry McCloskey. She must have been temporarily insane to have gone out with him last week, but he had caught her off guard. Anyway, a James Bond film and dinner at a mesquite grill had seemed innocuous enough.

Against her better instincts, Lisa twisted the volume control in time to hear him apologize. "Oh, yeah, and I'm sorry about last Saturday night. I guess I just can't get it into my head that things aren't ... well, aren't the same between us. But let's try to be friends, okay, Lisa? If you get home in time, how about a drink tonight? Give me a call."

Lisa scowled at the answering machine as if Jerry were imprisoned inside its narrow box, watching her through the tiny speaker grid. Their relationship had never been a smooth one, and since her decision to break it off, Jerry's persistent belief that she would one day see the light and welcome him back into her life had proved extremely annoying. Every time she gave him an opportunity to "try to be friends" their old problems had quickly butted in and spoiled things. No, it was painfully apparent—to her, at least—that they weren't going to be able to see each other successfully, not for a long time.

The tape recorded an irritating blip where someone had phoned but decided not to leave a message. The utterly ridiculous thought that perhaps, just maybe, Rob Randolph had called to inquire after Randolph's progress flitted across her mind for a moment, but only for a moment. No one would be so silly as to phone back within an hour of leaving the center.

Like pages turning in a photo album, the vision of Rob preparing dinner for his little girl took form in her head. On second thought, he would probably be as reluctant as she to cook after a busy day. They would most likely pick up a pizza on the way home; afterward they would watch a *National Geographic* special on television, and Karen would tell him again how she wanted to work with animals when she grew up. Lisa had little trouble imagining the Randolph's cozy den, comfortably furnished and free of the stacks of partially read journals and ungraded lab exercises that perpetually threatened to crowd her out of her own living quarters.

"When are you ever coming home?" Anne Torrence fairly shrieked from the machine, bursting the lovely mental bubble that Lisa was admiring. Feeling caught in the act, Lisa cast a sheepish look in the direction of the phone. "I've been trying to get you all evening. Listen, I hate to bother you on Sunday night and I know you must have a zillion things to do, but if you could spare a couple of minutes to give me a hand with these damned kitchen shelves, I'd really appreciate it. I've practically killed myself trying to hang these things, but I'm not getting anywhere. See ya!"

Lisa listened to the blank hiss for a few seconds before trudging to the utility closet to fetch her toolbox. After living next door to Anne for four years, she knew by now that giving her a hand meant doing a job while her vivacious neighbor made coffee and filled her in on the latest gossip. Anne might be a very capable paralegal, but changing a light bulb was the extent of her practical skills. Armed with the metal box and an electric drill, she warned Chuck not to wait up for her and headed out the back door.

"I heard your door slam," Anne explained, throwing open her own door before Lisa had a chance to nudge the buzzer. "I really appreciate this, kid," she repeated, running her fingers through her cropped red hair as she led Lisa to the kitchen.

"No problem," Lisa assured her friend. "What on earth did you do? Hold a firing squad in here?" She nodded toward the kitchen wall that was riddled with pilot holes. "Actually, this doesn't look too formidable." She stooped to examine the tangle of metal brackets and runners piled in front of the stove.

Anne groaned and scooted the Mister Coffee to the front of the counter. "I hoped you'd say that. Honestly, I was about ready to throw those things in the trash." She shoveled an extra scoop of coffee into the paper filter, still shaking her head.

"Do anything exciting today?" Lisa asked as she stretched her tape measure the width of the wall.

Anne gave her an indifferent shrug, but she placed the coffee mugs on the counter with telling vehemence. "Pete called this morning from Dallas to say he was held up and would have to take a later flight home, so we had to cancel our dinner plans. Same old story. I've decided that dating Pete is sort of like getting a glimpse of Halley's Comet: you've got to be there at the right time and learn to cherish the memory. Anyway, I salvaged the afternoon by going to the health club and letting Sue slaughter me on the racquetball court before I came back here and tried to drive myself nuts with those shelves."

"Sounds like a productive day," Lisa mumbled with a pencil clamped between her teeth.

"Scoff if you will, but I did just happen to meet a really pleasant attractive man at the club. He was swimming laps," Anne added archly, as if that achievement strengthened her opinion.

"You met him underwater?"

"I met him in the juice bar, Dr. Porter. And for the record, we had a very enjoyable chat. His name is Craig Stewart, and it turns out he's the owner of that new camping supply store on Selwyn. When he asked for my number I didn't hesitate," Anne confessed proudly.

"Good for you, Anne. Since you and Pete have agreed to date other people, it's high time you started meeting some new men."

"Amen. So, what about you? Anything worth reporting from the wilderness?" Anne folded her arms and slouched against the counter.

Lisa squinted at the phosphorescent yellow bubble in her carpenter's level and tried to line up the pilot holes evenly. "Nothing out of the ordinary," she fibbed. The strong impression Rob Randolph had made on her during their brief association was entirely out of line, and she was determined to tone down her interest in him. "We did get a new patient, a red-tailed hawk that had been shot. A man and his little girl brought him in this evening. By the way, the fellow mentioned that he was an attorney. Ever hear of someone named Rob Randolph?" Not waiting for Anne's answer, Lisa leaned against the whirring drill.

"Rob Randolph!" Anne shoved herself away from the counter as if the drill had been aimed at her backside. "You've got to be kidding!"

The drill fell silent, as Lisa turned to blink at her astonished friend. "No, I couldn't be more serious. Is there something I should know about him?" She was almost afraid to ask.

"Only that he's just about the toughest defense attorney in North Carolina." Anne whistled under her breath for emphasis. "I mean this guy has the reputation for being one of the meanest, no-holds-barred..." She paused, searching for a suitable superlative to describe Rob.

"He certainly seemed mild mannered enough when I met him today," Lisa commented, fiddling with the drill's screwdriver attachment. For some reason she felt defensive about the handsome, kindly man who had brought the injured hawk to the center. If his professional persona had some rough edges, she didn't particularly want to hear about them tonight.

"I've never met him myself, and I'm sure he's a different person out of the courtroom." Correctly reading Lisa's tone, Anne deftly maneuvered the conversation into more tranquil waters. "I hear that he's been widowed for a few years now," she added lightly.

"His little girl alluded to that today," Lisa conceded over her shoulder. She took a step backward and surveyed the metal tracks running along the wall.

Fragrant steam curled from the two mugs as Anne filled them with fresh coffee. "Like I said, I don't know him personally, but I've heard he's really good-looking."

"What do you think?" Lisa asked, ignoring Anne's last comment. Her interest in Rob Randolph was disproportionate enough without Anne's pestering to egg her on.

"I think you should call him up. Say you want to ask him some questions about the hawk or something." Anne's opal-green eyes narrowed slyly as she lifted a mug to her lips.

"I mean about the shelves!" Lisa glowered at her friend.

"The shelves look great," Anne replied without even glancing at them. She shoved a mug into Lisa's hands. "But let's get back to Mr. Randolph."

"There's nothing to get back to," Lisa insisted testily. "Besides, he knows where he can reach me." She fought to control the smile twitching at the corners of her mouth.

"Okay. That's all I wanted to hear. Just making sure you don't overlook any important details." She nudged Lisa's arm, sloshing a puddle of coffee onto the counter. "You ought to know: a bird in the hand is worth two in the bush."

"Anne, sometimes I'm not sure about you." Lisa rolled her eyes, but she couldn't help joining in Anne's laughter. For all her interest in Lisa's love life, Anne had come closer to the mark this time than she suspected.

Chapter Two

One thing about red lights, they did give you a chance to take care of certain things. Like digging an antacid tablet out of the glove compartment. Lisa glanced away from the traffic signal long enough to examine the assorted junk spilling out of the dashboard. She managed to rip the cellophane from a chalky pink tablet and pop it into her mouth just before the beacon changed to green.

As she edged into the entrance lane spiraling down to the Interstate she mentally added another rule to the ever-expanding "Porter's Axioms for Life." *Number 324: Never order the "Lotta Taco" for Monday's lunch.* Especially on a Monday like this one. She had been functioning in high gear from the beginning of her eight-o'clock Introduction to Biology right on through one of the two-hour labs she conducted three days a week; if breathing weren't a reflexive process, Lisa was sure she would have overlooked that necessary function during the morning's turmoil.

As his recorded message had forewarned, Jack Mayhew had been waiting for her when she finally made it to her office. She had spent thirty minutes listening to his litany of excuses for muffing the exam; it took another thirty for her to explain why she couldn't let him take the test again. The sophomore's woeful, bespectacled face had lingered in her mind during lunch; no wonder the plate of spicy Mexican food had wrought such havoc with her digestive tract. Then there had been a seemingly interminable committee meeting after lunch. What a relief it had been when she finally ducked into the rest room and exchanged her silk blouse and challis skirt for the army-surplus garb she wore at the center. Lisa blew out a long, tired breath and signaled her intention to squeeze into the left lane.

Maybe I should have gone to law school, she mused, echoing her mother's oft-repeated sentiments. But a lawyer wouldn't be headed for the Wildlife Rehabilitation Center right now, she was quick to point out to herself. Unless he were bringing in an injured bird or animal. As if playing instant association in her head, she flashed on a darkly handsome face with crystal blue eyes.

At the appealing thought of Rob Randolph, Lisa was reminded of her concern for the injured hawk he had delivered into her custody the previous evening. She always looked forward to her rounds at the center, but she was especially eager to monitor this hawk's progress in recovering from his gunshot wound. For some inexplicable reason Randolph the red-tailed hawk had already come to occupy a special place in her heart.

A Ford sedan of indeterminate vintage was the only vestige of human life at the Wildlife Center when Lisa pulled into the lot. The sight of Sam Wheaton's old clunker always brought a smile to her face. Ever since his retirement from the university's biology department, Sam had faithfully manned the center's office three days a week. "My real work has just started" was his stock answer to those who suggested that fishing or lolling in a hammock were more appropriate activities for a man his age. Like his trusty car, he stubbornly refused to act his age.

"Good day, Lisa," Sam greeted her as she entered the office. Even in retirement he had retained his gallantry.

"Hi, Sam. Got any good news for me? Anyone call to say they wanted to give the center a quarter of a million dollars or so?" Lisa tossed her shoulder bag onto the windowsill and began to shuffle through the mail addressed to her.

"No," Sam said slowly, as if he were actually pondering her last question. "You did get a call around noon today. From a young man."

Lisa looked up from the bulletin she was perusing. "Did he leave a message?" She tried to sound offhanded, but at the fleeting thought that Rob could have called she immediately pricked up her ears.

Sam's chin dipped, allowing him to peer over his bifocals. "'Call Jerry McCloskey.'" He retreated behind the thick glasses as a scowl darkened Lisa's pretty face.

"Huh!" Lisa grunted, and impatiently shredded the brown paper cylinder taped around a naturalists' periodical.

Silence reigned for a moment as Sam pretended to organize papers with the aid of rubber bands and paper clips. As Lisa continued to frown over her magazine, he cleared his throat ceremoniously. "Are you going to?"

"Going to do what?" she asked, knowing full well what was coming.

"Call Jerry," Sam said, tipping the old desk chair back as far as caution would permit.

Lisa closed the magazine and propped herself against the sill. She had been blessed with parents who never meddled in her love life, but Fate had found a way of exacting a price for that benevolence in the form of Sam and Ellie Wheaton. Not that she wasn't grateful for the Wheatons' warm friendship, but the retired couple never let the opportunity slip by to encourage Lisa's social life. She could see that today's conversation with Sam was going to be no exception.

"No, Sam, I'm not. At least not right away," she added in response to the older man's injured look. The moment the words were out of her mouth she could have bitten her tongue. "Look, don't you think I wish things had worked out differently between Jerry and me?" She paused for rhetorical effect. "I can tell you why he's calling. It's because of the argument we had last week when we went out for dinner. We can't even agree on which table to choose in a restaurant, much less on more important things. Besides, as long as I continue to see Jerry I probably won't start dating someone else." This was her trump card, and she laid it on the table with a triumphant flourish. "Jerry is a dead end for me, Sam; he's too jealous to date along with other men, and he's too scared of commitment for the long haul."

"It's his loss," Sam commented gruffly, apparently persuaded by Lisa's skillful presentation of the facts. "If someone could talk some sense into that fellow's head, he'd be thankful for it ten years from now. Why, the first time I met Ellie, I knew she was a prize. Would have been a doggone fool to dillydally around with her the way this Jerry has with you. I've a good mind to tell him that the next . . ."

"Oh, no, you don't, Sam," Lisa warned. She didn't need to push her imagination to envision Sam lighting into Jerry the next time he phoned her at the center. "Believe me, I've made the issue perfectly clear to him." She shook her sleeve back and checked her watch. "Well, enough chitchat for now. I need to get to work."

Walking briskly toward the birds-of-prey trailer, Lisa found it difficult to slough off the news that Jerry had called. Damn it, why did the wrong ones show such dogged persistence while the right ones—she refused to personify any of these with a name—usually remained as elusive as a will-o'-the-wisp. Her mind continued to wrestle with these apparent truths as she made her rounds through the cages of injured birds.

She deliberately left Randolph until last to allow extra time to examine him carefully. Pat had made a note on the chart that the hawk had refused to eat so far, but that was not unusual. Lisa took a stealthy peek through the grid in the side of the darkened cage. A large, sharp eye regarded her warily, but the injured bird remained unmoving, his pathetic left wing encased in a white bandage. After double checking the temperature reading and antibiotic dosage that Pat had recorded, Lisa decided to leave Randolph alone for the evening. The poor creature had endured quite enough during the past twenty-four hours; for now a tranquil environment was as necessary to his recovery as food and medication. Still, it might not be a bad idea to have Sam take a look at him.

Quietly closing the front door behind her, she stuck her head into the office. "Sam, I'd like your opinion on that new red-tailed..." she began, but stopped as the elderly man swung around from his desk, telephone receiver cradled in one of his large hands.

"Lisa, I'm so glad you're back! It's for you," he announced in a stage whisper.

"Hello?" Lisa took the phone and sank onto the corner of Sam's desk.

"Dr. Porter, Rob Randolph here." Even though they had met only once, Lisa immediately recognized the clear, resonant voice. "I hope I didn't pick a bad time to call?"

"Oh, no. Not at all," she assured him with uncharacteristic brightness. Take it easy, she cautioned herself, letting a wary eye travel to Sam's corner. But the checkered flannel shoulders were hunched purposefully over the typewriter.

"I just wanted to check on the hawk—Randolph." A touching element of warmth colored his tone as he called the bird by name, and Lisa could imagine the gentle smile on his face. "I hope he's doing all right."

Lisa bit her lip, wishing she could offer a rosy prognosis. "He seems to be in fairly stable condition. In fact, I checked on him just before you called."

"I tried to tell Karen that you might not see much progress for a few days, but she's so concerned about her hawk. She even called me here at the office as soon as she got home from school this afternoon." Rob sounded as if he were apologizing for intruding on her time.

"You can tell Karen that Randolph is getting lots of rest, that he's taking his medicine just like he should." Lisa groped for something positive that wouldn't be an outright lie.

"She'll be pleased to hear that."

A moment of silence followed, but before Lisa could think of a way to steer the conversation onto a less serious topic, Rob went on. "Well, I know you need to get back to your work. And—" he sighed wearily "—the stack of legal briefs on my desk doesn't seem to have shrunk any since we've been talking. But thanks a lot, Dr. Porter."

"Sure." *Call me Lisa. Call me again.*

"Goodbye."

"Bye." Lisa held the receiver, listening to the dull hum that had displaced Rob's pleasant voice. Rob Randolph—the same affable, handsome Rob Randolph who had occupied her thoughts for a significant portion of the past twenty-four hours—had called her, and what had she done? Barely managed to stammer out a few platitudes for his daughter's benefit. She had gotten her chance to chat with him, show him that there was another side to her besides the serious-minded academic who reserved her charm for Brownie Scouts and injured wildlife, let him know, subtly, of course, that her interest in him went beyond his role in rescuing the hawk. She had gotten her chance, and she had muffed it.

No, she thought, later that evening as she leaned against her kitchen counter and waited for the microwave to revive a dish of frozen lasagna. The social ploys that seemed to come so naturally to other women just never seemed to work for her. Take Anne Torrence, for example, who could come up with a witty opener if she were being hauled into the emergency room on a stretcher. Or her own mother. Since Lisa's parents had divorced, Sarah Porter had channeled most of her energy into her now-thriving business, but her circle of friends included several attractive men who would probably have pushed for a more intimate relationship if given half the chance. But then her mother didn't really need a man to fill out her life, Lisa thought with a twinge of envy.

Nor do I, she added fiercely, dumping the gummy mass of noodles and tomato sauce onto a plate. Lisa stomped past

Chuck and out into the living room where she listlessly nibbled at her dinner while leafing through the mail. To judge from the envelopes, it promised to be as uninspiring as the lasagna. Tossing aside an unopened American Express bill and a bulging magazine sweepstakes offer, she slit the remaining envelope with her thumbnail. Well, she consoled herself, at least the electric blanket she had ordered from Sears two weeks earlier was ready to be picked up. An electric blanket to keep a lonely woman warm, she added in a mirthless stab at humor.

Lisa's glum mood did not improve as she forced herself to prepare her classes for the next two days. Her limbs felt numb with fatigue when she at last clicked off the end-table lamp and plodded into the bedroom. Zombie fashion, she brushed her teeth and lathered the day's grime off her face before falling into bed.

Rolling onto her back, she fought the tangled sheets wrapped around her legs. For the past two hours she had been struggling to keep her eyes open, and now that she was finally free to sleep, she couldn't hold them shut. What was wrong with her? She glared at the neon-bright digital clock and let her arm fall heavily across the pillow beside her. Teaching, keeping up with research, writing articles, doing volunteer work at the center, not to mention trying to juggle the more mundane things like eating and doing laundry—the life she had chosen for herself left few hours unfilled. And, even in her present ruffled state of mind, she admitted she wouldn't want to part with any of it. She didn't need anyone to support her or tell her what to do. But if only... She hesitated before allowing the carefully guarded fantasy to evolve a little further. If only someone were there, just to hold her and tell her she was doing okay. Someone special. Someone she would want to do the same for. Rob's sun-warmed face drifted across her consciousness, a face as good-humored and kind as it was handsome, and she did not chase it away. Taking some comfort from his image if not his presence, Lisa carried the memory of his chiseled face into her dreams.

SUN FILTERED THROUGH THE PINES, dappling the rich brown of the eagle's outstretched wings, carving a moving shadow of the bird onto the ground below. Lisa's eye followed the gliding bird, gauging the exact moment to begin her retrieval. Responding to increased pressure on the line, Regina banked gracefully before settling onto Lisa's gloved hand with a whooshing flap of her powerful wings. Everyone in the audience seemed to be holding his breath during the eagle's flight; her spectacular landing elicited a collective gasp. Lisa smiled at the magnificent bird grasping her hand. As familiar as she was with birds of prey, she still shared the crowd's awe at the sight of one in flight.

"On behalf of the Piedmont Wildlife Rehabilitation Center, Regina and I want to thank everyone for coming out today." A patter of applause rose from the spectators as Lisa signaled the end of the exhibition. "Before I return our star to her dressing room, I'd like to take this chance to remind you that, in addition to our birds of prey, we have many other interesting exhibits that are open to the public. There are plenty of volunteers on hand today who will be happy to show you around and answer your questions. And thanks again for your support." More exuberant clapping followed, but the visitors were quick to clear a respectful path for Lisa as she carried the impressive bird out of the ring.

"So tell me who you like best, William or Regina?"

Lisa's attention was focused on the eagle riding her hand, but at the sound of an elusively familiar voice she was immediately on guard.

"Both of them. I like them both." The small voice bore an uncharacteristic trace of pique at the unfair question, but left no doubt in Lisa's mind as to the speaker's identity.

Rob and Karen Randolph were within earshot, somewhere in the smiling throng of Sunday visitors. To her consternation, Lisa felt the same silly confusion creeping up on

her that she had experienced the first time she saw Rob
climb out of his car, and she stepped up her pace in the
direction of the trailer. How on earth had she failed to spot
them during the exhibition, she wondered as she replaced
Regina on her comfortable indoor perch. As Lisa mechan-
ically put away her creance and gloves, a tumult of con-
flicting thoughts stampeded through her mind. To think
how she had struggled all week to put Rob Randolph behind her, ascribe her infatuation to a moment's weakness,
and write their encounter off as a chance meeting without
postscript. And now, a week later, he had unexpectedly
turned up again with his little girl! Despite her well-intended
resolutions to keep a level head, Lisa almost bounded out of
the trailer in her eagerness to get back to the exhibition ring.

She had little difficulty spotting Rob. He was standing
near the empty performance ring, arms folded across the
chest of his gray leather aviator's jacket. When he caught
sight of Lisa, he threw up a friendly hand. As she cut across
the parking lot Lisa took the time to refresh her memory of
him. He had seemed tall last week but not as tall as the lanky
six-foot-plus man she was now admiring. Her eyes traveled
up the long legs, sheathed in stone-washed denim, to the
trim hips tapering beneath an obviously well-developed
torso. When her gaze reached his face she started, partly at
the unexpected blue of his eyes that seemed to reflect the
unclouded Carolina sky, partly because he seemed aware of
her appraisal and not at all shy of it. Lisa felt another
treacherous bout of confusion coming on, and she moved
quickly to counter it with her most casual smile.

"Hello, Lisa." With a split second decision Rob resolved
to dismiss with "Dr. Porter" once and for all. "When we
drove out today, we were hoping to catch your show with the
birds. We were in luck."

"I hope you enjoyed it. I'm glad you decided to visit the
center again," Lisa said in what was surely the understate-
ment of the year.

A grin—an unexpectedly boyish one for such an obviously successful man—creased Rob's bronzed face. "With such beautiful weather it seemed a shame to spend the day indoors," he explained, lifting the camera dangling from his left hand. "I think I got some good shots of you and Regina in action."

"That's nice," Lisa commented. Her hands instinctively dived for the comforting depths of her pockets, only to slide lamely down the legs of her brushed cords. At least the cords looked better than the fatigues, she thought, even if they offered no shelter for nervous hands.

"Regina was won-der-ful, Dr. Porter," Karen cried, suddenly popping into view from behind a pine.

A child is indeed a blessing, Lisa thought, especially when two adults have no idea what to say to each other. "Did you enjoy the show?" she asked, stooping to catch the little girl's answer. If she'd had eyes in the back of her head, she could not have been more conscious of Rob's penetrating gaze resting on her, but she was determined to make the most of this pint-size icebreaker.

Karen beamed and nodded enthusiastically. "It was won-der-ful," she repeated. "I liked the raccoon family and the flying squirrel nests, too. Daddy, can we look at the birds back there?" A chubby little hand pointed to a rustic sign with Birds of Prey carved into its surface.

"We could drop by and visit William the owl, if you like," Lisa offered.

"Why not?" Rob agreed with a laugh, but Karen was already skipping down the pine-needle strewed path.

"It sounds as if you've managed to see a lot of the center already," Lisa said, falling in step with Rob.

Rob nodded. "Everything from the opossum habitat to the migration charts. Karen is nothing if not thorough." His firm, well-shaped mouth curved fondly as his eyes followed the dark head bobbing ahead of them on the trail

"I'll bet she keeps you on your toes. A bright child at that age must be quite a handful," Lisa remarked.

"Yeah. You know, sometimes I can't tell if I'm striking the right balance between my work and my responsibility to her, but I guess all parents worry about the job they're doing with their kids." Rob maintained his resolute smile, but a cloud briefly darkened the cheerful blue eyes.

The thought that he might have interpreted her comment as criticism of his daughter's behavior spurred Lisa to add, "Well, you must be doing something right. Karen is a delightful little girl."

"I think so, but then I'm prejudiced." Rob's eyes lingered gently on Lisa's upturned face, and she felt a tremor of emotion ripple through her. Then he turned to call after his daughter. "Wait for us, Karen."

Sweeping her tawny blond ponytail over her shoulder, Lisa led the way into the raptor exhibit building. "I am happy to report that William has made quite a name for himself since he made his stage debut in front of your Brownie troop, Karen. He must have liked the rousing welcome you gave him because he's turned out to be a real star."

"So I'm finally going to meet this William I've heard so much about," Rob teased.

"Right this way." Lisa wheeled and led her audience down a row of wire cages. "Recognize him?" she asked Karen, stooping to catch her reaction.

"Of course. Do you think he remembers me?" The little girl leaned closer to the cage to allow William a better look.

"Owls are supposed to be wise, aren't they?" Rob Randolph shot Lisa a conspiratorial wink. "I'm sure he never forgets any of the children he meets in his business."

William chose just that moment to blink solemnly, winning a delighted giggle from Karen.

Both Randolphs seemed intrigued by the center's resident raptors. Outside the building Rob snapped several shots of his little girl as she paused to observe the flightless eagles in their open-air pen. Lisa was as familiar with the educational birds as with the members of her own family, and she happily provided a running commentary for her two companions. When the winding path at last led them to the parking lot, she was surprised at how quickly the time had passed.

"That was really interesting," Rob said with genuine enthusiasm. "I hope we haven't kept you from your other duties."

"Not at all. When I do an exhibition I always come in early so that I can head for home right after the show."

"Then we've tied up your whole Sunday! That's even worse," Rob moaned, trying to seem contrite.

"Oh, no. It was my pleasure. Really." Lisa hoped her conversation wasn't sounding as banal to Rob Randolph as it seemed to her; she feared the only marginally intelligent comments she had made that afternoon were about the birds, and with the tour now behind them she was floundering once again.

But then Rob didn't seem to be doing much better. "We brought a picnic lunch with us. I parked up the road a bit, and we ate off the hood." He wound the camera strap around his wrist and watched the black Nikon slowly twirl in a circle.

That must have been fun. What a neat idea! Lisa grasped for possible responses in her mind; each rivaled the last in corniness. Her hands wandered to her belt, latching onto the belt loops in lieu of adequate pockets.

"What are we going to do *now*?" Karen came to the rescue once again. Not waiting for the plodding adults to mull over the possibilities, she suggested, "Let's go exploring!"

"I'm game as long as we don't need life jackets or hip waders." Rob tousled the smooth dark head that just skimmed his waist.

"You know what I mean!" Karen giggled. "We'll stay on the trail. I promise. You'll come too, won't you, Dr. Porter?"

In a sudden burst of daring Lisa looked straight at Rob. "Sure, if you won't make me hike too fast." The warmth emanating from Rob's ruggedly handsome face told her that she had chosen the correct answer. "And if you'll start calling me Lisa. Dr. Porter makes me feel like a granny."

With a delighted hoot Karen skipped ahead of them down the drive leading out of the center. "Watch for cars on the drive, Karen!" Rob called after her, and succeeded in slowing her pace only a fraction.

Falling in step with Rob's brisk strides, Lisa took the chance for closer observation of this man whom she knew so slightly yet who held such an attraction for her. His shapely mouth was still smiling, but the taut lines of his jaw revealed an unmistakable tension as he craned to keep sight of Karen. He worries about her, she thought, maybe more than he should. A single parent faced a host of unenviable pressures, and Lisa felt a warm empathy for the broad-shouldered man walking at her side. If Anne Torrence could only see her tough attorney now!

But Lisa was glad that no one else was there to see them, glad that she had Rob Randolph all to herself. When they reached the end of the winding drive, they let Karen choose one of the many trails snaking off into the extensive state forest surrounding the Wildlife Center. With a child's sense of purpose, she marched determinedly ahead, pausing only now and then to examine an unusual plant or insect more carefully. Lisa and Rob somehow managed to keep the little red down vest in view without quickening their leisurely pace.

They had been ambling along in silence for some time before Rob spoke. "I can see why you enjoy your work out here so much." He pulled a hand from his jacket pocket long enough to give the air an appreciative sweep. "This is a long, *long* way from downtown Charlotte. Think the center could use a volunteer lawyer's services?" He cut a humorous sideways glance in Lisa's direction.

"You'd better be careful," Lisa warned with a laugh. "We snatch up unsuspecting volunteers just like that." She snapped her fingers for emphasis. "But I know what your talking about. I'm sure my job isn't as high-pressure as yours, and I still find myself itching to get out here before my last class is over. Although I do enjoy teaching," she was quick to add.

"How long have you been at the university?" Rob's low-pitched voice did not intrude on the subdued woodland sounds. Since they had been walking, he had noticeably relaxed.

Lisa held up four spread fingers. "Four years, ever since I completed my dissertation. Two more and I'll have tenure." She crossed two fingers for luck.

"Then you'll be a lifer?"

Lisa nodded. "Yep. That's the way it works. At least, I *hope* it does for me. Besides feeling pretty entrenched in the biology department, I have the center to keep my heart in Charlotte."

"I gather you aren't a native, then?"

"I was born in Lynchburg, but I learned to like North Carolina when I did my graduate work at Duke." Lisa's initial awkwardness with Rob seemed to have stayed behind on the parking lot, and she was enjoying the chance to open up to him. "What about you? Are you a born-and-bred Charlottean?"

"Hardly. I'm more of a Chicagoan than anything, I guess. At least, that's where my dad's company finally let him settle down when I was a sophomore in high school. I ended up here in much the same way you did: after studying law in Chapel Hill I got a good offer from a Charlotte firm." Rob paused, keeping one eye on Karen who was hopping between two stumps up ahead. He smiled as he went on. "Of course, when I realized that you can't even *buy* a snow shovel here, I didn't need much persuading to stay."

"You don't like snow?" Lisa leaned against a convenient broad-leaf pine, a teasing smile playing on her face.

"Snow is something you should have to get in a car with a pair of skis lashed to the roof and drive to. And then leave behind," he added with a husky laugh.

Rob propped one hand against the pine's stout trunk, not more than a few inches from Lisa's shoulder, so close that they almost touched. Their eyes met, and, for a moment she was sure that he *would* touch her, touch her face or her hair or her shoulder. But he pulled back as quickly as he had leaned toward her. "Karen?" he called, a concerned frown furrowing his brow. "Karen, where are you?"

Lisa pushed reluctantly away from the tree. As she scanned the trail up ahead, her heart quickened its beat: the bright red down vest was nowhere in evidence. "There's a bridle path that intersects the paths on this side of the road, but I doubt if she would have wandered off onto another hiking trail." She tried to sound calm for Rob's benefit, but he had already broken into a run.

"Karen! Come here this minute!" Rob's voice rose to a nervous shout as he reached the edge of the sawdust-strewn bridle path.

As Lisa caught up with him she was relieved to see Karen perched on a flat stump at a bend in the trail. One of the many Sunday afternoon riders had reined her horse up for the little girl's inspection, and Karen was patting the animal's sleek neck with childish absorption.

"Look, Daddy! Isn't he beautiful?" Her little hand continued to smooth the velvety neck as she called to her father.

Despite the alarm Karen's sudden disappearance had caused, Lisa couldn't resist smiling at the touching picture the tiny girl made stretching to pet the big animal. Unfortunately Rob found nothing cute or appealing in the scene. To Lisa's amazement, he made a headlong dash to his daughter's side and snatched her off the stump into his arms. His maneuver left the unsuspecting horse prancing sideways and its perturbed rider struggling with the reins, but Rob didn't bother to apologize. He was too absorbed with the small red-clad figure he clutched in his arms.

"You could have been hurt, Karen," he whispered harshly into the shiny dark hair beneath his chin.

"I was okay, Daddy," Karen insisted in a near whine. "I just wanted to pet the horse."

"I'm sure you didn't mean to slip out of our sight," Lisa interposed. She reached out to place a comforting hand on the child's back, but almost drew back as Rob's eyes met hers. The stricken look registered there could not have been more real if Karen had actually been injured in some freak accident.

"Let's just head back to the car," Rob suggested through tight lips. He let Karen slip to the ground but kept a sure grip on her hand.

No one talked, not even Karen, as they walked back to the parking lot. Lisa tried her best to think of something cheerful to say, anything to dispel the sober mood that had fallen over the little party, but her reserve of small-talk topics seemed even skimpier now than it had earlier that afternoon. And she was finding it hard not to be irritated with Rob. After all, Karen had only wanted to pet a very docile saddle horse—under its owner's supervision, at that—surely nothing to provoke such a reaction from her father. She tried to remind herself that if she had kids someday she would probably overreact to imagined dangers in much the same way, but right now Rob's fears looked disproportionate, even foolish.

"Do you have to feed Randolph his supper tonight?" Karen interrupted Lisa's thoughts from out of the blue.

"No, Karen. Someone else will." Bless this little imp for bailing them out every time the conversation lapsed! "But I bet you'll be glad to hear that his appetite has perked up a lot. He's even been eating some chicken all by himself.

Karen nodded her approval without comment. Then she halted abruptly on the path and signaled her father with the wiggle of one small finger. When Rob obediently bent she whispered raspingly in his ear.

"Why don't I ask her?" he said as he rose, and Lisa was pleased to notice that whatever Karen had said had returned the now-familiar jaunty smile to his handsome face. "Since you don't have to hang around here and feed Randolph tonight, Karen and I are wondering if you'd like to join us for some barbecue. I'll give you directions to the restaurant, but you could just as easily follow our car back to the city. And we promise not to keep you out too late," he went on, sewing up his case in his best lawyer's fashion.

"I'd love to," Lisa agreed immediately. Her warm brown gaze moved from Rob's roughly chiseled features to the smooth oval of his little girl's face.

If she had written the script herself, things couldn't have worked out any better, Lisa marveled as she rolled out of her parking place and waited for the big Mercedes to take the lead. After the private torment—and it *had* been torment—she had put herself through that week, Rob had surfaced again without warning. He *must* have felt some of the same interest in her that she had in him; it was too much of a coincidence that he had brought Karen back to the center so soon. She smiled to herself as a hand waved from the window on the driver's side. And it hadn't just ended on the hiking trail with the exchange of inane pleasantries and a "well-I-hope-I-see-you-again"; they were going out to dinner. Okay, so what if Karen comes along, so what if it's just a family restaurant. Lisa was enjoying herself, and she was not going to qualify that enjoyment.

Although she had driven by Jeb's Barbecue Shack many times, Lisa was content to follow the Randolph's car as they exited the highway and wove their way through the Charlotte suburbs. When they at last pulled onto the crowded parking apron, she realized with a shock that this was the first time she had been out with a man other than Jerry in over two years. Anne had often referred to the process of regaining her "sea legs" after dating Pete Rossi for so long;

now Lisa understood what she had meant. Maybe it's just as well to have Karen along for starters, she mused. That little bundle of energy had certainly saved them before when the conversation began to lag. Rolling up her window, she spotted the Randolphs in the rearview mirror and scrambled out of her car.

Inside, the restaurant was brightly lighted and crowded; a cloud of irresistibly sweet hickory smoke hung over the Formica-topped tables and red vinyl seats. While they were lingering in the entryway, scouting a suitable table, a waitress in a blue nylon uniform huffed by, her arms loaded with overflowing plates of ribs and coleslaw. "Just take a seat anywhere, honey," she advised. Lisa wasn't sure if the comment had been directed at her or at Karen, but when Karen exclaimed "There's one!" she followed blindly.

"Is this okay?" Rob asked as he helped Karen slide across the seat into the corner of a booth.

"Sure." Lisa sidled next to the little girl and plucked a menu from behind the stainless steel napkin holder. Pushing up the sleeves of her sweater, she surveyed the menu. "Got any recommendations?"

"Anything and everything. Seriously, I think I've tried just about everything they serve, and I've never been disappointed. They have takeout, so this is a good place for me to hit after work," he explained.

"Sometimes he brings home pizza or stuff from McDonald's," Karen announced, folding her chubby hands on top of the menu.

"So you want bread and water maybe." Rob fixed narrowed eyes on his daughter in an attempt to look offended.

"I *like* McDonald's," Karen reminded him gently, eliciting a peal of laughter from Lisa.

Rob let the menu fall and threw up both hands. "I don't cook," he confessed. "We do have a housekeeper who usually puts dinner together during the week."

"Casseroles," Karen interjected with a wrinkling of her pug nose that eloquently stated her opinion of those concoctions.

"But on weekends..." He gestured toward the paneled ceiling.

His revelation had been so different from the cozy family dinners that she had pictured the Randolphs having in her mind, Lisa was moved to tell him that her distaste for cooking often prompted her to contemplate eating cat food, but before she had the chance the waitress appeared with her order pad.

"And three iced teas?" the friendly waitress—the same one who had greeted them at the door—asked as she scribbled Rob's order on her pad. "Or does the little gal want a glass of milk?"

"Iced tea!" Karen proclaimed emphatically without so much as a look at Rob.

"Two teas and one milk. We don't want our guest to get the impression that I let you load up on junk, do we, Karen?" He shot Lisa a quick wink.

Lisa rested one elbow on the table while her free hand drummed time on her knee with the country song wailing from a jukebox across the room. While she listened to the Randolphs debate the merits of sundry junk foods, her eyes lazily appraised her surroundings. There were a lot of couples scattered around the dining room, but most people had brought children along. To the casual observer, Rob and Karen and she probably looked like a family, a happy family joking and cutting up in their gleaming little red booth. A pang stung Lisa for a moment, but fortunately the waitress arrived just then with their order.

"This looks terrific!" Lisa appreciatively eyed the generous serving of chopped barbecued pork with corn on the cob and coleslaw.

Rob managed a smile, albeit with a full mouth. He still seemed a little uncertain as to how she was responding to their outing. *He's probably one of those men who thinks he*

*has to book reservations at a fancy restaurant every time a
woman is involved,* Lisa thought. Safely hidden behind the
corncob, her lips twisted into a smirk as she thought of Jerry's elaborate efforts to impress her in the early days of their
relationship. Poor Jerry, he had always invested an inordinate amount of time in "Keeping up." Everything from the
sleek leather-and-chrome furnishings of his condo to the
fashionable pleated pants and Panama print shirts he wore
had been purchased only after careful analysis, respectively
of *Architectural Digest* or *Gentleman's Quarterly*. The net
effect of his efforts was pleasing to the eye, that she had to
admit; if only Jerry weren't so damned conscious of what
other people thought of him. If Rob shared some of his
concern over the choice of restaurants, he definitely scored
points over Jerry in another matter; if Jerry had a child,
nothing, absolutely nothing, could ever have persuaded him
to bring her along if he was trying to impress a new woman
friend. But then maybe Rob wasn't trying to impress her, she
reminded herself cautiously.

"Think you might have room for dessert, muffin?" Rob
leaned over his plate to meet Karen on eye level.

The little girl nibbled the remains of a roll and shook her
head slowly. "I'm full," she said with the air of one
conceding defeat.

"That makes two of us," Lisa chimed in. "Whoo! We
need to take another hike to work this meal off." She blotted stray dots of russet-brown sauce from the table's edge
with a balled-up napkin.

"I have an idea!" Karen exclaimed with a renewed burst
of energy.

"I ought to know better than to ask, but let's hear it."
Rob chuckled, sliding comfortably down into his seat, hands
clasped behind his dark head. The look he exchanged with
Lisa clearly said that he, like she, would be perfectly content to spend the next hour lolling in the booth over mugs of
coffee. Both of them knew that Karen wouldn't.

"Let's go roller-skating." Karen gripped the edge of the table and pushed herself up, not taking her eyes off Rob. "Okay?"

"Roller-skating? You mean in a rink with lots of kids and a Wurlitzer in the background?" Rob's face contorted in mock pain.

"Uh-huh." Karen swayed from side to side, still clutching the table.

Offering a silent prayer of thanks that, so far, at least, none of his opponents in court had tried this pleading, big-eyed approach with him, Rob fumbled for an excuse. "Karen, I don't know if Lisa would be all that excited about roller-skating."

"It would be fun," Karen insisted, refocusing her considerable charm on the woman seated next to her.

Lisa threw up her hands with a laugh. "Wait a minute, folks! I'm not going to be the tiebreaker. If you want to skate tonight, I'm game. If not . . ."

Her alternative was drowned out by Karen's jubilant cry.

"But we can't stay too late," Rob warned the triumphant little girl as Lisa helped her into her down vest. "Tomorrow's a school day, remember."

"You don't mind too much about the skating, do you?" Lisa asked as they jockeyed for the check at the cash register.

"What do you mean, if I mind? I was afraid you'd be bored to death." He took advantage of Lisa's surprise to wrest the check from her hand and thrust it, along with several bills, at the cashier.

Karen's favorite skating rink was located a short drive from the restaurant; Lisa spotted the extravagant neon sign before the Randolphs' Mercedes in front of her signaled a right turn. As they purchased tickets and were issued skates in the appropriate sizes, she couldn't suppress a chuckle. If the barbecue diner had been a far cry from Jerry's haunts, it was hard to imagine this garish roller rink and Mr. Mc-Closkey sharing the same planet. A pervasive smell of hot dogs and spilled soft drinks filled the air, along with the peppy tootling of a concealed organ.

Karen was obviously an old pro around skating rinks; she twisted impatiently on the bench while Rob struggled with the laces of her scuffed white shoe skates.

"Let me give you a hand," Lisa offered tactfully. She propped one of the child's feet against her knee and accomplished the task with a feminine efficiency that Karen did not fail to notice. Flashing Lisa a conspiratorial girl-to-girl grin, Karen hopped onto her wheeled feet and glided effortlessly out onto the rink.

The rink itself was filled to overflowing with skaters who exhibited wildly varying degrees of proficiency; some jumped and pirouetted while others wobbled nervously along the wall. *I'm about to make a royal fool of myself*. Lisa thought as she nervously tested one foot. She would be doing well just to stay on her feet and avoid a collision, but to her surprise, Rob snaked a strong arm around her waist and guided her firmly into the middle of the droning crowd.

"You must have had some practice with this." After a turn Lisa dared to take her eyes off the swaying corduroy hips directly in front of her long enough to look up at Rob.

His bronzed face was a picture of serene good humor. "Karen's taught me a lot" was all he said, but the corners of his generous mouth twitched suspiciously.

Lisa laughed, a little too heartily, for her feet suddenly outdistanced her torso by a good foot. "Yipes!" she cried, but Rob caught her easily, pulling her so close she could feel the throbbing muscles of his leg as he propelled them along. "It's been about fifteen years since I've had a pair of skates on my feet," she apologized.

"Don't try to skate. Just stand still and I'll pull you along," Rob advised.

"Drag would probably be a more appropriate word," Lisa commented dryly, but she was only too happy to take his lead. More than her fear of falling flat on her rear, the pleasant closeness of him gave her little inclination to skate

on ahead. Despite the carnival atmosphere, she felt an odd
intimacy with the tall, good-looking man at her side. And
judging from the possessive grip he maintained on her waist,
he wasn't having such a bad time, either.

"Ready to take a breather?" he asked as they glided toward the gate. Lisa nodded, and he skillfully piloted them
out of the rink. When she swayed unsteadily, he gave her a
look of supreme amusement. "If you can't walk in those
things, I'll be glad to carry you."

"Just get us some coffee, why don't you?" Lisa brushed
off his not unappealing suggestion and tottered gingerly toward a bench on the sideline.

In a few minutes, Rob clunked back with two steaming
Styrofoam cups. Settling himself next to her, he dropped a
handful of sugar and creamer packets into her lap. Lisa took
a careful sip of the scalding hot coffee. "There she goes."
She pointed as Karen sailed by, her pretty dimpled face
flushed from exertion. "She's quite a little skater, isn't
she?"

Rob nodded, swirling sugar into his coffee with a plastic
swizzle stick. "A child of many talents, if I may say so. At
least she probably won't get hurt in here." He grasped the
cup with both hands and smiled wryly.

"I imagine watching your child skate or swim for the first
time is a little like the way I feel when I release a bird after a
long convalescence. You try so hard to make everything
right, but in the end you're never *really* sure."

Rob lifted the cup to his mouth, throwing his free arm
lightly over the back of the bench behind Lisa. "I know I
got too upset today when I saw her petting that horse," he
said quietly, reading her thoughts. "But I had a reason, you
see." He spoke haltingly, as if he were having difficulty
choosing the right words. "It's only natural that Karen
should be interested in horses. They were her mother's passion. But every time she even mentions learning to ride, all
I can see is that big bay stumbling and falling into the fence.

And Sylvia lying there, just lying there. She never got up again.''

He fell silent, his eyes still fixed on the crowded rink, but there was no joy now in their azure depths, just a weary sadness. Lisa licked her lips, trying to find a word of comfort to offer him, but none came to mind. Instinctively she placed a hand on the arm resting behind her, digging her fingers into the smooth leather sleeve in a gesture of silent consolation. Rob didn't speak, but his hand dropped to her shoulder, giving it a grateful squeeze. They were still sitting that way when Karen clumped up from behind.

"Daddy, can I have a soda?" she chirped, her remarkable energy reserve not in the least depleted by an hour's skating.

Rob pulled himself up and quickly released his hold on Lisa's shoulder. "I'll tell you what, kiddo. Let's get these skates of yours off, and then you can go buy yourself something canned to drink in the car while we turn in the skates. Your old dad will keel over on his face in court tomorrow if you keep him out much later."

Karen giggled at the comical image he suggested and willingly accepted the dollar he handed her. In a few minutes she returned with a bright orange can clutched to her chest, and the three of them stumbled to the counter to exchange skates for shoes. As Lisa stooped to lace the little girl's sneakers, she smiled to herself. An hour earlier she had been anticipating a struggle to get Karen pointed toward home; now *she* was the one who—secretly, of course—wanted to prolong the evening. But when they reached the two parked cars outside, all she could think to say was "Thanks for including me in your plans tonight." That sounded so noncommittal and pointedly neutral that she instantly regretted not saying something more personally aimed at Rob.

But Rob seemed to understand. "Thank *you* for being such a good sport." Karen was already safely strapped into the car, and he didn't hesitate to reach for Lisa's hand.

Lisa closed her grasp over the long, tapering fingers. They were standing very close, so close that if she had stood on tiptoe her lips could have easily touched his. But she remained sedately rooted to the ground. "Good night, Rob," she said in a very low voice.

His head inclined slightly forward, narrowing the space between them, but then an invisible wire seemed to catch, pulling him up short. "Good night, Lisa" was all he said before climbing behind the wheel.

While she was unlocking her car Lisa saw the Mercedes brake for the light at the corner. On impulse she tossed her hand up in a little wave, but in the darkness she couldn't tell if either of the Randolphs saw her or responded.

Chapter Three

"See, Daddy? It says right here that we can get a special map of hiking trails."

Rob Randolph's neck stiffened as he tried to focus bleary eyes on the granola box that Karen had thrust between him and his cup of coffee. A weak smile struggled to brighten his unshaven face as he groped to regain consciousness.

"'Your own official map of America's most beautiful nature walks.'" Karen's voice was unnervingly chipper as she read from the back of the cereal carton. "We want one, don't we, Daddy?" She regarded her father intently, waiting for a response. When none was forthcoming she leaned as far across the table as her small torso would permit. "Don't we, Daddy?" she prompted.

"Sure, sweetheart. That would be real nice," he managed to mutter, lifting one hand weakly to forestall another intrusion of the cereal box. *How do kids do it?* he wondered. This one in particular rarely rested and never tired.

"Are you finished?" Karen's voice prodded him again.

What did she mean by "finished"? Good Lord, at six o'clock in the morning he wasn't aware he'd even started anything yet. Rob looked up to find his daughter glaring at the wedge of toast remaining on his plate. Slowly he comprehended. "Just clear off your own place and give me a few more minutes, okay?"

The little girl nodded before carrying her empty cereal bowl and milk tumbler into the kitchen. Rob heard the rattle of dishes in the sink followed by a violent gush of water. Shortly afterward the swinging door whooshed on its hinges, and small sneaker-shod feet raced up the carpeted stairs. Taking a listless bite from the cold slice of toast, he reflected that he had never had that much energy, not even when he was a kid. At least his memory seemed to recall it that way now. Karen was such a sweet little girl; if only her body clock were set at a slower pace.

Rob planted an elbow on the table and scanned the folded newspaper. A candidate for the county commission smiled confidently up at him as she signed her filing papers. Even in the grainy photograph her relaxed self-assurance and unflappable poise were apparent. A woman like Lisa Porter; the thought flitted idly across his mind, but the little squirt of adrenaline that her image released helped him open his eyes a fraction wider.

Feeling slightly self-indulgent, he let his mind conjure up Lisa's lovely golden tanned face, Lisa smiling up at him as they wobbled around the roller rink, Lisa's enormous soft brown eyes brimming with humor as she regarded him across the table at Jeb's.

Rob slumped back in his chair and took a sip of lukewarm coffee. *Go on, admit it; you're attracted to her,* he chided himself. *And why not?* his rational legal brain argued defensively; she was, after all, an uncommonly beautiful woman, the type of woman that most men would find hard to forget. But there was more about Lisa that drew him to her than her perfect, even features or the thick ponytail cascading down her back like spilled honey. Maybe it was her obvious intelligence or her calmness in the face of an emergency, or her unruffled manner that proclaimed she was in control and everything would be all right, at least, if she had anything to say about it. Maybe it was a combination of all of these factors, but for whatever reason Rob was too honest with himself to deny the unfamiliar emotions she had stirred to life.

"Are you about ready, Daddy?" Karen's little-girl falsetto carried down the stairs.

"I'm getting there," Rob called back. Taking advantage of the energy he had summoned to answer his daughter, he pushed himself up from the table and shuffled into the kitchen.

Rob poured himself another cup of coffee, trying to keep his eyes selectively trained on the Pyrex carafe and the earthenware mug. The rest of the kitchen was too much of a mess to contemplate on a semiempty stomach. Stray flakes of granola crunched under his moccasins as he turned his back on the overflowing sink and headed upstairs.

Trying to maintain the same tunnel vision that had helped him get through the kitchen, he ignored the partially dismantled bicycle that took up most of the den floor and gingerly sidestepped the muddy hiking boots booby-trapping the stairs. One thing he would lay money on: if Lisa Porter ever got a good look at this house, she would be off in the opposite direction at a dead run. Single people never could understand how impossible it was to keep things immaculate with an active child around.

Karen was sitting on the top step with a book open in her lap. Her Day-Glo-pink school bag and denim zipper jacket lay neatly at her side. When Rob approached she greeted him with an impatient frown.

"I'm hurrying. See, this is what happens when you take me skating on a school night." Rob clung to the banister and pretended to pant for breath; the act set Karen off in a chorus of giggles.

He had better step on it, he reminded himself. A glance at the bedside clock revealed that it was almost seven, and he still needed to shave and shower. With a manful burst of speed Rob brushed past the unmade bed and closed the door to the adjoining bathroom. Fifteen minutes later he emerged with the morning's ablutions behind him; another five and he was almost dressed, that is if he could just find the partner to this black sock. A quick cut of Lisa's face with its direct, open gaze flashed across his mind. Damn it, if he would quit mooning like a teenager, maybe he could manage to do something right this morning.

Rob ripped the sock out of the dresser drawer and threw it on the bed next to its mate. He scowled into the mirror and wrestled the silk St. Laurent tie into a knot. As his impatient fingers shoved the knot into place, his eyes caught sight of another face that made him stop short. The face was immortalized in a color photograph that stood, framed in austere sterling silver, keeping watch over the dresser mirror and all that passed before it. The smooth cheeks were as delicately pale as antique bisque, and the clouds of blond hair that billowed around them almost matched the silver of the frame. The face of a princess, Rob thought. He had thought that the first time he had seen her at the party her father had given for some of his fledgling legal clerks; she had been a princess then, too, Judge Max Cheatham's only precious daughter. Even after four years of marriage she had retained the aura of a doted-upon child, a little spoiled perhaps, but her charm had made him overlook that. Most of the time.

Why did you leave us alone? Rob's eyes implored the picture and as usual got no answer. *Didn't you know how hard it would be for me to raise a little girl by myself? If only...*

"Dad-dy!" Karen's childish voice interjected itself into his thoughts with a new note of urgency.

"Let's hit it!" Rob cried as he dashed out the master bedroom with his jacket draped over his arm.

Father and daughter pelted down the stairs and out the back door leading into the garage. It was always the same Keystone Kops sequence, every morning of the week: doors flying open on both sides of the Mercedes, the garage door gliding up and descending again almost before the car had cleared the portal. And always the same traffic. Karen kept up a steady stream of prattle, oblivious to the competition the drive-time disc jockey was giving her on the car radio, while Rob gritted his teeth and swallowed curse words as he battled the crush of automobiles.

"Have a good day, sweetheart." In one of the few pleasant morning rituals, Rob offered his cheek to Karen before she hopped out of the car and scampered across the school parking lot. He always allowed himself a few minutes in the lot, just long enough to see the glossy dark head and bright pink book bag disappear through the double doors before he tore out into the traffic again.

When Rob finally reached his office, he was no more frazzled than usual, but for some reason he was feeling very annoyed. Without much effort he pinpointed the source of his irritation. Everything he did, everything he saw somehow reminded him of Lisa Porter—Lisa Porter eating breakfast, Lisa Porter getting ready for work, Lisa Porter, for heaven's sake, taking her morning shower. Rob was so thoroughly disgusted with this adolescent lapse, he wished he could have angled his foot into the appropriate position to give himself a good, solid kick.

But if Rob had wanted to boot himself for his idle musings over Lisa, the frantic activity that always characterized his office soon left him little time for daydreaming. Although there were no court appearances on the day's schedule, the morning's calendar was dark with scribbled-in appointments, and the afternoon, when he dared to look, was just as packed.

Eleven o'clock had rolled around before it even occurred to him to phone Mrs. Elliott. Rob expected to be home later than usual today, and he needed to let Mrs. Elliott know. He had employed that stout, kindly lady as housekeeper since Sylvia's death. Mrs. Elliott was as slow as she was stocky, and in truth performed only the minimal housekeeping chores, but a warm and loving relationship had developed between Karen and her very early. She was unflaggingly dependable, always met Karen at the bus stop and remained in

the house until Rob arrived home, priceless duties that could
not be compared to mere vacuuming and dusting.

"I'm just fine," the housekeeper's flowery Southern voice
wafted from the receiver, giving her perennial response to
Rob's greeting. Yes, her daughter Gladys could pick her up
at six; no, he wouldn't have to drive her home but thank you
anyway.

After Rob bid Mrs. Elliott goodbye, his hand clung to the
receiver like a kid's hand lingering in a cookie jar. *C'mon,*
he thought. *You just saw her last night. Besides, she's a
professional like you, with an overloaded schedule that
doesn't permit chitchatting on the phone in the middle of
the day.*

Rob continued to argue with himself while he flipped
through the directory and scanned the university's listing.
When the Arts and Sciences switchboard answered, he asked
for Lisa and, propping his heels on the wastebasket, waited
for her to pick up.

"Lisa Porter!" Her voice was slightly breathless, as if she
were in the middle of doing something both irritating and
demanding. Rob guessed the slight fuzziness on the line
meant that she was cradling the phone under her chin while
her hands continued their task.

"Lisa, this is Rob. I hope I didn't choose a rotten time to
call." Saying that was always an admission that you know
you have, Rob thought. He was already beginning to rue the
bad timing of this call.

"Oh, no. I... uh, I'm just trying to get some of these papers under control." Her soft laugh was interrupted as she
shifted the phone to her other shoulder.

"I won't keep you long, but I just wanted to..." Rob
cleared his throat and, following Lisa's cue, shifted the
phone to his left shoulder. Damn it, what *did* he want?
What on earth had possessed him to pick up the phone and
call her without the faintest notion of what he intended to
say? "I just wanted to see if we could get together again.

Soon. I had such a terrific time last night, even if it was just barbecue and roller-skating."

"So did I! That was really..." Lisa sounded encouragingly enthusiastic, but unfortunately the phone slipped from beneath her chin and banged against the desk, cutting her off in midsentence.

Waiting for her to recover the phone, Rob tried to think of a suitable activity to suggest. Never before in his life had he called a woman for a date without having a few possibilities in mind, but he realized now how rusty his once well-honed dating skills had grown from disuse. Suddenly he felt as if he had stepped into a courtroom with a dubious client, a hostile jury, a beady-eyed judge and an opponent with bared fangs. And he had forgotten to prepare his case.

When Lisa returned to the line she solved the problem for him. "Sorry about that. But, yes, I'd love to plan something. Why don't we shoot for this weekend?" she suggested in a tone that would have bolstered the most sagging male ego.

"This weekend?" Rob repeated, stalling for time as he plundered the open briefcase for his pocket calendar. "Uh-oh. I forgot, but this Saturday Karen has her big Brownie Scout cookout, so I'm going to be roasting hot dogs and handing out Band-Aids all day." He forced a chuckle, the standard ploy of a stand-up comedian with bad writers.

Lisa seemed unfazed. "What about Sunday?"

"Sunday we're driving to Winston-Salem to see her grandparents. They've been expecting us for weeks," he added, hoping to strengthen his case, but the cheer in his voice was beginning to wear thin.

"It sounds as if this weekend is out."

"Yeah." Rob wheeled in his chair, upsetting the pencil cup with his elbow. "Well, then why don't we have lunch?" He stooped to retrieve the stray ballpoints and felt tips that were rolling helter-skelter across the floor like the disorganized thoughts in his mind. "This week," he managed to throw in as he straightened himself and stuffed the pens into the cup. "Today," he added in a final stab at decisiveness.

"Today?" Lisa pecked at the word as if she were startled by its novelty. "I'd really like to, but I have such a tight schedule, driving downtown is out of the question. We could meet somewhere up here, though. Say, at one o'clock?"

"Sure. Name your place, and I'll be there at one o'clock sharp." He would drive, walk, roller-skate to the most far-flung corner of Charlotte. That was the least he could do after botching the weekend date.

"Good. How does one o'clock at Luigi's strike you?"

"One o'clock at Luigi's it is."

"I'm looking forward to it," she added in parting. She sounded as if she really meant it.

MAYBE LUIGI'S HADN'T BEEN the best choice, Lisa fretted. Nervously clutching her shoulder bag with both hands, she scooted closer to the streaky plate-glass window, trying to clear a path for the ravenous horde of college students pressing toward the salad bar. But she had been so surprised and pleased when Rob had called, she had not wanted to forfeit the chance of seeing him. Especially when she knew that next weekend would be her last fully free one for a month. The image of an obsessive career woman who gives her social life short shrift was one she did not care to foster, particularly with someone who seemed to manage both career and family as successfully as Rob did.

Her hand fluttered in recognition as she spotted the blue Mercedes wedging itself between a beat-up Volkswagen van and a red Mustang. When Rob climbed out of the car he seemed to spot her immediately. His hand shot up in greeting, and his generous mouth broadened into that charming grin that Lisa now considered his trademark.

"Am I late?" Rob looked crestfallen as he charged through the door.

"No, I'm early," Lisa corrected him. "I hope you didn't have any trouble finding this place," she added as they jostled their way to a window table.

"I just let my nose follow the oregano."

"Their pizza is really good," Lisa began apologetically before she caught the teasing expression in his eyes. "Sort of like Jeb's barbecue."

Rob nodded, but he was already scanning the paper place mat that doubled as a disposable menu. "Do they mean what they say with this one called 'The Works,' or are they just bluffing?"

"Let's try it and see," Lisa ventured. She relayed their order to the waiter who had just dropped napkin-wrapped cutlery onto their table. Only when she looked up beyond the tomato-stained apron did she recognize Jack Mayhew's perpetually mournful face.

"Would you like a couple of beers to go with 'The Works,' Dr. Porter?" Jack asked, invoking her title as if she were the sort of doctor who committed people to padded cells.

"Two large lemonades," she insisted quickly without even consulting Rob. "I don't drink on the job," she explained when Jack had shuffled back to the order counter.

Rob rested one arm across the back of the booth. His impeccably tailored pin-striped suit stood out in bizarre contrast to the cutoffs and jeans favored by the college crowd, but he seemed to feel right at home. "I guess a lot of your students eat here, too," he commented with a mischievous twinkle in his blue eyes.

Lisa nodded, but before she could comment a youthful baritone hailed her from behind. She twisted in her seat and cringed as she recognized one of her senior honor students bearing down on them.

"Dr. Porter, am I glad I ran into you!" a young man with a white-blond surfer cut and loud Hawaiian-print Bermudas exclaimed. "You know that fungus I was trying to cultivate? Well, you'll never guess what I discovered."

Commandeering a chair from a nearby table, he angled up to their table and deposited a half-filled beer mug squarely between Rob and Lisa.

"Don, I don't really want to discuss fungi over lunch," Lisa told him bluntly, taking some satisfaction from the way her disinterest drained the joy from his face. "Stop by during my office hours tomorrow, and we'll talk about it, okay?"

"Well, okay. See you then," he agreed after some hesitation. He reluctantly scraped the chair back to its rightful table and retreated to the bar.

"And I thought lawyers were bad about talking business over lunch." Rob chuckled. He leaned back to allow Jack room to slide "The Works" onto the table.

"At least legal shoptalk doesn't involve fungi," Lisa countered, trying not to look at the mushroom slices liberally scattered across the pizza.

"There is a bit of your business I wouldn't mind discussing, and that's the subject of Randolph."

"Oh," Lisa began, letting her voice fall more than she had intended. She lifted a slice of pizza onto her plate, tugging at the stubborn strand of mozzarella that was anchored to the pan like an umbilical cord. When she looked up at Rob she realized that he had already guessed the worst. "I didn't want to alarm Karen on Sunday, but he had stubbornly refused to eat for most of the week. We finally decided to force-feed him, but, thank heaven, he's eating on his own now." She looked at the bite perched on her fork before returning it to her plate.

"What about the fracture?" Rob chewed thoughtfully, mulling over the information she had just relayed.

"I'm planning to take him back to Neil for another X ray this Saturday. After I see how the break is mending, I can decide what sort of therapy will be best for him. I'll keep you posted." Lisa tried to smile, but the topic of Randolph's questionable chances for recovery had chased her cheerful mood away along with her appetite.

"Both Karen and I would really appreciate that," Rob said quietly, but he was quick to sense the need for less serious conversation. "I'm really impressed with the Wildlife Center. It's always nice when parents can enjoy an outing as much as their children do." He raised his voice in a valiant attempt to compete with the music that suddenly blared from the mammoth speakers suspended over the bar.

"We're always glad to hear that at the center," she told him, but even her lecture-hall delivery was no match for this punk-rock vocalist who seemed to have a particularly large chip on his shoulder. Defeated, Lisa sank back in her seat and focused her attention on the remaining slice of pizza.

"Yours or mine?"

"Excuse me?" She looked helplessly from Rob to the two speakers menacing them.

"Yours or mine," Rob repeated, indicating the remaining pizza slice. His voice boomed as if he were questioning an evasive witness, but he had obviously never cross-examined anyone playing a high-powered synthesizer with a frenzied drummer and two guitars to back him up.

"Yours," Lisa shouted. She managed to grin in spite of the singer's ravings about fire and death and the end of the world.

Rob smiled back, but he apparently had written off any more attempts at conversation. He dispatched the slice of pizza in three bites before balling the soggy paper napkin into a knot and tossing it onto his plate. "I'm afraid I've got to head back to my office," he announced, as he checked his watch.

Lisa searched for a note of regret in his voice, but the competition coming from the speakers rendered all but the most primitive analysis impossible. "Me, too," she agreed wanly, assuming that, if nothing else, he had learned to read lips during this lunch. She watched as Jack Mayhew swooped by to retrieve Rob's credit card. The bright thought that she should say "next time, it's on me" occurred to her, but the resounding crash of an upturned pitcher accompanied by raucous guffawing from the adjoining booth cautioned her not to push her luck. What with fungi, obnoxious music and rowdy students, this lunch date had been anything but an auspicious occasion.

"I'll have to remember 'The Works' the next time I get a yen for pizza," Rob told her before he unlocked the door of the Mercedes. His grin was as persistent as ever, but dark sunglasses concealed his eyes from her scrutiny

"I'm sorry the place turned out to be so noisy. To tell you the truth, I usually stick to take-out orders," Lisa confessed. In the glaring sunlight Rob's dignified pinstripes seemed to stand out even more than they had inside the pizzeria.

"So do I, but this was fun for a change. Especially with you." He added this last comment as he stuck his head through the car window, but Lisa was now certain he was only trying to make her feel better.

"Take care," she called. She prodded herself to throw him a passably jaunty wave.

Rob tooted the horn before he pulled out into the four-lane roadway and was swept away by the oncoming tide of traffic.

"Ooooh!" Anne Torrence clutched the doorknob and took a shaky step backward.

"May I come in?" Lisa asked uncertainly. She pulled back as her neighbor's usually sunny face contorted in pain. "Good Lord, Anne, are you dying or what?"

"My feet are," Anne moaned. Leaving the door open for Lisa, she limped back into the living room and dropped heavily into the tub chair. "Look but don't touch," she cautioned as Lisa stooped to inspect the feet in question. They looked normal enough, burrowed inside house shoes that resembled two industrial-size pink mops, but when Anne lifted them testily onto the ottoman, she winced in pain.

"What happened?" Lisa perched on the edge of the couch, still not taking her eyes off the hot-pink dust mops.

"You know Craig had invited me to go hiking Sunday?" Her eyes narrowed as Lisa nodded agreement. "I had these lovely visions of a pleasant stroll through the woods, right? A bottle of wine in the knapsack, a checkered cloth on the mossy bank, birds twittering in the trees and all that. Well, I couldn't have been more wrong." She let out a disgusted sigh. "I swear, Lisa, this guy must take his vacations with the marines on Parris Island. First, we got up at the crack of dawn so we could drive for miles until the road literally vanished. Here I am not even awake yet, and he bounds out of the Jeep—four-wheel-drive, naturally—and announces that we've reached the T.A. or the A.T."

"The Appalachian Trail," Lisa offered helpfully.

"Whatever. Anyway, then the real fun began. We walked and we climbed and we crawled until I thought I was going to drop from sheer exhaustion. Every now and then, he'd stop and offer me this yucky concoction of nuts and raisins he carried in his pocket, and while I was trying to choke the stuff down, he'd drag me to the edge of a gorge to see something. You know how I am about heights, Lisa." She waited for a sympathetic nod before continuing. "This was instant vertigo. The crowning blow came when we finally got to whatever was supposed to be our destination, and I pulled my new boots off to discover my feet were in the process of melting."

"Anne, you didn't go hiking in brand-new boots?" Lisa sounded appalled.

Anne regarded her coldly. "Purchased especially for the big occasion. What did you expect me to wear? These things? No matter now; the damage is done." She slumped deeper into the chair, the picture of a woman in defeat.

"I'm sorry Craig's idea of a good time turned out to be so...strenuous. But you did meet him at a health club," Lisa reminded her gently.

"You call this healthy?" Anne lifted one foot far enough out of the slipper to reveal a maze of jumbo Band-Aids.

"You know, Anne, I think you might prefer a man who's a little more sedentary than Craig."

"Yeah, like a pen pal." Anne's mouth twitched into a grumpy smile. "But enough of my woes! What are you up to today?"

"Neil Clark has kindly agreed to X-ray one of my patients for me after his regular office hours today, but I'm free until then. I was going to challenge you to a game of racquetball . . ." Lisa tried to keep a sober face.

"Don't even think of asking me to bounce around on my feet for a year or so," Anne warned her. "But, of course, you could always call up Rob Randolph and invite him. I bet he plays a wicked game of racquetball."

"Anne!" Lisa exclaimed, letting her mouth drop open for an instant. "Don't be ridiculous! I hardly know him." She fostered a skeptical laugh, but the uneasy feeling that her perceptive friend had been reading her mind put her on guard.

Anne was unperturbed. "Racquetball might be a nice remedy for that problem."

"I would think that after your recent experience you'd be the last person to recommend sports as a way of getting acquainted," Lisa retorted. "Anyway, I really ought to look over my research paper instead of going to the club with anyone." Jingling her keys in her hand, she sprang up from the sofa and sidled toward the door.

"For heaven's sake, Lisa, it isn't as if you were asking him to the prom. I'm sure he'd be delighted to hear from you." Anne twisted around in the tub chair as far as she could without moving her feet.

He's busy today, Lisa almost blurted out, but caught herself in the nick of time. If Anne found out she had actually seen Rob since their first meeting, her needling would become unbearable. "I've worked on this paper so sporadically, I'm afraid I've overlooked something important,"

Lisa went on smoothly, trying her best to talk around Anne. "Let me know if you need anything for those feet," she added just before she ducked out the door.

"Coward!" she heard Anne cry through the closed door.

She was not a coward, just a realist, Lisa thought as she unlocked her door and stooped to stroke the ball of yellow fur brushing her ankles. Rob was a very busy man; not only did he have a very demanding profession, but his responsibilities as a parent constituted another full-time job. Not the sort of person whose schedule left him available for impromptu games of racquetball, she reminded herself.

Lisa dropped onto the sectional and flipped listlessly through the typed manuscript lying on her coffee table. The last thing she needed was to let this infatuation overrule her common sense, she told herself sternly, pausing to scrutinize one of her diagrams. The skating expedition had been fun, but it had been Karen's idea to include her in the first place, hadn't it? Of course, Rob had taken the initiative to call on Monday, but the resulting lunch date had given them little more than the opportunity to watch each other's lips move while gobbling down pizza. Even a casual dating relationship could not be expected to flourish under those circumstances.

Lisa bit her lip and rested the fat document on her knees. It had been a long time since she had considered anything more than a simple dating relationship with a man, but Rob Randolph had awakened a suppressed craving in her, a deep yearning for intimacy and sharing that would span the full spectrum of human emotions.

He's a warm, sensitive, intelligent, attractive man, and he's interested in you. Even thinking about him in those terms sent an instant pleasant sensation rippling through her. Just as quickly, Lisa moved to stifle the daydream. She had been listening to Anne Torrence too much these days. In any case, only time would tell if Rob shared the attraction, she decided as she patted the papers into a neat stack.

If only she could order her life with the same precision she applied to the scientific data in her charts, Lisa mused as she slid behind the wheel of her car later that afternoon and headed for the Wildlife Center. So many things seemed to be out of her control these days, not least of all, Randolph's troublesome injury. The red-tailed hawk had been at the center for two weeks now, and although she had closely monitored his condition, only Neil's X ray could determine if the broken wing were mending properly. She had both longed for and dreaded the day when the veterinarian's foggy gray film would reveal how well the break had fused and if the joint had suffered in the process.

Turning off the Interstate, she caught a glimpse of a hawk circling overhead, effortlessly riding the air currents that carried it between the soaring pines. The contrast between that graceful silhouette and Randolph's pathetic bandaged figure flashed before her eyes with cruel irony. At the same time, the images of Rob and his little girl rose in her mind—Karen's sweet face grown serious with concern, Rob's sea-blue eyes full of compassion for the wounded bird. Regardless of what the future held for any of them, one thing was certain: the stricken hawk had united them in a bond of mutual caring that would not be easily broken.

When she reached the Wildlife Center, Lisa did not stop by the office to exchange pleasantries with Pat Taylor but went straight to the raptor ward. Except for a new screech owl that stirred its wings in a defensive posture, the intensive-care room was very quiet. Almost too quiet, she thought as she gently loaded the unresisting Randolph into a carrier and carried him back to her car.

Driving to the emergency animal clinic, she kept glancing at the carrier nestled in one corner of the back seat. She rolled her shoulders, trying to loosen the strained muscles, but her hands continued to clutch the steering wheel with a white-knuckled grip.

Neil had apparently been watching for her car; he waved to her as she pulled up beside the clinic's ramp. "Is our patient coming along okay?'' he asked, holding the door open for her.

"That's what I'm here to find out.'' Lisa mustered a nervous laugh, but she felt oppressed by the clinic's sterile white corridors and antiseptic smell.

Neil gave her an understanding nod. Inside the clinic's radiology center, the two of them spoke barely above a whisper, Lisa crooning softly to Randolph as she steadied him on the table, Neil giving her his terse instructions while he performed the X ray. The young veterinarian seemed to take an hour in the laboratory processing the two exposures of Randolph's wing; when he returned, Lisa leaped up from the folding chair where she had forced herself to wait for him.

"How's it look?'' she demanded. Her anxiety had mounted to the point where she could no longer wait for the verdict, however crushing it might be.

"I'll let you see for yourself'' was all Neil said as he perched the two X-ray films in front of the viewer.

Lisa leaned over the viewer, studying the ghostly outline of the hawk's wing structure. "There's no problem with the break; as you can see it's healing pretty nicely. But the joint worries me a little bit...." She heard the veterinarian's youthful voice drift off uncertainly.

"It's going to calcify, isn't it?'' Lisa's voice was surprisingly steady as she acknowledged what they were both thinking.

Neil nodded slowly, venting a long sigh of frustration. "It might,'' he hedged. "A lot depends on how long the wing remains out of use. You know, it's sort of like an athlete's injury.''

Lisa straightened herself and took a deep, calming breath. For some reason she was at a loss to pinpoint, her nervousness had subsided noticeably. Perhaps it was the uncompromising reality of the X ray in front of her, perhaps it stemmed from having to confront the problem she had wanted to avoid, but Lisa felt a renewed determination to defy the odds. "Randolph is going to get the best therapy I can give him. I'm going to manipulate that wing for him until he can do it himself. And he's going to fly again, Neil, so help me." Looking up from the X ray, she fixed her intense dark eyes on the young veterinarian.

Neil lifted his horn-rimmed glasses and rubbed the bridge of his nose thoughtfully. "I hope so, Lisa. I really do."

SLIPPING THE PINK RIBBON MARKER between the pages, Rob slowly closed the colorful book resting on his knee. "And that, folks, is all for tonight. Be sure to tune in tomorrow for another exciting installment."

Karen giggled, a plush animal firmly nestled in the crook of each chubby arm. No matter how often he used that line to conclude his bedtime reading, she always laughed.

"Did you enjoy yourself today, sweetheart?" Rob gently stroked Karen's thick bangs away from her brow.

The dark head nodded emphatically. "I can't wait to show Grandma and Grandpa my prize badge. You had a good time, too, didn't you, Daddy?"

"I sure did." Rob smiled. All the spilled mustard and boisterous sack races and scuffed knees in the world could not detract from the joy he experienced in sharing Karen's world.

"I bet Lisa would have had fun, too. She likes to do neat things." Karen made this pronouncement as if she were letting her father in on a special insight of hers.

"Yes, she does," Rob agreed. He hoped that his reply was sufficiently neutral to disguise the turbulent feelings Lisa's name evoked. "And now I think it's about time to shut those eyes." Karen's eyes obediently clamped into a tight squint. "You don't want to be tired and sleepy at Grandma's tomorrow, do you?" Eyes still firmly closed, Karen shook her head.

"Sweet dreams, muffin." Leaning over his daughter, Rob thought how much she looked like a little angel fallen from heaven, propped up on the daintily sprigged pillows with her stuffed menagerie. His hand rested lightly on her dark head as he kissed the downy cheek. Straightening himself carefully, he fumbled with the pulley dangling from the Winnie-the-Pooh lamp.

"Good night, Daddy." The little voice was drowsy, and Rob instinctively rose onto tiptoes as he left the room. From the stairs he glanced over his shoulder at the half-opened door. He could imagine Karen's gentle breathing, her heart-shaped face now relaxed as she drifted into a child's untroubled sleep.

She was such an innocent little girl, it always amazed him how perceptive she could be. With her infallible antenna attuned to the slightest shift in his moods, she had picked up on his interest in Lisa right away. For some obscure adult reason he had avoided mentioning the pizza lunch he and Lisa had shared, but he had managed to look guilty when Karen had questioned him about Randolph.

"Is Randolph getting better?" she asked with unfailing regularity. And when she deemed his spotty reports inadequate, she always demanded, "Why don't you call Lisa then?"

Well, he had called her; he had even made a stab at asking her out. But he was certain that even his own daughter would take a dim view of his inept handling of that matter.

Rob twisted the dimmer switch in the hallway, adjusting the light to a soothing level, when the telephone jangled. Hoping that Karen was still sleeping soundly, he dashed into the study and caught the phone on the third ring.

"Rob? Hi, this is Lisa."

Her voice sounded even more low and feminine than he had recalled; its unexpected music seemed to cast a soft focus over the businesslike room.

"I know you must be worn out from your cookout," she went on. "I'll only keep you for a minute."

"I've gotten my second wind," he insisted. *Just about two seconds ago, when I picked up this phone,* he added to himself.

Her laugh was soft as a caress. "I just wanted to let you and Karen know that I had Randolph X-rayed today. And," she drew a deep, resolute breath, "it looks as if there's going to be a bit of stiffening at the joint. But I think with therapy he just might have a chance of flying again."

"That's wonderful!"

"We still have to be cautious," Lisa reminded him, and Rob could tell she was making a great effort to curb her own expectations.

"I don't know anything about healing, really, but I'm sure of one thing: if I were in that hawk's place, I'd want your kind of determination pulling for me. Surrender just isn't in your vocabulary, is it?"

"I may have to learn it someday." Lisa laughed, a self-deprecating laugh that, Rob was sure, accompanied a soft flush warming her cheeks. "Anyway, I wanted to let you know because—" she paused for a moment "—well, just because you care. Be sure to tell Karen," she added quickly, as if some preassigned time for her call were running out.

"I will," Rob promised.

"Good night, Rob."

She was still holding the phone, waiting for his reply. "Lisa?" Rob began, and then hesitated. For his entire life he had always regarded the phone as a sterile tool of commerce, at best a handy if impersonal link to clients and auto mechanics and far-flung acquaintances. But right now, leaning across the big desk in the unlighted study, it was as if Lisa's presence had somehow defied the space separating them. Her dark eyes, full of courage and incredible gentleness, the perfect oval of her face, her small, strong hands— all of Rob's senses tingled with the awareness of the total that was Lisa.

"Yes?"

"Good night, Lisa." Rob heard the click at the other end signaling she was gone. With deliberate care he gently replaced the receiver. He did not want to do anything that might dispel the image of Lisa Porter remaining there with him in the dark room.

Chapter Four

Chin propped on one hand, Lisa hunched over the desk. Outside the window in front of her, streaks of violent russet and amber slowly drained from the darkening sky, but they were wasted on her today. Her fingers doggedly rummaged through the file cards, but her eyes scarcely registered the information they contained. Finally she snapped the plastic lid of the little file box shut, rubbing her forehead as if to banish the fatigue that thwarted her efforts to concentrate.

"I'll bet you've had a tiring day, haven't you, Lisa?" Sam Wheaton wheeled his desk chair away from the bookcase and regarded the young woman slumped over her cluttered desk.

The dark blond head nodded weary consent. "Things have been terribly hectic lately," she conceded. "And last night I made the mistake of staying up until two trying to review my paper for the conference next weekend."

Propelling the ancient desk chair forward with his heels, Sam rattled toward Lisa's desk. "How many times do I have to tell you to quit worrying about that doggoned paper?" His bushy gray brows knit in the closest semblance of a frown that Sam could manage. "Confound it, Lisa, your work is as solid as any I've seen in my career, and we're not talking about just a few years in biological research, mind you." Lisa's sheepish smile must have placated Sam somewhat, for he continued in a less riled tone. "If it will make you feel any better, bring your paper in on Wednesday, and I'll have a look at it before you take off for Minneapolis."

"Would you, Sam? Your stamp of approval would really bolster my confidence when I make my presentation to all of those raptor experts."

"I'll read your paper," Sam repeated. "But only on two conditions: you've got to promise me that you won't re-write a single word on the plane. Ellie can tell you that I always found something to change in my papers even while I was walking to the podium to read the blasted things." The wrinkles framing his bright blue eyes crinkled as his mouth drew into a wry smile.

"Biologist's honor." Lisa clapped a hand over her heart. "But maybe I shouldn't agree until I've heard your second condition."

"I want you to go home right now and get yourself some sleep." Sam jiggled the arm of Lisa's chair as if to spur her into compliance.

"No fair, Sam. I swear, I'm not as tired as I look, and I'm scheduled to leave in an hour anyway," Lisa protested. She squared her shoulders and blinked brightly to underscore her point. "Besides, I have no one to blame but myself for going roller-skating two weekends ago instead of working on my paper as I'd planned."

"Roller-skating?" Sam's feigned pique vanished instantly as he pounced on this unusual bit of information.

Seeing the interest growing on his face, Lisa immediately regretted the slip. All she needed was for Sam to get wind of her interest in Rob Randolph, and there would be no peace in the tiny office they shared three afternoons a week. Sam was a dear, but his fatherly concern for her bordered on the meddlesome. "Uh-huh. I read somewhere that skating is good aerobic exercise," she mumbled. Grabbing the card file, she began to pore over the cards as if both their lives depended on it.

"Roller-skating!" Sam shook his head as he swiveled to the typing stand. "Well, I guess it's about time that a lively young woman like you got out and had some fun."

Lisa waited until Sam's hunt-and-peck typing struck its familiar syncopated rhythm before she chanced a glance in his direction. She was relieved to see him hunched over the machine, critically reading each line as it was tapped onto the paper. That had been a close one; she vowed on the spot to exclude any references to Rob from her conversations with Sam, at least for now.

Lisa was composing a list of questions for her weekly veterinary consultation when the telephone's shrill buzz cut through Sam's jumpy typing. She spun around in her chair, but Sam beat her to the receiver. She turned back to the file cards spread across her desk, trying to ignore the one-sided conversation taking place behind her. The Wildlife Rehabilitation Center received dozens of routine calls every day, and this was probably just another one.

But she was wrong. "It's for you, Lisa," Sam announced cheerfully, too cheerfully for the call to involve an injured bird.

Before she had even stretched across to Sam's desk and pressed the blinking button on the telephone, Lisa's sixth sense anticipated the deep voice that would greet her on the line. "Hello?" she murmured, doing her best to disguise the annoying tremor in her voice.

"Well, you've finally lighted long enough in one place for me to catch you." Rob's throaty chuckle rolled over the wire, and Lisa could imagine the striking contrast of gleaming white teeth against tanned skin as he laughed.

Lisa giggled self-consciously before answering. "Am I that hard to track down?" She tried to avoid looking at Sam, who for some reason had abandoned his typing for the time being.

"I called the university three times, only to be told you were in a class or a meeting or the lab, take your pick. I knew if I waited until tonight, I'd risk talking into that damned machine you use to censor your calls at home, so I dashed out to a phone booth the minute court adjourned." Another resonant laugh punctuated his good-natured complaining. "You know, I really appreciated your call the other night."

"I couldn't wait to tell you. I'll bet Karen was glad to hear some news about Randolph." From the corner of her eye she watched Sam's mock perusal of a reference book. Although he pretended to squint over the fine print, she could see that he sensed this was no ordinary inquiry.

"She was pleased as punch. We both have a lot of faith in your therapy, Dr. Porter. But, you know, I actually called to discuss something besides Randolph with you. Now, I know Jeb's and Luigi's are hard acts to follow, but I'm willing to give it my best shot. How about taking in a film and having dinner with me on Friday night? I promise we'll go a little more uptown this time," he added, as if she needed extra persuasion.

"Friday? Let me see." Lisa licked her lips, trying to scan her mental calendar and avoid Sam's sly scrutiny at the same time. If only the phone weren't anchored so firmly to her co-worker's desk! "Oh, I almost forgot, but I'm flying to Minneapolis Friday morning. I'm giving a paper at a conference on birds of prey," she hastened to explain, watching Sam's beetle brows rise. She could imagine his mental computations: if the caller were sufficiently interesting to distract her from the conference that had been her obsession for the past two months, he must be someone very special indeed.

"When will you be coming back?"

"Saturday, but I've forgotten when my plane gets in. Can you hold on?"

"Sure."

Lisa punched the hold button and trundled her chair back to her desk. She heard Sam mutter something about making tea, and when she returned to the phone with her purse calendar in hand, he had disappeared into the office kitchen.

"Let's see." Lisa cradled the phone under her chin and flipped through the smudgy pages. "I'm scheduled to arrive at seven forty-five. That means by the time I get my bags, it will be at least eight-thirty. Doesn't sound too encouraging, does it?"

How many weekends did she spend in Charlotte with nothing to do but grade papers and commiserate with Anne Torrence, and this one evening she wanted free was unalterably taken. Worse yet, the image of a superbusy career woman rushing from one commitment to another with a carefully designed fortress of answering machines to shield her from interference was not exactly the one she wanted to cultivate with Rob. "What about the following weekend?" she suggested.

"I haven't given up on this one yet. We could forego the movie this time; if you don't have any objections to hopping off the plane and heading straight for a restaurant, I'd be glad to pick you up from the airport." Lisa heard another coin slide through the digestive tract of the pay phone as Rob waited for her answer.

"That would be great, if you don't mind plowing through that airport traffic." Despite her buoyant spirits Lisa managed to keep her voice at a discreet level. Sam's tea preparation was progressing with a suspicious absence of noise, but she was determined to make his eavesdropping as difficult as possible.

"I'll line up a baby-sitter for Saturday night and meet you in the baggage claim at eight o'clock sharp. And now I've got to get back into court. Don't want my client to get packed off to jail behind my back." He chuckled briefly before adding, "Oh, and have a good trip, Lisa."

"Thanks, Rob," she responded, but before the words were out, the phone had already clicked. As she slowly replaced the receiver, her mind tried to deal with the unfamiliar emotions Rob's brief call had stirred to life. She had met an attractive man; he had called to invite her out to dinner. Simply put, that was all that had happened. It was a scenario that could be applied as readily to her relationship with Jerry McCloskey as to the one with Rob. But much as she wanted to tell herself that this was business as usual, something warned her that Rob Randolph was not a man to be pigeonholed into a convenient category.

Lisa was still smiling to herself when a cup of tea appeared at her elbow. "Thank you, Sam," she muttered before lifting the cup to savor its tangy fragrance. Through the cloud of steam she watched Sam struggle to find the right opening line.

Taking a sip of scalding tea, the older man returned to the fat volume opened on his desk. As he ran a pencil through the cowlick of wispy gray hair dipping across his forehead, he seemed to be deep in thought. Finally he pushed back from the desk and looked straight at Lisa. "You feel pretty good about your paper, don't you?"

"Yes, I do. In spite of my last-minute jitters." Lisa nodded, tracing the rim of her mug with one finger.

"Just wanted to be sure. Because, you know, you can always talk with me about your work. Or whatever," he added, clearing his throat.

"I know that, Sam." A fond smile warmed Lisa's face. It was impossible to resent Sam's interest in her life, especially when she was reminded of the genuine concern that spawned it. "That's why I'm grateful that you're my friend."

"Just wanted to be sure," Sam repeated. A satisfied smile warmed his face as he returned to his typewriter.

MAYBE IF SHE HAD TALKED with Sam a little about her attraction to Rob, she wouldn't have spent so much time thinking about it during the next few days, Lisa later mused. The memory of his handsome face—wearing that gently amused expression that, during their brief acquaintance, she had come to regard as his trademark—seemed never to stray far from her consciousness. At least his distraction served to defuse some of the tension surrounding her appearance at the conference. Sam was right, she had concluded as she pecked out her concluding remarks on her skittish little portable typewriter. She did need to get out and have some fun, and as soon as she had the Minneapolis conference behind her she intended to do just that.

But when Lisa finally boarded her flight back to Charlotte on Saturday evening, the first thing she did was snap off the piercingly bright light over her seat. At that moment the only activity that seemed within the realm of possibility was sleep. Easing her feet out of her pumps, she let herself sag against the armrest. She had not been allowed to sit quietly for more than two minutes all day. First, there had been the reception the night before, then a too-early breakfast that morning followed by her panel's presentation. And then there had been discussion groups and lunch and then more discussion groups. At least her paper had been well received, she thought through her fatigue-induced haze. Sam would be glad to hear that. And Rob, too.

Rob. Lisa shifted uncomfortably to one side and tugged at the seat belt. She had been so looking forward to having dinner with him, it would be a shame to fall asleep over the appetizer. Like a fairy godmother eager to transform pumpkins and mice into wondrous things, a smiling flight attendant chose that moment to appear with a steaming pot of caffeine-laden brew. Lisa managed to gulp two cups of coffee before the plane landed, and by the time they had taxied to the gate she was beginning to feel herself again.

That she had even considered the need for an artificial stimulant seemed foolish when she caught sight of Rob from the escalator. His rangy frame was propped against a column strategically facing the escalators, and he spotted her right away. When he threw up his hand in greeting, Lisa felt her pulse quicken. It was crazy, she freely admitted to herself, but just the sight of him had transformed the professionally competent but exhausted biologist who had climbed onto the plane three hours earlier into an excited, radiant woman.

Rob was waiting at the foot of the escalator, and he immediately took her carry-on bag, expertly linking arms with her at the same time. "You look as if you had a pretty good flight. Or are you still beaming from your latest academic triumph?"

"Everything went very well, thank you, but I think 'triumph' is going a little too far." Lisa looked up at him with what she hoped was a serene smile. If he had thought she was glowing with excitement on the escalator, she could only imagine the sort of Cheshire-cat grin that had been plastered across her face. *Watch it, Porter,* she cautioned herself. Adolescent gaping is unbecoming to thirty-year-old college professors. "Did you get back to court the other day in time to save your client?" Keeping the conversation in the professional realm would help sober her up.

Rob let out a laugh hearty enough to turn a few heads at the baggage carousel. "I think so, but it'll be another few months before I can be sure. Sometimes I wish cases would resolve themselves the way the old Perry Mason shows did. You know, the attorneys argue back and forth for about fifteen minutes, and then a witness suddenly cracks on the stand, confesses everything, and, bang, that's it."

"You mean it *doesn't* work that way?" Lisa regarded him with a look of mock amazement that elicited another roar of laughter from him. "I guess the Perry Mason court scenes are about as realistic as my imagined academic triumphs." She reached for a blue nylon garment bag only to have Rob neatly intercept it. He swung the bag over one shoulder and quickly rejoined arms with her. As they emerged into the crisp night air, she thought she detected a tightening of the arm looped through hers, pulling her closer to the inviting warmth of his husky body.

When they reached the parked Mercedes, Lisa settled comfortably into the leather seat. She watched Rob as he circled the car, deposited her bags in the trunk and then slid behind the wheel. She was grateful for the darkness that masked any uncertainty between them, grateful for the sol-

itude of the sleek car that separated them from everyone else
for the time being. They had talked enough already for her
to have formed a sense of who he was, but this was only the
second time she had seen him without his small daughter at
his side. The role of father now receded into the background, allowing a new aspect of Rob's personality to
emerge. The man piloting the smoothly running car seemed
less concerned with the weighty burdens of life. His keen
blue eyes narrowed against the stream of oncoming head-
lights, but when he cut an occasional glance at her, they
glowed with unabashed masculine appreciation.

He feels it too, Lisa thought. A charged atmosphere had
developed in the car, even as they continued their pleasant
small talk. She had just finished giving him a detailed report on Randolph's therapy program, and Rob had picked
up the conversation with an account of Karen's plans for a
show-and-tell about North Carolina's wildlife.

"Tell her I'll be glad to give her a hand. I'm sure I have
some old nature journals with pictures she could cut out and
use," Lisa offered.

"She'll take you up on it; I can guarantee that much."
Rob took the opportunity to caress Lisa with another smile
before turning into a parking apron lined with replicas of
old-fashioned gaslights. "This is it," he announced, shoving the gearshift into park. His voice bore a trace of disappointment, as if he wished they could continue driving and
talking on into the night.

"I've never eaten here, but I've heard such good things
about this restaurant," Lisa commented. She, too, was in no
hurry to leave the cozy togetherness of the front seat, but she
was impressed with Rob's choice.

"That makes two of us. A law school buddy of mine
swears they offer the only authentic nouvelle cuisine in
Charlotte, and his dad was in the restaurant business in
Chicago, so I guess he's qualified to pass judgment." Rob
had sprung out of the car and reappeared on Lisa's side,
helping her easily to her feet.

Even before they had seen the menus, Lisa was certain that Rob had made the right choice for their first evening together. The waiter who greeted them at the door led them through a tastefully lighted dining room to a table tucked in a quiet corner. With smooth efficiency he lighted the pale pink tapers nestled in a bouquet of fresh flowers before presenting Rob with a leatherbound wine list. Looking around the spacious room with its dark green walls and crisp white-skirted tables, Lisa could just pick out the subdued notes of a Duke Ellington tune coming from a piano in the adjoining cocktail lounge.

"We can hit Jeb's later for a beer and some fries." Rob winked at Lisa after the waiter had delivered a chilled bottle of white wine.

"Maybe next time," Lisa ventured. For the first time she felt emboldened to suggest that there would, indeed, be a next time. Relations between men and women had always seemed so fragile to her, she seldom risked the temptation to think beyond a pleasant evening shared under mutually convenient circumstances, but she sensed that Rob operated on terms slightly different from those of most men. As if reading her thoughts, he lifted his glass to hers, clicking the rim lightly in unspoken agreement.

Lisa took a sip of wine and leaned back to allow the waiter to serve the Shrimp Rémoulade appetizers. "I've been looking forward to this all day," she confessed. "Just the chance to relax with a glass of good wine and good company." Her eyes swept the room, resting lightly for a moment on Rob.

"I gather you don't care much for the academic limelight?" Rob pulled a chunk from the crisp baguette on his bread plate and thoughtfully dabbed it with butter.

Lisa uttered a low groan. "I rate it only slightly higher than strolling across a bed of hot coals. In that respect, I'm definitely not my mother's girl. She's a born performer. When she was eighteen and fresh out of boarding school, she shocked her entire Tidewater clan by running off to New

York, determined to make it on Broadway. I can remember the tales she used to tell me when I was a kid, about living in a funky cold-water flat and going to all the casting calls." Lisa chuckled softly, aimlessly rearranging the silverware surrounding her empty plate.

"Did she make it?"

"Only to the chorus line. Actually I think she had what it takes to succeed on the stage, but things changed, as they have a way of doing. She made the mistake of coming back to Lynchburg at Christmas, and she met a nice young man who later went on to become my dad." Lisa's shoulders rose and sank in resignation.

"That's doesn't sound like such an unhappy ending. Especially in light of the end result." Rob looked up from the platter of Chicken Kiev that the waiter had just slipped in front of him.

Lisa prodded one of her veal scallops with the tip of her knife. "Their marriage turned out to be a flop." The words sounded especially flat and harsh uttered against the carefully orchestrated elegance surrounding them. What had started as a lighthearted little vignette about her mother had definitely taken a wrong turn somewhere along the way. And the last thing she had wanted to do was to strike a sour note during their festive evening.

Rob must have sensed her consternation, for he obligingly came to the rescue. "And I suppose the sequel to that episode has your mother going back to New York and making a name for herself after all?" He smiled briefly before lifting his wineglass to his lips.

"Almost. She went to Miami Beach and opened a fancy boutique." Lisa laughed, glad to have the conversation back on more pleasant terrain. "Actually she's become a star of sorts, jetting around to the big fashion shows. And she keeps her daughter in decent rags."

"What about your father?" Rob ventured.

"Dad remarried, and he still has his little engineering firm in Lynchburg. I ought to go up and see him at Thanksgiv-

ing, but I haven't decided yet if…if I'm going to be able to."
She let her voice trail off. Enough of her private concerns
had been aired for one evening, and she was ready to turn
the tables on Rob. "Here I've given you a complete geneal-
ogy on me, and I still don't know anything about your
background." She narrowed her eyes and leaned across the
table, pretending to scrutinize him closely.

"I have one father, who's a corporate exec, one mother,
who's a housewife, and one brother, who's still sweating his
way through medical school. The only thing remarkable
about my childhood is its numbing uneventfulness." Rob
rolled his napkin and stuffed it under the edge of his plate
as if to signal an end to the matter. "You've probably
guessed already that I went to law school; at one point I
married and had a child. And that, my dear lady, is about
all there is to be said about Robert Jennings Randolph."

"I don't buy that for one minute," Lisa countered, giving the tabletop a playful slap that brought their waiter
scurrying to the table.

"Care for dessert?" Rob smiled wickedly, obviously
proud of his success in thwarting her curiosity.

"Coffee and chocolate mousse, thank you, but let's not
change the subject. Surely you have some charming anec-
dotes from your school days." His wavy dark head moved
slowly from side to side as he scanned the menu's dessert
offerings. "An eccentric great aunt who always pulled a
marvelous stunt at Christmas gatherings?" Rob shook his
head again. "Nothing?" Rob nodded agreement, a slow
smile enlivening his face.

"Hate to disappoint you," he said with unconvincing remorse. After giving the waiter his order he propped both
elbows on the table and fixed Lisa with a riveting gaze that
she imagined was at least partially responsible for his numerous successes in court. "Besides, I've revealed quite a bit
of my recent history, which is more than I can say for you."

Lisa thrust out her chin, striving for a suitably defiant
stance. "I'm Bird Lady; you know that."

"Not twenty-four hours a day." Unclasping his hands
that cupped his chin, he let them settle lightly on Lisa's bare
arms. A delicious shiver ran through her as his fingers
played with the gold bangle adorning her wrist, slipping
between the cold metal and her warm skin. "I want to know
when you feel happiest, what lifts your heart, what makes
you sing. Those are the important things, not a court case
or a biologists' conference."

"I like music, mostly classical and the jazz they played
when my parents were kids. Movies that make me cry, and
books that make me laugh. Wild birds and my cat, Chuck."
She looked down at the strong tanned hands enclosing her
arms. Rob really did want to know what was going on inside her, something that no man had asked of her before,
and what was even more unnerving was the temptation to
tell him. *You. I like you, Rob Randolph. Just the thought
of you, and my heart bursts with song.* But ingrained caution held her back, and she continued her litany of prefer-
ences. "And, believe it or not, I like good food, although I
hate to cook. I'll bet you know all of the good restaurants
in Charlotte." She deliberately grinned more broadly than
usual. Her efforts to lighten the serious tone that Rob had
struck succeeded; his hands slid free of her arms and bus-
ied themselves with the convenient napkin ring.

"Besides Jeb's?" Rob twisted his mouth to one side in a
grin, as if he were giving the matter careful consideration.
"Any place with a good steak where you can take a kid or a
client, I guess."

Lisa giggled as she spooned a dollop of velvety mousse
into her mouth. "You have unusual criteria."

"Not really. When I eat out it's usually with someone
connected with my work or with Karen. Not that I don't
appreciate a meal like this—" he spun the napkin ring
around one finger "—but I seldom have the occasion to rise
much above the Jeb's level."

Lisa concentrated on the sweet morsel melting on her
tongue. That an attractive, desirable man like Rob Ran-

dolph rarely went out to dinner with a woman was too far-fetched for her to believe, but that seemed to be what he was saying, at least indirectly. She studied the man seated across from her. His personally tailored gray herringbone jacket, pearl-gray shirt and designer tie made him look right at home in the elegant dining room, and Rob certainly appeared to be enjoying himself that evening. No, she concluded, Rob was more of a man-about-town than he was willing to admit; all of his banter about barbecue joints was just a guise he fostered for amusement's sake.

Rob was quick to interpret Lisa's silence. Folding his arms across his chest, he smiled as he picked up the lapsed conversation. "Having a child to look after changes your perspective. But Karen has been worth it; I've never regretted having that little angel for a minute," he added with a vehemence that left no doubts. "Funny, though, the things you learn to enjoy after you've become a parent."

"Like roller-skating?" Lisa laughed, but secretly she had to admit that, childless as she was, she had enjoyed the skating quite a bit.

"Roller-skating and helping someone discover life and grow. Not exactly the fast track by a single person's standards perhaps, but watching Karen grow up has been one of the most rewarding things in my life. Much more rewarding than any coup I've pulled off in the courtroom." As he spoke, Rob's velvety blue eyes followed the brass napkin ring that he turned between his fingers, as if he were fascinated by the sparks of candlelight reflected in the burnished metal.

"A person doesn't have to have children to understand the feelings you've just described," Lisa interposed gently. She didn't want to appear defensive, but the line he had just drawn between what he believed to be her world and his own was unnecessarily stark. "I've always maintained that I prefer my work with the center's birds to any other aspect of my career. Being able to apply my knowledge to help a creature recover the use of its wings or its talons, nurturing a bird until it can manage on its own again—those are the skills I spent so many years buried behind a book to gain. I would never have worked as hard to get where I am today if my only successes were in a lecture hall or a conference room.''

"Touché." Rob's hands enfolded hers again, and when he looked up from the gleaming ring his eyes carried a flicker of that brilliant light with them.

They sat there for some time without speaking, reading in each other's eyes the thoughts and desires that live without words. If a giant guardian had clamped a crystal bell jar over their table, Lisa could not have felt more intimately sequestered with Rob than she did in the corner of the now almost deserted restaurant. There was so much she wanted to tell him—how much he had come to mean to her, how deeply she understood the thoughts he had shared with her, how he touched her as man to woman in a way that she had never experienced before; if only she had the courage. And for a while, as his strong, tapered fingers smoothed and warmed her hands, she almost believed herself brave enough to let him see the vulnerable woman hiding behind the competent professor and healer of birds.

Their waiter had to glide past their table three times before either Rob or Lisa paid him any notice; on the fourth sally he finally managed to make eye contact with Rob.

With a sigh loud enough to reach the waiter's ears, Rob reluctantly released Lisa's hands and signaled for the check. "I hadn't noticed, but we appear to be the last ones in the whole restaurant." He scanned the empty tables around the dining room, some of which had already been stripped of their starched cloths. He whistled softly as he glanced at the slim Rolex encircling his bronzed wrist. "It's past midnight! I should feel guilty for keeping you out so late after the long day you've had."

"But you don't?" Lisa smiled impishly at Rob over her shoulder as he draped her coat around her.

"Not in the least." Rob stooped to whisper in Lisa's ear, and she could feel his hands tighten through the fluffy pile of her coat.

Only when they reached the car waiting on the empty parking lot did he relinquish his grasp, but then just long enough to clamber behind the wheel. Inside the car, his long arm encircled her shoulders once again, pulling her to his side, and Lisa willingly snuggled her cheek against the nubby tweed shoulder. Through half-closed eyes she watched the bright blur of lights pass outside the windows. A mellow fatigue had settled over her, tempering her senses so that her awareness of Rob had blended into a sensual mélange of tweed and warm skin and tart citrus after-shave.

Like a cat uncoiling from a nap, she tensed and then relaxed her muscles; she felt his sinews beneath the expensive tweed flex before drawing her even closer. Through a curtain of hair, Lisa glanced up at Rob and was rewarded with his familiar smile, but a new tenderness seemed to have loosened the taut lines of his face, smoothing the tension from his rugged contours. She imagined how nice it would be to touch that sun-warmed face, let her fingers pirouette along the sculpted jaw with its prickly dark shadow, up to the temple and into the thicket of black hair framing his high brow. She imagined, too, his hands taking a cue from hers, the way they would feel against the delicate skin of her throat, the contrast of their cool touch, as they invaded the layers of clothing, to her heated body. His lips would follow, offering another kind of touch, arousing her in a different way.

Through the dreamlike cloud surrounding her, she felt Rob's hand cup her jaw, angling her face toward him. His lips were gentle and pliant as they first grazed her cheek and then caressed each closed eyelid. "My sleeping beauty," she heard him murmur. She lifted heavy hands to embrace his neck, but she resisted opening her eyes; this dream was too tantalizing to let go of so readily. The next thing she dreamed was that he was holding her, lifting her gently so that her feet scarcely touched the ground. She was vaguely aware of a chilling gust, but the bulwark of his solid, masculine body shielded her well.

"Your keys are in here, I bet," she heard him whisper as he gently slipped her bag from her shoulder, but the damp, coffee-scented breath caressing her ear was far more interesting than the location of keys or anything else, for that matter. "Poor, tired baby," he crooned. She leaned, unresisting, against the muscular plane of his chest. A lock clicked somewhere off in the distance, and then they were once again engulfed in warmth and darkness.

Lisa blinked and recognized the bamboo-patterned wallpaper of her own foyer. "I must have fallen asleep," she mumbled, lifting a hand clumsily to massage the drowsiness from her eyes.

"There's no need for you to wake up now," Rob assured her. With a deft sweep he lifted her off her feet and into his arms. "You're home, and I'm going to tuck you in, all safe and sound," he promised.

A curious excitement mingled with the heavy grogginess Lisa was feeling, a feeling akin to the state she imagined certain drugs induced. Part of her was responding to his sensual closeness while another part of her was content to be cuddled and pampered by this very caring man.

Her hand remained clasped behind his neck after he had placed her on the bed. In the darkness she glimpsed the even row of teeth revealed by his smile just before his lips descended on hers, covering her mouth in a kiss that sent tingling waves undulating through her relaxed body. Another kiss followed, this time more lingering, a good night kiss. His fingers gently caressed her brow, smoothing her tangled hair and closing her lids with a stroke as delicate as the brush of a butterfly's wing.

"Good night, Lisa." His soft voice drifted into her dream, bringing a smile to her lips. "Good night, my love."

Chapter Five

Anne Torrence frowned and waved her bright magenta nails briskly. "Can you get this one, Lisa?" Still holding her splayed hands in front of her, she jerked her head toward the front door.

Lisa shoved herself up from Anne's well-cushioned sofa. "You're the only woman I know who would try to give herself a manicure on Halloween night," she grumbled good-naturedly, grabbing the bowl of chocolate kisses on her way to the door. "I'm coming!" she cried, loudly enough to silence the impatient youngster leaning on the buzzer.

"How's our candy supply holding out?" Anne asked when Lisa returned from the foyer a few minutes later.

Lisa jiggled the bowl and pretended to count the foil-wrapped candies. "If you quit snitching them, I think we'll have enough."

"In the event we do run out, you can always trot into the kitchen and make some popcorn." Anne smiled sweetly; with her hands dangling limply in front of her, she looked like an oversize red-haired puppet.

"Get serious! I'm not cooking anything tonight, not even popcorn. And you'd better start blowing on those nails because the next time that doorbell rings, you're on." Lisa flopped solidly onto the sofa, signaling her intention to remain there for some time.

"What a mean friend you are!" Anne teased. "Ever since you broke up with Jerry, you've been…shall we say, rather moody."

"That's nonsense, Anne, and you know it. I was a hell of a lot meaner when Jerry and I were always squabbling than I am now." Unable to resist her friend's ribbing, Lisa narrowed her eyes mischievously. "In fact, I do not think I am mean at all, although Jerry would probably have a different opinion," she added, cuddling one of the chintz throw cushions against her stomach.

"Speaking of Jerry—or the devil, if you wish—reminds me of something I've been meaning to tell you." In response to the doorbell Anne hoisted herself to her feet and gingerly picked up the candy bowl. "I almost forgot to mention the party Lois and Steve Watson are planning for next Saturday. I promised them I would be sure to let you know."

Lisa heard the rustling of costumes and a chorus of thank-yous before Anne returned to the living room. "Sounds like fun," she commented. Disregarding her own dictum, she selected a chocolate and thoughtfully peeled away the foil wrapper.

Anne's brow knit as she inspected her lacquered nails for damage. "I think I'm going to invite Larry to come with me. I'm sure he'd love to see the work Steve and Lois have done on their house."

"Larry?"

Anne smiled a little self-consciously. "I guess I forgot to tell you about him."

"Yes, you did, but that's all right, as long as he doesn't share any of Craig's enthusiasm for wild and woolly weekends."

Anne grimaced as if Lisa's words had reopened an old wound. "None, as far as I have been able to determine after two dates. He's really a very interesting person, has a company that specializes in remodeling old houses. In fact, I met him in the drugstore while I was buying plasters for my

poor, mangled feet. He had smashed a finger while putting
in a skylight and asked me what sort of bandage I would
recommend.''

"That's nice that you two had something in common
from the very start." Lisa picked over the remaining choc-
olates, tossing aside the balled-up foil wrappers.

"Don't try to be a wise guy. By the way, you can bring a
guest along with you, if you like, you know." She dabbed a
thumbnail with more polish, not looking directly at Lisa.

"Okay."

A perplexed look spread over Anne's face as she replaced the cap on the nail polish bottle. "'Okay'? Just
'okay'? No lengthy explanations of why you won't call
Jerry? No painful soul-searching about why you might call
him after all? No veiled threats that you just might come
alone?''

"I hate to disappoint you." Lisa's smile could only be
described as smug as she tossed the cushion aside and pulled
her stockinged feet up under her. "You see, dear Anne, you
have made one fatal mistake in assessing my social life: you
automatically assume that when a male companion is
needed, I will of necessity turn to Jerry." She dropped another chocolate kiss into her mouth with dramatic flair.

"There's someone new! Someone I don't know about!"
In her excitement, Anne completely forgot about wet nails.
Her elegant hand curled into a fist and pounded the sofa
arm, demanding more details.

"New, yes, but you know about him already." Lisa
smiled coyly. Anne always knew so much about everyone's
affairs, it was going to be pure bliss to torture her.

"What *are* you talking about? I mean, you live right next
door to me; I see you almost every day, and I have noticed
nothing even remotely male anywhere in the vicinity since
the fortunate departure of Jerry McCloskey." Anne's
translucent green eyes snapped indignantly.

"I guess I'm just very discreet." Lisa grinned.

"Enough cat-and-mouse, Porter. I want a full report, on the double," Anne demanded.

"You don't want to wait and meet him Saturday?"

"No! That's for normal people."

"I took your advice, Anne." Lisa waited for the gears to begin grinding inside Anne's tousled red head. "I've started going out with Rob Randolph."

"Rob Randolph!" Anne gaped at Lisa and fell back in her seat, almost upending a bottle of polish remover. "Our little Lisa and big, mean Rob Randolph?"

"He's really a marvelous person. The more I learn about him, the better I like him." Lisa's voice softened, and the impish glint that had sparked her dark eyes suddenly vanished. Even the thought of Rob seemed to transport her into another dimension.

"And I gather the feeling is mutual?" Anne was smiling now. No amount of bantering could conceal the glimmerings of love revealed on her friend's face, and Anne was genuinely pleased at what she saw.

Lisa nodded a little shyly. "I'll risk jinxing the whole thing, but, yes, I think so. He's so remarkably tender, Anne, without any of the usual pretenses I always seem to run up against with men." She tried to restrain the dreamy smile that the vision of his deep blue gaze and rugged, tanned face prompted.

"How long has this been going on?" Anne's question bore a tinge of reproach at having been left ignorant of the exciting developments in her next-door neighbor's life.

Lisa gave her friend a brief summary of the relationship that had blossomed so unexpectedly during the past few weeks, with heavy emphasis on the lighthearted aspects. Her account of their visit to the roller rink elicited howls of laughter from Anne, and somehow Lisa was relieved that the very serious emotions she had been forced to sort through lately remained safely concealed behind this amusing anecdote. "We went out to dinner a couple of weeks ago, but actually, most of our contact has been limited to phone calls. His little girl is simply too young to fend for herself yet. But he's so thoughtful; he always manages to call even when his day has been a killer."

Lisa paused. No one, not Anne, not any other living being would ever understand how much his husky voice, filtering like a familiar melody from her phone recorder, meant to her when she finally staggered home after a long day's work. When she was too tired to eat, too tired even to look at another ungraded lab, almost too tired to sleep, his loving good-night always soothed her like warm balm. That Rob could scarcely conceal the fatigue in his own voice made his unfailing call all the more touching.

"This all sounds very nice, but I still want to get a good look at you two together, so by all means bring him with you on Saturday," Anne ordered. She slid the candy dish to her side of the end table and frowned over its dwindling contents. "I suppose he can get a baby-sitter, can't he?"

"I'm sure that will be no problem," Lisa assured her. "He just can't leave Karen with a sitter every night of the week. It wouldn't be fair to her."

"That's really tough, raising a kid by yourself. My hat's off to him if he can make time for a social life and still be around when his little girl needs him. I guess it'll get easier as she gets older." Anne chewed the chocolate thoughtfully, rolling the foil wrapper into a tight silver pellet.

"I guess it will," Lisa agreed. For some reason the exhilaration that had buoyed her when she was telling Anne about the relationship had subsided, leaving her feeling vaguely depressed. She wrote her sinking spirits off to fatigue; a ferocious day lay behind her, complete with a disastrous Biology 101 lab and a new kestrel with multiple wing fractures at the center. "I think I'm going to climb on my broomstick and head for home," she announced, reaching for her keys on the coffee table.

"It looks as if we've had our last trick-or-treater anyway. I'll turn out the porch light when you leave." Anne rose and followed her into the foyer. She held the door half-open, leaning against the frame as Lisa skipped down the steps. "Good night. And congratulations!" she hissed.

"Thanks, Anne. Sleep well," Lisa called over her shoulder. She turned to flash her a smile just before the curly red head retreated behind the door. Anne was a dear, she reflected as she let herself in the back door of her apartment; she was glad to have had the chance to share the good news about Rob with her, now that it appeared he was not just a flash in the pan. It would be fun to take him to the party, too.

Maybe she would call him tonight, she mused, stepping out of her shoes as she entered the bedroom. She certainly wasn't too tired for *that*. The feathery brush of warm fur announced Chuck's arrival, and Lisa squatted to give him a generous stroking. After a brief interlude of loud purring, the cat continued on his way, leaving his mistress sunken on her knees beside the bed.

Lisa rested her back against the bed, pulling her knees up under her chin. It was no use anticipating the party or thinking about calling Rob; a decidedly glum mood had overtaken her, one that was not going to take flight in the face of naive distractions. She had never been any good at denying her emotions, at least not to herself; she was depressed tonight, and she knew exactly why. It had only taken Anne's comments to underscore the reason. Wonderful as her relationship with Rob had been in the past weeks, the conflict between fatherhood and his own needs was ever present, even if carefully suppressed.

Lisa bit her lip, trying to fight the wave of guilt coming over her. Heaven knew she didn't begrudge the little girl her father; that young life had been shadowed by tragedy already. Karen was a very sweet, lovable child, she told herself honestly; it was impossible to resent her. But no amount of pleasant fantasies could erase the inevitable circumstances of such a relationship. Casual dropping-in was something you didn't have much time for if you had a child to feed and deliver to piano lessons and Brownie meetings.

Baby-sitters usually looked askance at staying on the job until four o'clock in the morning, so the conclusion of an evening date was pretty well defined from the start. The mere thought of spending the night together, of sharing coffee and the Sunday paper in bed the next morning was unthinkable. As Lisa pondered these unavoidable realities, an unseen force began tenaciously tugging the corners of her mouth downward.

Her unhappy musings were mercifully cut short when a short buzz, followed by two prolonged ones, sounded from the front door. Still scowling as she scrambled to her feet, she padded barefoot down the hall. "Who on earth is that? Halloween is over," she muttered with more than a trace of lingering ill temper.

Lisa squinted through the peephole; despite her earlier annoyance, her face broke into a wide grin at the sight ballooning in the wide-angle lens. A black bat about three and a half feet tall spread its shiny taffeta wings and extended a small plastic jack o'lantern toward the door. Hovering close behind the bat was a strapping six-footer of a ghost wrapped in the most clumsily designed sheet costume that Lisa had ever seen.

"What are you two doing here?" she exclaimed, throwing the door open to Karen and Rob Randolph.

"It's an old American custom," Rob explained. "We ring your doorbell, and you put candy in our bags." As he lifted the black mask that had concealed his eyes, his wide mouth relaxed into a grin.

"Come in!" Lisa commanded. She stepped back to make way for them, flipping the overhead light on in the process. The minute she saw her living room, illuminated in all its chaotic disarray, the urge to snap the light off seized her, but the Randolphs were already making themselves at home on the sofa. Neither the ghost nor his bat-child seemed at all put off by the four textbooks, empty mixed nuts canister, broken umbrella and catnip toy that took up most of the sofa's available surface.

"It's so late, I guess we should have called first, but Karen wanted to surprise you." Rob tried not to look at Lisa's bare feet as he continued, "Her school class had its Halloween party tonight, and yours truly was a chaperon."

"I'm glad you stopped by," Lisa assured him. "Karen, you'll have to give me a minute to see what I have tucked away in the kitchen for little goblins." Karen gave her an understanding nod; her attention was now focused on Chuck who had ventured onto the back of the sofa to check out the unexpected visitors. "Would the big goblin like something to drink?"

"If I can manage to drive home safely afterward." Rob's grin expanded a little wider. "Let me give you a hand." Looking like a very awkward sheik, he gathered up his sheet and followed Lisa to the kitchen.

"You know I've never actually seen much of your apartment beyond the living room. And the bedroom, once." Rob cleared his throat noisily at the memory of the night he had carried Lisa's half-sleeping form from his car to her bed. "You really have a nice, homey place." He leaned against the counter and watched her dig a Sara Lee pound cake out of the freezer.

Lisa grimaced. "What little you can see of it beneath all the mess is pretty nice." She popped the cake into the microwave and turned back to the refrigerator. "You've got a choice: apple juice or white wine."

A long arm draped in white snaked between her shoulder and the refrigerator door. Seizing the jug of wine, Rob pushed the door shut and ensnared Lisa with his free arm in one fluid motion. He spun her around, maneuvering her close enough to the counter for him to get free of the wine bottle. Then he clasped his hands behind her, rocking her playfully back and forth.

"You're in a good mood. That must have been some party tonight." Lisa smiled demurely, but her eyes sparkled with mischief. She ruffled his hair with her hand, dislodging some of the baby powder that was responsible for its ghostly cast.

"No party is any good without you." Rob's fingers dug gently into her back as if to emphasize the point.

"How do you know? We've never even been to a party together," Lisa chided. Pretending to brush away the powder that clung to his costume, she let her hands rest lightly on his shoulders. Rob's nearness, his overwhelmingly masculine presence, seemed to heighten all of her senses, and only the thought that his six-year-old daughter might scamper in on them at any minute held her back.

Rob apparently shared none of her reservations. Without further ado he let his hands slide down her hips and lifted her easily onto the counter. "That's better," he murmured in a voice so low and seductive that Lisa impulsively reached up to stroke his cheek. The faintest trace of a heavy beard tickled the skin on the back of her hand, sending prickles of excitement dancing down her spine. Rob's hands cupped her rounded hips as his lips began to nibble their way along the curve of her jaw. At the first gentle pressure of his mouth on hers, Lisa closed her eyes and surrendered herself to the magic of the moment. She was still holding her breath when he at last withdrew. Rob planted a few whisper-soft pecks on her cheeks and the tip of her nose before drawing back to regard her appreciatively.

"Karen is going to wonder where the goodies are," Lisa felt compelled to remind him, but her hands remained firmly fastened around his neck.

"Adults have a right to some goodies, too," he countered with a devilish smile, and Lisa could tell by the seductive look in those hooded blue eyes that he intended to have some more very soon.

"Lisa?" Karen's childish voice carried from the living room. "Is it okay if I watch TV?"

Steadying herself against Rob, Lisa made a jack-rabbit bound off the counter. "Sure, honey," she called with a breathless cheeriness that anyone but the most guileless child

would have found suspect. "See! What did I tell you?" she
scolded Rob in a raspy whisper. In an effort to reestablish
propriety, she tried to busy herself with the refreshments.

"That we've never been to a party together," Rob replied with boyish ingenuousness as he filched a slice of
pound cake from the plate Lisa was preparing. With cha-
meleonlike talent he had replaced the sensual expression on
his face with one of disarming innocence.

Lisa thoughtfully licked crumbs from her fingers as if a
bright idea had suddenly struck her. "That's true, and I intend to do something about that. Some friends of mine are
having a party next Saturday evening, and I thought you
might like to come." She had never felt very adept at asking a man out, not even one as unpretentious as Rob; she
managed to blurt out her invitation while rummaging
through the cupboard in search of two wineglasses.

"I'd love to." Without turning around, Lisa could feel
Rob behind her. When he began to toy with the hair bundled at the base of her neck, she felt another giddy rush
mounting within her. With the two glasses clasped stiffly
between her fingers, she had no choice but to turn and face
him, knowing full well that those smiling lips would be
waiting to capture her.

"You're missing a real scary movie," a small voice reminded them. Lisa swallowed a gasp as she caught sight of
a very large bat with dark brown pigtails standing in the
kitchen door. Its wings drooped comically as it clutched the
counter's edge and squirmed from one foot to the other.
"It's too scary to watch by myself."

"If you'll help me carry some of this stuff, we'll join
you." Lisa tried to assume a suitably prim expression. As
she handed the little girl a tumbler of apple juice she shot
Rob a look that plainly said "I told you so."

But if he felt in the least repentant, he staunchly refused
to show it. "Remind me to get a baby-sitter for Saturday"
was his only comment as the three of them trooped back to
the living room.

"I'LL BE BACK BEFORE ONE, but if you need to get in touch with me for any reason, you can reach me at one of these numbers." Rob clamped a scrap of paper to the refrigerator door with a banana-shaped magnet.

The gangly teenage girl grazing from a bag of potato chips at the kitchen counter didn't bother to remove the earphones clamped over her head; for all Rob knew, they had permanently grown into her ears. But he was in a hurry, and just watching her feet shuffle in time to an unheard beat fanned his irritation. "Okay, Leslie?" he repeated, a trifle louder.

"For sure!" Still swaying to the beat, the girl grinned, revealing a set of braces that resembled the supports on the Brooklyn Bridge.

With a quick kiss for Karen, Rob grabbed his keys and made a dash for the car. At least Karen liked this baby-sitter, he consoled himself as he glanced over his shoulder before tearing out of the driveway. The thought that his own daughter might even pass through a similar stage herself when she reached her teens was too dreadful to contemplate right now, and Rob quickly turned his thoughts to the good time that lay ahead.

Incredible as it seemed, he couldn't recall ever anticipating seeing a woman quite as much as he was now looking forward to seeing Lisa's sunny face, so full of life yet so serene, greeting him in the arched doorway of her little duplex. He could imagine her wide smile slowly stretching across her face like a ray of sunshine, could see her shake back one of the stray tendrils of honey hair that always persisted in falling across her smooth brow. And her laugh . . . He could have gone on, but after a turn at the next light he would be only a few minutes from having her in flesh and blood and all her vitality. That, unknown to him, he had coexisted in the same town with such a marvelous creature for so many lonely years seemed a lamentable waste of time. And now that he had found her, he was determined to make the most of it.

Although it was still light when Rob turned into the drive, he noticed that Lisa had already switched on the porch light. In response to a brief buzz, her light footsteps sounded on the hardwood floor.

"You're right on time," she welcomed him. Standing a little behind the door, she looked even more attractive than in his imaginings. She was dressed in taupe gabardine slacks and matching silk blouse with a wide leather sash that called attention to her tiny waist and pleasantly curved hips.

Rob seized the edge of the door, leaning around to plant a kiss on her lips. "You look terrific," he commented in a low voice. "Especially up close." He added an extra kiss on her forehead to emphasize that point.

Lisa returned his kiss before gently pushing herself away from the door. "I'll just fetch my bag, and we can get going."

The thought that he would actually prefer to spend the evening cuddled up with her in her cozy apartment was one that Rob had manfully put aside by the time she returned with a burgundy suede bag slung over her shoulder. As he opened the door of the Mercedes for her, he sternly reminded himself that he had really been looking forward to the party until her captivating little form had set his imagination running back there in the hallway.

"Any problems getting a baby-sitter?" Lisa asked after giving him directions to the Watsons' house.

"None. One my law partners has a teenage daughter who was free for the evening. She's a pretty reliable kid, although you might have some doubts if you saw her. God, to think how hard I worked to put together those Halloween costumes for us, and this kid manages to come up with weirder clothes every time I see her."

"The important thing is how she interacts with Karen," Lisa reminded him.

Rob frowned into the rearview mirror before signaling a turn. He had hoped that his juggling act with Mrs. Elliott and the assorted baby-sitters he employed had somehow escaped Lisa's attention, but apparently it had not. It was bad enough that he had to wrestle with his own divided responsibilities without troubling her.

"How's Randolph doing these days?" he asked, eager to change the subject.

"I'm almost afraid to say so, but I think he's coming along better than I actually expected. I've been manipulating his wing for him, regularly, and he's already regained a wider range of motion. Let's just keep our fingers crossed." Lisa leaned toward the dash and pointed. "Their house is the rock-and-shingle bungalow on the left."

Rob managed to squeeze the car into one of the few available parking places on the block. Before he could clamber around to the passenger's side, a redheaded woman dressed in a slinky emerald-green jump suit had bounded down the rock walkway and flung open the door.

"Hey, Lisa! I'm so glad you could make it," she exclaimed, almost dragging her quarry out of the front seat.

Lisa settled a steady hand on the redhead's arm. "Anne Torrence. Rob Randolph." She nodded to each of her companions in turn.

"I bet you know Malcolm Walker," Anne bubbled to Rob, giving his hand the sort of shake usually reserved for slot machines. "I'm his legal assistant."

Rob smiled and nodded, but before he could think of a witty comment to make about the portly, combative Walker, Anne was herding them around the house to a torch-lit patio. Somehow he had been expecting a small, casual gathering, but when they entered the glassed-in sun room adjoining the patio, he found himself surrounded by a throng of well-dressed guests. Fortunately, Anne seemed blessed with a bouncy personality to match her redheaded pixie's good looks; she wasted no time in hailing their host and hostess and making the necessary introductions. As she led them to the wet bar, her eyes continued to scan the crowd. She looked relieved when an agreeable-looking man with sandy hair and a neatly-trimmed mustache to match waved to them from the sun room door.

"Larry O'Neil," he volunteered. His right hand—swathed in a cumbersome white bandage—was thrust out before he even reached the bar. "Annie, you didn't tell me what a terrific attic Steve and Lois had," he chided Anne after exchanging minimal pleasantries with Rob and Lisa.

Anne looked nonplussed. "To be honest, I didn't know they even had one, but if you say it's terrific, I'll take your word for it."

"I just took a look up there. It would make an ideal loft, you know, for a study or an extra bedroom. Or you could knock out the ceiling here." He rolled his eyes heavenward, gesturing with his cocktail glass. "That would give this whole room incredible drama."

"I think razing the roof might be a little too dramatic for tonight, okay?" Anne tried to look perturbed, but broke into a grin when Larry latched a long arm around her shoulders. She shrugged helplessly as he led her off in the direction of the buffet.

"Anne told me that Larry renovates houses." Lisa seemed to feel obligated to provide an explanation.

Rob nodded. "Do you know many of these people?" He bent over Lisa to whisper in her ear while they wandered around the crowded room.

She shook her head, tickling his nose with the strands of hair curling around her ear. "A few." In the muted, indirect light, her soft brown eyes glowed warm and golden as they swept the crowd.

"Lisa? Lisa Porter?" An incredulous voice boomed from across the buffet table. Rob and Lisa both swung around to face a short, flushed man ambling toward them. He was clutching a beer bottle to his chest as if it were a teddy bear.

"Oh, hi, Hamp," Lisa said coolly, and Rob didn't have to be too astute to detect a slight strain dampening her smile.

Hamp spread one hand on the table to steady himself; his bleary eyes seemed to be having difficulty focusing, but he managed to give Lisa a crooked smile. Although his college years were a good twenty years behind him, he reminded Rob of a certain type of fraternity man he had always tried to avoid when he had been a student. "Well, tell me. Where's ol' Jerry?" Hamp's thickened tongue had a hard time getting the *l*'s out.

"I'm not keeping tabs on him these days," Lisa replied a little tartly. Out of the corner of his eye Rob saw her lips tighten although she still maintained a resolutely polite smile. "How have you been?" she asked in a transparent attempt to move the conversation in another direction.

Hamp ignored her ploy. "Jeez, I almost didn't recognize you without Jerry." Consternation wrinkled his jowly face, and he squinted at the beer bottle in his hand as if he hoped to find some news of Jerry in its sudsy contents.

Seeing what was threatening to happen, Rob sidled closer to Lisa and, ignoring Hamp entirely, dropped a more-than-friendly arm around her shoulders. "Say, don't I know you from somewhere? You were skiing last January in Vail, right? No, now I remember!" His handsome face brightened, and he clicked his old-fashioned glass against her wine goblet. "It was in Palm Beach!"

Lisa looked startled for a minute, but not as startled as Hamp, who swayed slightly as he looked up at Rob. Quickly picking up the game, she wrinkled her nose and snuggled into Rob's embrace as she said in a kittenish voice, "Wrong again. Does the name Aristo Cruises ring a bell? You can't have forgotten the ship captain's costume party?" Her sensuous mouth feigned a charming pout. "You have a short memory."

"I'll never forget that moonlight dip in the pool." Rob's eyes swam dreamily in pretended recollection of the tantalizing memory as he skillfully turned Lisa away from the buffet—and from Hamp. The dull sound of an empty beer bottle dropping onto the table followed them across the room.

"I didn't dare look back, but I wish I could have seen his face!" Lisa giggled uncontrollably when they were finally out of Hamp's range of vision. "You were absolutely masterful!"

"You learn to think on your feet in court." Rob rocked back on his heels, his hands clutched modestly behind him.

"Hampton is such a boor." Lisa shook her head, but she was still laughing over the joke they had played. "Every time I'm unlucky enough to run into him, he seems to have a beer bottle in his hand. It's his security blanket, I guess. Ever since Jerry and he worked together at the same ad agency, Hamp has pretended that they're good friends, but Jerry can't tolerate him." She cut a glance at Rob, who was nodding with interest. "In case you're wondering, Jerry is a man I used to date."

"I sort of figured that one out already."

Lisa licked her lips, trying to tame the uproarious grin twisting her lips. "Yeah. Well, we, uh, we broke up several months ago."

"I sort of figured that out, too."

"You're pretty good at figuring things out," Lisa teased. "No telling what other conclusions you've drawn."

Rob gave one of the stray wisps at her temple a gentle tug. "Let's see," he began, but at that moment Lois Watson shouldered her way up to them.

"Ready to eat?" she asked brightly. Not waiting for an answer, she herded them to the tables nested around the built-in gas grill. "Rare steaks on that platter; these are medium, and the black things down there are well done. Just help yourselves, and don't forget the bar's still open," she instructed them gaily before flitting off to round up other guests.

As they moved around the tables Anne interrupted them over a casserole of baked beans. "Has either of you seen Larry?" she asked.

Lisa shook her head. "The last time I saw him he was with Steve, but you need to find him so we can all eat together. We'll be in the dining room."

Anne frowned, hands braced on her slim hips. "Save us a place" was all she said before marching off across the room.

"I don't care if it is supposed to be an informal affair, I like the looks of those chairs," Lisa remarked as she led the way into the bungalow's deserted dining room.

"So do I," Rob agreed. He also liked the idea of getting away from the crowd for a while, just the two of them.

Lisa smiled warmly at his enthusiastic reply. She was so lovely, it was pointless to apply superlatives to her beauty. But tonight she seemed to glow with a new radiance, as if her sophisticated clothing and the convivial party atmosphere had allowed another aspect of her complex personality to come into play.

"I guess Anne and Larry decided to eat somewhere else," Lisa remarked when they had finished dinner and were lingering over their wine. "I don't suppose we're very good guests, hiding out here all by ourselves."

"No, I don't suppose we are," Rob agreed with a placid smile that said he intended to do nothing to correct matters, either.

Lisa leaned an elbow on the table. She was so close to him he could smell the sweet fragrance of her cascading hair, feel the warmth emanating from her body. He was about to part the thick hair obscuring her face, with the intention of kissing the mouth so tantalizing concealed from him, when an exasperated voice abruptly interrupted his fantasy.

"See, Larry, they're already finished." Dinner plate balanced on one hand, Anne Torrence gestured dramatically toward Lisa and Rob with the steak knife she held in the other.

"I'm glad you didn't wait for us," Larry O'Neill told them. As he seated himself at the table, he looked a little sheepish, like a tardy kid on the first day of school. Rob thought he detected a film of cobwebs clinging to the top of his sandy head.

"I don't know why you and Steve had to go poking around in the attic right when dinner was being served." Anne was sawing furiously on her steak, her pert mouth set in a distressed line.

"Steve wanted me to look at his joists," Larry contented, managing to sound both offended and repentant at the same time.

Lisa exchanged a knowing look with Rob. "I think we're going to get some dessert," she announced. "We'll catch you later." When they were back in the sun room, she leaned her head close to Rob's ear. "Poor Anne! I know she was really looking forward to having an enjoyable evening with Larry."

"I'm sure they'll work things out before the night is over. But for now I am solely concerned with your wishes." Rob looked down at the burnished gold hair billowing over his shoulder. "What would you like to do? Stay a bit longer and have some dessert, or shall we head homeward?"

Lisa thought for only a moment. "Let's go," she said softly. Her small, strong hand found his and clasped it firmly.

They relinquished each other's hands long enough to thank the Watsons for their hospitality, but when they were alone again on the front walk, Rob did not hesitate to encircle Lisa's shoulders with his arm, leading her to the waiting car.

"That was a good party tonight, wasn't it?" He glanced at Lisa as he steered the car away from the curb. The streetlight cast a pale glow over her face, throwing her full, dewy lips and short, straight nose into delicate relief.

"Uh-huh," she murmured, sliding comfortably down into the leather upholstered seat.

Rob's free hand crept along the front seat until it found hers; enclosing her small hand in his grasp he stroked the cool, slim fingers tenderly. They rode along without speaking, just enjoying the stillness of the empty streets and the solitude they shared in the car. Even after he had turned into Lisa's drive and shut the motor off, he did not relinquish his hold on her.

"Do you have time for a nightcap?" Her voice scarcely rose above a whisper, and he could feel her fingers curl around his as she spoke.

"I'll make time." Only the promise of a brandy shared with her could persuade him to free the hand he held.

In the living room Lisa paused only long enough to switch on a table lamp before heading for the kitchen. Rob had just flicked the three-way bulb back to its softest level when she reappeared with a bottle of Grand Marnier and two glasses.

"I'm really glad you could make it tonight. I wouldn't have begun to enjoy the party half as much without you." Lisa handed Rob a glass of mellow amber liquid, letting her fingers caress his like an elusive butterfly.

Rob hesitated before speaking, testing the words taking shape in his mind like the warm, sweet liqueur on his tongue. "I don't care which restaurants or parties we go to; I'm just happy I met you. That's all that's important to me." He watched her over the rim of his glass, sensitive to any sign of hesitancy, but the gaze of her large brown eyes did not waver. Perhaps it was the effect of the drink, but Rob felt his senses sharpen, as if his body could actually feel her barely audible breathing, feel the heady warmth emanating from her, flavored with the delicate floral perfume she wore. His eyes didn't stray from her lovely face as he slid the glass onto the edge of the end table and then gently took hers from her unresisting grasp.

The passion that had been simmering somewhere beneath the surface suddenly flared with an urgency that Rob could not remember ever having experienced before. This woman with her tenderly beautiful face, her dark, liquid eyes, her taut, nubile body beckoned to him in a way that words could not express.

"Oh, Rob," he heard her murmur softly, but Rob didn't take his eyes from the small hand he held. As if discovering those strong yet delicate fingers for the first time, he carefully kissed the tip of each one before moving on to the palms, then her wrists. Only as he slowly worked his lips along the soft curve of her arm did their eyes meet. Her moist lips moved, forming silent words; her hands, now free from his mouth's probing, traveled up his back. The strength with which she gripped his head, digging her fingers deep into his hair, told him clearly what she had been unable to speak. She wanted him, he dared think, as much as he wanted her. Still clasping his head, Lisa stretched back on the sofa, pulling him gently down with her.

"You're beautiful, Lisa, incredibly beautiful," Rob whispered when his mouth brushed her ear. She responded with a pleased sigh as she kissed his chin and then nuzzled into the warm cleft below his jaw.

If a malicious spectator had chosen that moment to pitch a bucket of cold water over the entwined lovers, it would not have been any more unsettling than the abrupt telephone buzzer that rudely intruded on them.

Rob could feel Lisa's body tense inadvertently, and on the third ring he lifted his mouth from hers long enough to mutter, "I thought the damned answering machine was turned on!"

With one arm still thrown around his back, Lisa propped herself on one elbow. "I left it off in case the baby-sitter needed to get through," she explained in a voice equally weighted with concern and annoyance.

The baby-sitter! Rob had so completely lost himself there on the sofa, had allowed the pleasure of being with Lisa to transport him so far from his normal, mundane concerns that he had entirely forgotten the gum-chewing New Wave kid keeping watch over Karen. As he jumped up from the sofa, he glanced at his watch. It was two o'clock in the morning! "Damn it!" Rob spat the words furiously before jerking the receiver up to his ear.

"Mr. Randolph? Mr. Randolph! Boy, am I glad to find you! This is Leslie. Listen, my dad just called, and he's on his way over here to pick me up 'cause he says I can't stay out any longer. He says he'll wait here until you get home, so don't worry 'bout Karen, but he told me to call you and find out—"

"I'm on my way, Leslie," Rob interrupted. "I just lost track of the time, but I'll be right there. Sorry if I caused any problems." He had to swallow his irritation to choke out the last sentence. He heard "No problem, Mr. Randolph" pipe from the receiver just before he let it drop onto the phone's cradle.

If Rob had ever felt as miserable as he did standing there staring at the phone with his hands hanging helplessly at his sides, time had mercifully erased the memory. When he finally dared to look at Lisa, she had already tidied and smoothed and buttoned herself back into the woman he had squired to the party several hours ago. "I have to go, Lisa." He almost gagged on the words, as he gave a halfhearted tug to his tie that her skillful hands had loosened only minutes earlier.

"I know," Lisa said quietly. Her voice bore no trace of rancor, but the brave little smile that quivered precariously on her lips said it all.

"I'm sorry," he began. Good God, he couldn't just go running out the door without saying *something* after the emotions he had experienced with her on the sofa.

But Lisa was now determined to conclude the evening as expeditiously as possible. The firm pressure of her arm at his waist as she led him to the door, the artificially cheerful expression she somehow held on her face, even her quick, nervous gestures as she unbolted the door told him that she was having difficulty mastering her emotions and wanted to be alone.

"Good night, Lisa." Rob started to kiss her again as they stood in the doorway, but the look in her eyes when he leaned toward her brought him up short.

''Good night, Rob,'' she said, and Rob imagined her lips trembled slightly on the words.

Rob walked slowly down the steps. When he reached the car he looked back, planning to throw her a wave. But the door was closed, the windows were dark and Lisa had vanished from sight.

Chapter Six

A horn squawked sharply from the driveway, freezing Lisa with one hand thrust inside her mailbox. Her face knotted into a scowl as she recovered herself and looked up to see who was pestering her.

"Hey, Lisa!" Anne Torrence was battling with her pencil-slim straight skirt as she emerged from behind the wheel of the Toyota hatchback.

"Hi, Anne." Lisa smiled briefly before returning to the handful of mail she had retrieved from the box. She was sorting through the abundance of "occupant" flyers when Anne staggered up the walkway, burdened with a bag of groceries and a bulging briefcase.

"If I hadn't noticed your lights going on and off this week, I would have asked the police to put out a dragnet for you. Where the hell have you been hiding?" the redhead demanded.

"I've been really busy," Lisa countered, slapping the mailbox lid shut. As she turned to open her door she could see that Anne had every intention of following her into the apartment.

Two navy blue pumps went sliding across the hardwood floor as Anne kicked her shoes off. Dropping the groceries onto the coffee table, she threw the briefcase on the sofa and, sitting stiffly, clutched her lower back. "Am I ever tried! Hope you don't mind if I just flop here for a sec, but somehow I can relax a little better at your place than at home. It always looks so much cleaner.''

"You need to get glasses," Lisa commented drily, dumping her mail onto the end table. She wadded a supermarket flyer into a ball and slam-dunked it into the wastebasket.

"I'd rather get a car." Anne stretched across the arm of the sofa to impart a loving pat onto Chuck's furry back. "Do you think I should get a cat, Lisa?"

"If you want one," Lisa mumbled, impatiently ripping open a business-size envelope.

"Boy, are we in a rotten mood or what?" Anne folded her arms across her chest and surveyed her friend with a critical eye.

"I'm sorry, Anne," Lisa apologized. "I've just had a hectic day. Would you like a glass of wine?" she asked in a more hospitable tone.

"Please." Anne accepted cordially. She idly flipped a magazine while the fingers of one hand plied kinks from her neck. "Cheer up, woman. At least you have Rob around to take your mind off sick birds and gawky freshmen who don't know an amoeba from a rhinoceros. You *could* be teamed up with a guy like Larry, you know. As if crawling around in that dusty attic weren't bad enough, he insisted on showing Steve how he could hook a deck onto the kitchen. Here were these two grown men stumbling around in the backyard in the middle of the night. Lois told me she nearly had a fit when she looked out the next morning and found her herb garden trampled into oblivion...." Her singsong litany of Larry's transgressions died as she glimpsed Lisa glowering in the doorway with a wineglass in each hand. "Uh-oh. Please, *please*, just tell me nothing's gone wrong with Rob Randolph. Just let me believe that occasionally things do work out with men. Please!"

Lisa interrupted Anne's histrionics. "There's nothing wrong with Rob," she said through unusually tight lips. "We're just experiencing a clash of life-styles, that's all. I'm not to blame; he's not to blame." The matter-of-fact way she presented the issue was a dead giveaway that she had spent hours mulling it over.

"His little girl is the problem, right?"

Lisa did not answer, but when she deposited a glass of wine at her friend's elbow, Anne seized the opportunity to look up into her face. "Yep. I thought so," she insisted, a trifle archly for Lisa's irritable frame of mind. "Well, Lis, you're just going to have to confront the problem head on, This isn't something two people in love can't work through, you know." She tipped her wineglass knowingly in Lisa's direction.

"I'm sure you're right. Too bad we're not in love, isn't it?" Lisa snapped.

Anne let her arm fall across the back of the sofa in a gesture of supreme weariness. "Lisa, you are a woman of many facets, but the hard-hearted type is one number you can't play worth a damn. I had a chance to observe you two last Saturday; he couldn't take his eyes off of you, and you were just as bad. If that's not what falling in love looks like, then it's a good enough imitation that I would settle for in a flash. So let's not have any of this studied indifference, okay?" Anne had roused herself from her slumped position long enough to deliver this speech; now she sank back, spent from the effort.

Lisa ran a finger around the rim of her glass. Anne was right, of course. She was anything but indifferent to Rob, and, as far as being in love was concerned, her extreme touchiness on the subject seemed rather suspicious, even to herself. "Don't misunderstand me, Anne. I like Karen a lot, and I've really enjoyed the time I've spent with her. But I want a woman-to-man relationship with Rob, and that means being alone without Karen some of the time. I know it must be awfully hard for him, but..." She bit her lip as if to check any further complaints before they were spoken.

"Sure it's hard for him, but it's not impossible. You both have a right to time together. Alone. Without the little girl. And the first thing you need to do is quit feeling guilty about wanting that. If Randolph is scared to death that he's going to scar his kid for life by leaving her with a sitter now and then, all the more reason for you to take the lead.''

"I can't tell him how to raise his child," Lisa pointed out.

"That's not what I'm talking about, and you know it. I bet you haven't mentioned any of this to him, have you?" Anne jabbed the air accusatively with a long burgundy red nail. When Lisa shook her head, she continued triumphantly, "There, you see! Discuss it; bring it out into the open. I can guarantee you, the one person who's not going to lose any sleep over a few nights with baby-sitters is Karen. While you two adults are muddling around with your forbearance and self-sacrifice, that kid would probably look forward to an occasional evening in front of the tube with a bowl of popcorn and someone closer to her own age.''

Lisa couldn't help laughing. "You're right, Anne. Maybe I'll breach the topic on Sunday. It's my weekend off from the center, and Sam and Ellie have invited Rob and me to have dinner at their place. I could bring this ticklish subject up afterward.''

"There you go. And now that we've settled that one, I think I'll just have another tot o' grog, if you don't mind.'' Anne wrenched the creeping skirt down and rose stiffly.

"Help yourself," Lisa called, turning back to her mail.

When Anne returned with the wine jug in hand, she found Lisa smiling over a postcard. As she bent to refill her friend's glass a low whistle escaped her lips. "Who do you know that's sending you cards from Capri?''

"My mother!" Lisa chuckled, shaking her head over the message scrawled on the back of the card in an extravagant, looping handwriting. "Sometimes I don't believe this lady's escapades. Listen to this. 'Was in Milan for next year's summer collection and thought I would drop down to this gorgeous'—that's in caps—'resort for a few days.' I want you to meet Mom someday, if she ever slows down enough to come to Charlotte. You two remind me a lot of each other.''

Anne picked up the postcard as Lisa opened another letter. "Just 'drop down' to Capri. I'll have to remember that one the next time I'm marooned on Park Road in rush-hour traffic."

"Oh, dear," Lisa sighed as she read from a neatly creased sheet of typing paper.

"What now?"

"Dad has written to ask if I'm coming up to Lynchburg for Thanksgiving."

"Why didn't he just call?"

"He says he knew I'd want to think it over, and that's why he didn't mention it the last time we talked. I feel like such a meany sometimes, but I really can't help it that I've never warmed up to Lucille. And Dad always acts so hurt if I don't spend a holiday with them; I can tell he thinks it's because of Lucille."

Anne rolled her eyes up to the ceiling. "What started out as a nice, calming drink together after work has turned into a guiltfest. Look, Lisa, tell your dad that you don't have anything against his second wife, but she's not your mother. That still doesn't change things between you and him." Anne paused and took a big gulp. She eyed the half-empty glass as if she wished it contained something more potent than white wine before continuing, "And tell Rob Randolph that you want a guarantee of some time for just the two of you."

"I guess I have my orders, Sergeant Torrence." Lisa's mouth drew into a lopsided smile.

"You bet," Anne shot back before draining her glass.

IF THE MATTER WITH ROB could not be resolved as simply as Anne implied, Lisa still had to agree that her pitch for an open discussion had been very persuasive. Rob suffered from the constant push-pull of his divided responsibilities, of that she was certain; as for herself, Lisa knew she would be unwilling to undergo very many repeats of last Saturday night's conclusion. By Sunday she was thoroughly convinced that they only needed to discuss their relationship in a mature, open fashion in order to work out an acceptable compromise.

"He'll be relieved when I bring it up," she told herself for the umpteenth time as she wove her hair into an attractive row of braids. Stabbing a bobby pin into the thick coil bridging her head, she checked the bedside clock reflected in the dresser mirror. Nine-thirty, early enough for her to have another cup of coffee and skim over the Sunday paper.

Curled up on the sofa with Chuck and the *Charlotte Observer* Lisa was reminded of her as-yet undecided plans for Thanksgiving when the phone rang. This was probably her dad now, she thought, scouring her brain for excuses with one hand poised on the receiver.

She started when, instead of Paul Porter's slow Tidewater drawl, Rob's voice greeted her. "Lisa, I hope I didn't get you out of the shower." Judging from the way he hesitated over that feeble opener, she knew that whatever was coming couldn't be good.

"No, I'm already dressed and ready to go." She waited for Rob to go on.

"Look, I hate like the devil to change our plans so suddenly, but I'm afraid I'm not going to be able to have dinner at the Wheatons. Karen is awfully sick; I've been up all night with her." He paused, giving Lisa the chance to commiserate, but she rewarded him with a stony silence. "I think it's just a case of mumps, but a pal of mine who's an M.D. promised he'd stop by this afternoon to have a look at her."

"That's too bad, Rob." Lisa swallowed slowly. This was her chance to show him how wonderful and understanding and supportive she was. *Of course I don't mind! Don't be silly; we can have dinner with Sam and Ellie anytime. Is there anything I can do to help?* But try as she might, Lisa couldn't force a single regret into words. "I hope she gets better soon" was the best she could manage.

"Lisa, I'm really sorry..." Rob began.

"Why? You couldn't help that she happened to come down with mumps this weekend." *The one weekend in the month that I have completely free.* "I'll talk to you later, okay?" Her exaggeratedly upbeat tone made her words ring all the more hollow.

"Tell your friends I'm sorry about this." Rob's dejected voice gave his parting comment the sound of a deathbed request.

"Sure." Lisa replaced the phone in its cradle and folded her hands in her lap. So much for Anne's squadron of baby-sitters. *What about the times a child is sick, Anne? You forgot about that,* Lisa thought spitefully and instantly repented her bad temper. The creeping certainty that she had thoroughly conveyed her disappointment to Rob on the phone added to her guilt pangs. She shouldn't have been so curt with him, especially since he must have felt every bit as lousy as she did. The phone was still within reach; she could call him back. But what could she honestly say? That she didn't mind being squeezed into his schedule whenever his six-year-old daughter didn't need him? The fear that another phone call would end even more unsatisfactorily than the last prompted her to leave well enough alone.

By the time she was driving toward the Wheatons' Lake Norman home, she had talked herself into enjoying the rest of the day or to die trying. But when the retired couple's expectant faces fell as she climbed out of the Chevette alone, she knew that having a good time today was only so much wishful thinking.

"Rob's little girl came down with mumps." Eager to get the necessary explanations out of the way, Lisa made her announcement from the driveway.

"What a shame!" Ellie's gentle gray eyes blinked sympathetically from behind her bifocals. "We were really looking forward to meeting him."

"It's just one of those things," Lisa muttered as she followed the Wheatons into their spacious paneled den.

She hesitated in the doorway. Sam had mentioned that their son and daughter-in-law would be coming, but she was not expecting the six people who looked up from the televised football game as she made her entry. It was what Anne would have described as a "Noah's Ark affair," everyone securely mated off with a member of the opposite sex. Everyone except herself. After mumbling a greeting to Terri Parker, whom she knew as a fellow center volunteer, Lisa nodded in response to Sam's introductions and headed for a captain's chair in the corner.

"I thought you were going to bring Rob," Marilyn, the Wheatons' daughter-in-law, asked, letting her eyes stray from the television screen for only a split second.

"He had to stay home with his little girl when she got sick," Ellie explained before Lisa could answer. Lisa hoped everyone in the room had heard so she would be spared further inquiries, but when they trooped into the dining room Ellie's haste to clear away the extra place setting reminded her once again that her plans had gone afoul.

She would try to concentrate on the delicious meal of smoked ham and fresh vegetables her hostess had prepared, try to join in the small talk around the table. She had come out here to relax and enjoy herself, not to brood over Rob, she told herself with the same grim resolution she relied on to change a flat tire or tell a student he was failing.

"Visiting you two is like taking a vacation," Terri Parker commented as she scooped another portion of candied yams onto her plate. "Speaking of vacations, did I forget to mention that Rick and I went to Edisto last month? We had a terrific time, didn't we, Rick?"

"Sure did," the square-shouldered young man seated next to her mumbled through a mouthful of ham.

Terri passed the yam dish to Lisa. "You and your friend ought to look into Edisto the next time you're in the mood to get away for a weekend."

Lisa smiled wanly and poked at the yams. "Maybe we will." *In twelve years or so, after Karen is off at college.*

Lisa knew she needed to snap out of it, but her spirits had not risen appreciably by the time Sam helped himself to the last slice of black bottom pie and Ellie circled the table a second time with the coffeepot. When everyone roared approval at Sam's suggestion of a walk along the lake, she was only too glad to volunteer her services in the kitchen with Ellie.

"You're sure you don't want to join the others?" the petite, gray-haired woman asked her as she pulled another apron from a drawer.

Lisa shook her head over the slices of ham she was piling into a plastic container. "I'd rather help you," she said with the most genuine smile she'd mustered all day.

"Something is on your mind, isn't it, honey?" Ellie asked. Her back was to Lisa as she bent over the sink, but Lisa could imagine the look of motherly concern clouding her face.

"Yes." Lisa sighed, wishing that her moods weren't so transparent. "Does it show that much?"

"You've been mighty quiet today." Ellie turned and began thoughtfully pulling on a pair of yellow rubber gloves.

"I just keep wishing Rob were here. If this were the only time we'd been forced to change our plans, I wouldn't mind so much, but it isn't. I'm beginning to think I just don't have what it takes to deal with a man who's someone's father, as well." Lisa hadn't intended to blurt out so much of her frustration, but it was pointless to repent her candor now.

"I don't know this young man," Ellie began after several moments' silent consideration, "but I'd be pretty surprised if he weren't having the same feelings right now. He's got to be father and mother to his little girl, even when he'd rather be with you. You might say he's torn between two kinds of love, the kind he has as a parent and the kind he has for you." She lifted a yellow rubber hand to ward off Lisa's protest. "But unless I'm dead wrong, he'll come through if you give him a chance."

"I care more for him than for any man I've ever known, Ellie," Lisa almost whispered. "I'm willing to do all I can to make things work, but a relationship on these terms isn't doing either of us much good."

Ellie smiled gently. "Just give it time. Patience is something you learn by the time you're my age. And don't think for a moment you won't have trouble juggling responsibilities after you're married, but it's worth it. It surely is worth it."

Lisa opened her mouth to speak but just as quickly closed it. It was one thing to wrestle with the complexities of her relationship with Rob, but the cavalier manner in which Ellie mentioned marriage had taken her totally by surprise. Marriage? To Rob? Lisa wasn't sure she was ready even to think about that possibility, and she was considerably less sure she wanted to be catapulted into overnight motherhood. But she knew Ellie would be unfazed by any protestations on her part, and she had appreciated the older woman's thoughtful counsel.

"Thanks, Ellie" was all she said in response to the gentle pat that Ellie gave her hand.

"I OWE YOU ONE, CLARK." Rob ran his fingers through his tousled dark hair.

"I'll remember that if anyone ever tries to sue me." The stocky man dressed in a dark blue warm-up suit chuckled as he leaned over the foyer credenza and quickly jotted a note on his pad. "Here's a prescription. You probably won't have much trouble keeping her in bed for the next few days, but our young lady should start to perk up pretty quickly. Her throat is going to be sore for a while, but that's the worst you can generally expect from mumps. Call me if you have any questions." He grinned, fumbling with his jacket zipper.

"Thanks again, Clark." Rob waved to the amiable doctor's retreating figure before quietly closing the door. On tiptoe he climbed the stairs and carefully stole a peek through Karen's half-open door. A night-light in the shape of a clown's grinning mask cast a dim glow next to the dresser, just enough illumination for him to see that Karen was sleeping now. Her usually rosy cheeks looked painfully swollen against the colorful print pillowcase, but her breathing was even, and she didn't stir as he stepped into the dark hall. "Sleep well, angel," he whispered outside the door before dragging his fatigue racked body into the master bedroom.

He could certainly use some sleep himself, he thought. Karen's fever had come up around midnight, and since then he hadn't relaxed for more than a few minutes. Rob collapsed onto the bolsters of the king-size bed, too tired even to remove his shoes. He stared, numbly and without focusing, around the untidy room until his eyes fell on the portrait of Sylvia. It was almost as if she were watching him, smiling that same competent smile she had bestowed on Papa and beaux and photographers alike. More frequently than any remnant of Sylvia that Rob carried in his memory, her triumphant, self-assured smile came most readily to mind. Sylvia rising from the piano bench to regard her awestruck audience, Sylvia springing from her mount after another flawless round in the show ring, Sylvia basking in the appreciative looks she garnered on the country club dance floor. And now that smile reminded him without remorse of his inadequacies as a parent.

Unable to take his eyes off the picture, Rob sifted through his memories of the time they had spent together. Sylvia had continued to smile after they were married. And why not? Rob's career had taken off like a meteor, and she had effortlessly assumed the role of young society matron, hostessing chic parties and taking an active part in the Junior League. To everyone, their's must have seemed the perfect marriage.

She had been a good mother; Rob was careful to remember that. But somehow she never seemed to give him what he wanted most from her, and her cool perfection prevented him from ever asking. Perhaps he had feared that any attempts at infusing their match with more warmth would have earned him only another one of her smiles. What would have become of their marriage in later years was something about which Rob never allowed himself to speculate; whatever the case, it was too late now to do anything differently.

Rob rolled irritably onto his stomach and tried to pummel the firm bolster into a normal, yielding pillow. At least he could turn his back on Sylvia's maddeningly confident portrait; his persistent thoughts of Lisa Porter were another matter altogether. Not that he wished to compare Lisa with Sylvia. Although she was beautiful and professionally successful, her warm and generous temperament rendered her approachable and infinitely appealing. He wondered if she had any inkling of how much she had given him during the few weeks since they had met, of how integral a part of his life she had become. Probably not, if she considered the way he had treated her as a reliable basis.

"Damn it all!" Rob coughed the angry words into the hard cushion. He had been granted a reprieve from his loneliness, finally met someone whom he could really love, and he had ruined it. His fist clenched beneath the bolster as he thought of all the times he had thought things were too hectic to meet her for a drink. He had put the demands of business associates and baby-sitters and the PTA ahead of Lisa; no wonder she had sounded so disgusted when he had broken their date that morning. He wouldn't be surprised if she never wanted to see him again; he certainly wouldn't blame her.

Not lifting his head from the uncomfortable bolster, Rob snapped the nightstand lamp off and waited for sleep to unburden his troubled mind.

THERE WERE FEW CARS traveling Providence Road on Sunday evening, something for which a driver trying to locate an unfamiliar side street could be thankful. Lisa shifted the car into second and strained to read the silver numbers angled across a sandblasted brick gatepost; she smiled in the darkness when the numbers tallied with those scribbled in her address book.

It seemed strange to be following the long graveled drive up to Rob's house, strange to be visiting, for the very first time, the home of a man whom she had been seeing for nearly six weeks. Theirs had been a haphazard affair, she reflected, but if the attraction had flourished under such trying circumstances, it must be more than a passing infatuation. At least, she was going to operate on that assumption.

The sprawling contemporary home was even more impressive than she had expected. Several strategically placed floodlights revealed a dramatic glass wall on one side of the house; a second-story deck was just visible through the magnolias flanking the house. When Lisa climbed out of the car, she almost expected a pack of barking guard dogs to appear suddenly out of nowhere, but the only sound was the muted crunch of gravel beneath her feet as she approached the front door.

Lisa had to depress the buzzer four times before arousing any signs of life inside the house. When the yellow porch light at last glimmered on, it occurred to her that perhaps this impromptu visit had not been such a good idea after all. The buzzer had probably awakened Karen, and Rob would be out of sorts.

But the haggard face that appeared in the doorway was anything but ill-tempered. "Lisa!" Rob exclaimed. "What are you doing here?"

"I came to see how Karen is doing and—" she ceremoniously swept a brown paper bag from behind her back "—to bring you both some homemade bread and jam, courtesy of Ellie Wheaton."

"Don't just stand there! Come in!" Rob shuffled clumsily back from the door, raking a hand across his uncombed hair.

"Thanks," Lisa said with an impish grin. Rob took the bag while she unbuttoned her jacket, and she couldn't help but think how comical he looked, standing there fully dressed but in his stockinged feet, with a look of rapt amazement on his face. "I'll only stay a minute," she promised him.

"Oh, no! I mean, yes, please stay. More than a minute." Hitching the bag under one arm, he met her grin. "C'mon. Let's take this out to the kitchen. I'll offer you a cup of coffee if it won't keep you awake all night."

"My system thinks caffeine is a sedative," she assured him with a giggle. Their soft laughter sounded almost boisterous in the hushed tiled corridor leading to the rear of the house.

"I've got instant, instant and instant," Rob announced sheepishly as he placed three flavored coffee mixes on the butcher-block counter.

"I'll take...that one." Lisa closed her eyes and pointed to one of the canisters. When she opened them again, Rob was already placing a copper kettle on the big six-burner range.

While she watched he slid two white mugs across the counter and began to count out spoons of powdered mocha. "Lisa, about today—" he hesitated, not taking his eyes off the mugs "—I'm really sorry."

"Shh!" Lisa leaned across the counter and placed two fingers on his lips. "There's nothing to be sorry about. Except that I was such a bear."

"You had every right to be upset. God knows my excuses are always getting in the way."

"A sick child is not a lame excuse, and I'm really ashamed of myself, acting like a big, spoiled baby." Lisa felt Rob's lips form a kiss on her fingertips; she was sure she would have thrown her arms around him if the jet of steam spurting from the kettle hadn't demanded his attention just that minute.

"How is she doing?" she asked as he filled the cups with hot water.

"Fine." Rob smiled and took a cautious sip from his mug. "In fact, if you're not afraid of mumps, you can help me rouse the little dear for her next dose of medicine."

"I think I'm past the mumps stage, and I have lots of experience poking medicine down reluctant patients, remember?" She chuckled as she slid off the bentwood stool.

Karen whimpered in her sleep when Lisa and Rob slipped into her room, but didn't wake up. Leaning over the bed, her father placed a gentle hand on her forehead.

"Time for some more of this icky stuff, sweetheart," he whispered.

Karen didn't reply, but obediently propped herself up on her little elbows and swallowed a teaspoon of bright aqua syrup without protest.

"Just call if you need me, okay?" Rob's hand smoothed the damp hair away from the little girl's brow.

"Sleep tight, Karen, and you'll feel a whole lot better in the morning," Lisa added, stepping out of the shadows.

"G'night, Daddy," Karen croaked hoarsely. "An' g'night, Lisa," she added as naturally as if she had been expecting to see her there all along.

"She's a little trouper, isn't she?" Lisa whispered after Rob had partially closed the door.

"More so than her old man, I'm afraid." Rob stretched his shoulder muscles stiffly and made a face.

"I'd better get going so you can get some rest. You look as if you're about to keel over in your tracks."

"I'm not all that tired," Rob fibbed. "At least let me give you a quick tour of the house before you leave. I'm really ashamed that I haven't invited you over before, but we always seem to meet somewhere out there, don't we?" He gestured toward the glass wall overlooking the drive.

"Uh-huh. I was thinking about dressing up as a witch and trick-or-treating you, just to get a look at your hideout, but you beat me to it." Lisa ambled alongside Rob, close enough to elbow him playfully.

"This is the guest room," he announced, flipping on a light inside a room papered with a sweet Laura Ashley print. He didn't even bother to glance at the comfortably furnished room with its coordinated comforter and drapes. "Do you think we're hopeless, Lisa?"

"Ummm." Lisa pursed her lips thoughtfully in order to suppress a smile. "No, 'hopeless' is a pretty extreme word for us, I think."

"But rather?" Rob snapped on another light, briefly illuminating a gray marble bathroom that needed no introduction.

"I'd say we're two people who have always had very definite ideas about how childless career women and solo fathers live their lives. And even when some of those ideas don't fit, we have a hard time letting go of them." Lisa spoke slowly; although the conversation was part jest, she was surprised at how neatly she had described her own perceptions.

Rob hooked his fingers over the frame of the master bedroom door. "What are we going to do about that?" His crystal blue eyes were twinkling, but the question was posed seriously.

Lisa needed no invitation to slip her arms around the stretched torso displayed so invitingly in the doorway. "Dump all our preconceived notions, for starters."

Her arms tightened their grasp as he bent to nuzzle her hair. His mouth buried gentle kisses in her hair, tracing the deep part until he found her face. As his lips savored the smooth skin, the intensity of their exploration mounted. The reservoir of powerful feelings that they had both restrained for weeks stirred to life, seeking physical expression.

Lisa's hands tightened their hold on his waist, begging for more, but he needed no prompting. As his mouth continued to tease her sensitive earlobe, his hands began to caress her shoulders, kneading the warm flesh before slipping into the inviting cleft of her blouse. She was clinging to him now; every caress filled her with such dizzying pleasure, she feared she would fall if she let go. But soon passion overrode caution; her hand was unable to resist the temptation of the firm buttock curving just inches below her grasp. As her hand tested, then squeezed him with unconcealed sensual delight, he let out a low moan.

For a moment, Lisa thought she was falling as Rob swept her into his arms. He carried her to the king-size bed dominating the room, letting her down gently as if she were the most precious treasure in the world. She lay back, her arms stretched out beside her, watching him undress with a slowness and a precision that fanned her passion to a feverish pitch. First he pulled the sweatshirt over his head, allowing her the first glimpse of the tautly defined muscles layered beneath the tanned skin. Then the shirt dropped to the floor, followed by his corduroys. The sight of his desire delineated beneath tight knit briefs escalated her simmering passion to new heights, and she knew she could hold back no longer. Pushing herself upright, Lisa hungrily enclosed his hands with her own, guiding them down past his waist until the last of his garments were stripped away.

"Oh, Rob," she murmured as he joined her on the bed. He stretched himself alongside her, pressing a lean thigh across her belly and down her legs. As his leg continued to stroke her, his fingers began the infuriatingly tedious job of undoing the tiny buttons of her blouse. Their labors were at last rewarded, and she rolled to face him, neatly unclasping her bra at the same time. Together they consigned her slacks to the same fate as his cords.

"You're so beautiful," he whispered. His mesmeric blue eyes traveled the length of her naked body before coming to rest on her glowing face. "So beautiful and strong and delicate." His fingers sent delicious chills racing through her as they played along the curve of her hip, dipping teasingly to her thighs before returning to her breasts. With ever-growing urgency his hands fondled her breasts, now relishing the satiny skin, now gently twisting the pale nipples until they were hard and rosy. Soft sounds mingled with the short gasps of her breathing as he mercilessly continued to ply her breasts, only relenting long enough to dive once more to her thighs that now seemed to ache with pleasure.

Gradually, like a burgeoning, irresistible torrent, a shuddering sensation of delight enveloped her. She cried out, her body rigid with ecstasy. She was still floating as he bridged her with his body, but her hands soon responded to his probing. With renewed urgency, she gripped his shoulders, pulling him to her in rhythm with his hungry thrusts. She felt another delicious shudder swell within her just as he threw his head back, his mouth opened in an unvoiced cry.

Lisa coiled her arms around Rob's neck, responding to the warm heaviness of his body as he stretched himself alongside her. Through half-closed eyes, she looked into his face, still flushed and damp. He smiled tenderly, letting his finger slowly follow the outline of her parted lips.

Sated from their lovemaking, they fitted their sweating bodies around each other on the bed. Rob neatly scooped Lisa into his lap sideways, closing his arms protectively around her while she wove her leg between his, her toes tickling the silky hair covering his calves.

"My precious Lisa," he whispered into her hair after their breathing had slowed to an even rhythm and their bodies lulled into supreme relaxation.

Lisa did not speak, but only tightened her fingers around the big hand she held and lifted it to her lips. With her mouth still formed in a kiss, she held it there long after sleep had overtaken both of them.

Chapter Seven

Flames crackled between the split logs, greedily licking at the fresh sap seeping between the chipped bark. Rob energetically prodded his latest addition to the heap of logs burning in the grate before returning the poker to its stand. "That should hold it for the night," he announced, brushing bits of moss and sawdust from his cords.

Lisa looked up from the row of marshmallows she was skewering with a bent coat hanger and grinned. "We could roast a suckling pig over the bonfire you've built." Her comment elicited a giggle from Karen, who was enthroned on the couch next to her, bundled up in a tartan lap rug with Chuck purring somnolently in her lap.

"Can I do 'em this time?" the little girl asked, eyeing the marshmallow-laden wire eagerly.

"Sure, sweetheart. Just be careful and hold it back here so you don't toast your fingers at the same time." Lisa demonstrated the proper technique before handing Karen the coat hanger.

Karen slid from under the afghan, taking pains not to disturb the sleeping cat, and padded to the flagstone hearth. In her red flannel jump suit and plush booties, she looked like a Christmas elf.

"Last batch of marshmallows before bedtime," Rob intoned. "Remember, you're still not completely off the sick list."

"But I'm lots better," Karen contended, not taking her eyes off the melting marshmallows. She carefully turned the coat hanger until the marshmallows had attained the desired beige hue. Her chubby face was flushed from the blaze when she trudged back to the couch, proudly displaying the crusty marshmallows.

"Not bad," Rob commented, pulling one of the oozing confections off the coat hanger. "And here's one for the cook," he popped a plump marshmallow into Karen's open mouth, "and one for the Bird Lady." Lisa opened her mouth, stealing a surreptitious lick from the gooey fingers that delivered her marshmallow. "And one for the kitty?" He cast a doubtful eye at Chuck's placid form.

"Cats don't eat marshmallows, Daddy," Karen informed him patiently. Licking the white goo from her fingers, she tried to conceal the yawn that threatened to stretch her mouth wide open.

"Looks like someone is about ready for bed." Rob scooped his unprotesting daughter, lap rug and all, into his arms and carried her toward the stairs. "I don't think this will take long." He tossed Lisa a wink over his shoulder.

"G'night, Lisa." Drowsiness had already taken the bright edge off Karen's voice.

"Good night, Karen," Lisa called before turning to the roaring fire. Listening to the receding sound of Rob's muffled steps as he climbed the stairs, she was reminded of what a pleasant ritual this tucking-in ceremony had become. She had come to see it as a fitting caesura between the pleasant evening the three of them spent together and the quiet time that she and Rob shared afterward. Nudging her outstretched legs a few inches closer to the hearth, she marveled over the two weeks that had passed since that night when she had driven from the Wheatons' to Rob's house on an impulse. For once in her life her impulse had been the right one. Call it magic, call it destiny, but since that night their relationship had moved into a new dimension, one more satisfying than Lisa had ever imagined possible. And although he had not said it in so many words, she guessed that the present state of affairs far exceeded Rob's expectations, as well.

What had happened to straighten things out so perfectly, all of a sudden? They had made love, just as they had continued to make love frequently since, but the wonderful harmony of their daily undertakings, the effortlessness with which they had merged their lives could not be attributed to a wonderful sex life, wonderful as it might be. They had talked a lot in the past weeks, each revealing things that had been suppressed for too long.

For the first time in memory, Lisa felt she had found a man who didn't expect her to be anyone but herself. Everyone else always seemed to want a science whiz or a perfect date to be seen with or an invincible superwoman; she had learned too well how to be all of those things. But Rob just wanted *her*, the person she was happiest being.

She hoped he felt as comfortable and secure with her as she did with him; happily, everything seemed to indicate he did. After all, he had been the one to suggest that she stay in his house. "It makes sense to set up our headquarters here for the time being," he had proclaimed the morning after their first lovemaking. "Karen's going to want a lot of my attention while she's recovering, and I'm going to want a lot of yours," he had added with a chuckle that Lisa had promptly smothered in a kiss. After leaving the center that evening, she had stopped at her apartment only long enough to throw a few outfits into a bag and collect Chuck.

It wasn't as if they were actually moving in together, she had told herself when the first attack of doubt hit her; that had occurred shortly after she had timidly scooted aside the shirts in Rob's closet to make room for some of her clothes. They were just trying to find a compromise between each other's life-style; this was only a temporary arrangement, designed to give their relationship the chance it deserved.

Lisa felt safe in congratulating herself that, at the very least, she had allayed most of Rob's fears about Karen's role

in their relationship. She had spent a great deal of time with
the little girl during her convalescence from the mumps;
often Lisa was the first one to reach the house after work,
giving her the chance to prepare Karen's dinner and regale
her with stories from the Wildlife Center while she ate. She
reflected that it would have been a real strain if she was
forced to fake her affection for the child, but fortunately
that wasn't the case. Lisa sensed that a strong bond was de-
veloping between her and Karen. In fact, tonight had been
one of the few that week when Karen had not requested Lisa
to do the honors of bedtime story and tuck-in ritual.

She misses having a mother. Lisa was touched by the realization, just as she shied away from the stifled memories
it summoned up from her own past. Memories of another
little girl who had both a mother and a father, but never in
the same place for very long. And when they were in the
same place, life was rarely as harmonious as the little girl
wanted it to be.

She remembered her eleventh Christmas, the first big
holiday after the divorce was final. Her mother had put up
a gigantic Christmas tree, bigger than any they had ever
decorated in Lynchburg; even with the humid Florida cli-
mate driving the thermostat above eighty, she had defiantly
sprayed the windows with swirls of artificial snow. And
Santa had been extra generous that year, something that
Lisa now realized her mother really could not afford after
her recent purchase of the closet-size boutique. But what she
wanted most had been missing, and, even as an eleven-year-
old she had been aware of how hard it was to feign delight
over the new cassette player and the Jack Kramer tennis
racket. She had called her father after dinner, but he had
sounded so sad that she had felt even worse after talking
with him. Later that night, after the sparkling tree lights had
been unplugged and the piles of torn wrapping paper cleared
away, she had curled up in the corner of her bed and cried
herself to sleep.

"If she keeps falling asleep so quickly, we're never going to find out where the wild things are." Rob had slipped up behind the couch, unnoticed by Lisa. She felt his hand knead the back of her neck for a moment before he tossed a lavishly illustrated children's book onto the end table and dropped down beside her. "Lisa! What's wrong, darling?" Concern modulated his low-pitched voice as he lifted her face and saw the tears trailing down her cheeks.

"Nothing, really." She smiled and sniffed, smudging the telltale moisture with the back of her hand.

"Baloney! You don't spend the evening toasting marshmallows in front of a cheery fire and then burst out crying for no reason at all," Rob insisted. He had already wrapped her in his arms and was rocking her gently.

"I was just thinking about my parents." Lisa swallowed a sob. Normally she would have felt pathetically foolish, whimpering over something that had been a reality of her life for a good twenty years, but the serious lines drawn in Rob's lean face told her she had nothing to be ashamed of. "The holidays always remind me that we aren't all together, the way we should be. And now, Dad wants me to come up for Thanksgiving, but I just can't decide. I've told you how I feel about Lucille...." The remainder of her sentence was lost in the downy weave of Rob's sweater as he pulled her head, unresisting, against his shoulder.

"I know the feeling," Rob said quietly, gently smoothing her hair.

A twinge of guilt pricked Lisa at this reminder. How could she, a grown woman with a basically happy life, complain about the complications of her childhood to someone who had suffered a loss as recent and painful as Rob's? "I'm sorry, Rob," she began, lifting her head a little to meet his eyes.

He gave her tumbled hair a loving pat. "But this year, I'm looking forward to a genuinely merry Christmas, and I hope you are, too." At this, Lisa squeezed the hand resting on her knee but didn't interrupt. "You know, we've probably been thinking about a lot of the same things, just from different angles. And I'd like to make a few suggestions." He looked down at the tawny blond head that immediately nodded approval. "First of all, I think you should take a chance and go to Lynchburg for Thanksgiving. From what you've told me, you don't actually dislike your father's second wife."

"No," Lisa agreed slowly. "She's just so different from Mother, always fussing over Dad as if he were a child." She tried to soften the edge in her voice, with mixed success.

"Okay, but remember she probably acts that way because she loves him. Hell, maybe he even likes it."

Lisa shrugged in Rob's arms, but his appraisal of her father's second marriage struck a chord of truth, mirroring her unacknowledged suspicion that her father was the sort of man who needed to be babied a little. And babying was one talent that Sarah Porter had never developed very highly.

"Mr. Randolph, you make a very strong case." Lisa shifted just enough to lace her hands behind Rob's neck. "I'll book a flight to Lynchburg tomorrow and give it my best shot."

"And then you'll come back here, and we'll spend Christmas together?"

"Just the three of us?"

"Four, if you count Chuck."

"It's a deal." Lisa loosened her fingers, the better to ruffle the little curls looping over his collar. "Is that an example of what they call 'plea bargaining'?"

"I prefer to call it friendly persuasion."

A simmering log split in two, sputtering a shower of sparks onto the hearth as Rob eased her back against the cushions and covered her receptive body with his own.

LISA KEPT IN MIND Rob's evaluation of the dynamics at work between Lucille and her father during the four days she spent in Lynchburg with them. Perhaps she had her own positive state of mind to thank, but for once she managed to accept Lucille's fluttering ministrations without protest. Then, too, she was surprised and a little embarrassed that she had failed to notice the way her father basked in the flowery woman's care.

"You go to too much trouble, Lucy," Paul Porter had admonished his wife as he stood, carving knife in hand, preparing to dismember the perfectly browned turkey. "This dinner looks fit for a king."

Lucille's plump cheeks dimpled, calling attention to the two determined dots of rouge adorning them. "I like a nice spread for Thanksgiving, especially when there's company," she demurred, with a sidelong glance at Lisa. "It wasn't any trouble at all."

Perhaps not for the restaurant staff of the Queen Mary, Lisa thought as her eyes roved across the numerous dishes testing the strength of the mahogany dining table's leaves. The peeling and slicing and chopping and basting that went into preparing such a meal were activities that she personally associated with the first circle of hell, but, to judge from Lucille Porter's beaming face, not everyone shared her conviction.

"This is quite a treat for me, Lucille." She smiled at the woman who had just thrust a broccoli casserole in front of her. Lucille responded with a grin that buried her pale blue eyes in laugh lines.

"Couldn't ask for a finer feast," Lisa's dad chimed in. The fond pat that he bestowed on Lucille's hand as she served him a hot biscuit was not wasted on Lisa.

"What a wonderful Thanksgiving dinner," Lisa repeated at the end of the meal as she folded her napkin beside her dessert plate. In response to the compliment, Lucille sprang to her feet, eager to threaten her with yet another slice of pumpkin pie. "No, thanks. I couldn't eat another crumb. Maybe later," she quickly added to forestall the crestfallen look spreading over her hostess's face. "But right now, I insist on giving you a hand with these dishes."

"No, no, dear. I can manage just fine. I'll only tuck these things in the dishwasher, and then I want to bone the turkey and put some up in the freezer. And this dressing, I guess I'll freeze it, too." Lucille's voice trailed off as she cocked a finger against one rosy cheek and frowned over the generous array of leftovers. "You two go make yourselves comfy in the den. This will only take a minute," she assured them, trotting off into the kitchen for what Lisa was sure would be three hours' work.

"I'm really glad you could get away from Charlotte for the holiday, honey," Paul Porter commented diffidently. He squinted at the heap of indistinguishable football players that had just popped onto the television screen before turning the volume down to a low hum.

Lisa winced inwardly, remembering the many phony excuses of job demands with which she had so often countered her father's invitations. "I'm having a good time, Daddy," she said sincerely.

"What with that young man you've met and all, I feel real flattered that you still can find the time to come visit your old dad." He tamped his pipe slowly and pretended to watch the ball game.

"That young man, as you call him, is the very person who persuaded me to fly up," Lisa retorted with a smile. Kicking her shoes off, she curled her legs up under her. The pleasant meal, the homey family room, and, not least of all, her father's undemanding presence had conspired to make her feel very relaxed.

Lisa's father appreciatively watched the fragrant puff of smoke spiraling from his pipe. "Well, having you here sure has brought back some old memories for me. Do you remember how we always started Thanksgiving Day when you were a little thing?"

"Of course I do!" Lisa countered, burrowing her feet under the latest example of Lucille's handiwork, a fluffy crocheted afghan. "We always watched the big Macy's parade."

"You'd be so bright eyed and wide awake when you dragged your mom and me out of bed. We would have given anything for another hour's sleep." Her father chuckled and gave his pipe a philosophical tap. "But, you know, after all this time, I still remember the one morning in the year that we watched the parade together, while I've completely forgotten all those other mornings I managed to sleep in."

A suspicious mist softened Lisa's gaze as she looked at her father. His thick shock of hair glistened beneath the floor lamp these days with a bit more silver, and his body had thickened to a more generous circumference, but he was still a remarkably handsome man, somehow even more handsome than she remembered him from her childhood. And he looked happy.

"I guess you've talked with your mother lately?" he continued. He always managed to find an opening to ask about Sarah, but today his face remained free of the usual tension that subject provoked.

"Miraculously enough, yes. The way she jets around, snooping out the latest designs for her shop, I'm amazed that she still finds the time to call or write, but she does.

"So she's doing okay?"

Lisa glanced at the calendar on her watch. "As we speak, she is probably stretched out on a beach in Capri. The last postcard I received from her mentioned her plans to tack an island vacation onto the end of her Italian buying trip."

"That's good. I'm glad to hear she's happy." The contented way Paul Porter sank back into the cushion of his leather easy chair vouched for his sincerity.

"You seem really happy now, Daddy," Lisa ventured.

The silvery head nodded slightly. "I have all any man has the right to ask for, sweetheart: the most wonderful daughter in the world, a woman whom I love and who loves me, and a community that I can call home. Yep, I think you'd have to call me a happy man." He let his head roll to one side and gave her one of his warmest smiles.

"I've always wanted to hear you say that..." Lisa began, but she hesitated as Lucille's round face peeped through the doorway.

"Excuse me," Lucille shyly interrupted, wiping her hands on the edge of her ruffled apron. "But you've got a call, dear, long distance. Oh, me, I hope nothing has happened." She followed Lisa down the hall to the telephone desk, still wringing her apron hem; she was the sort of person for whom long-distance calls could only mean illness or death.

"Still eating turkey?" Rob's resonant voice teased Lisa as she picked up the receiver.

"Rob!" she cried. She gave Lucille a reassuring smile of dismissal before continuing, "I wasn't expecting to hear from you."

"You thought I could go four whole days without hearing your voice? It's bad enough that I can't see you or touch you," he grumbled good-naturedly.

"I miss you, too," Lisa confessed. "Is Karen still going full steam?"

"You'd never guess she's been sick. We had dinner today with one of my partners and his family, and she managed to wear down both of his ten-year-old twins as well as the family St. Bernard. As a matter of fact, we just got home."

And you went straight to the phone and called, Lisa thought. That maddening tingle that Rob seemed to awaken in her with such ease suddenly rushed from her head to her feet. "I've had a very enjoyable visit here," she went on in a surprisingly even voice. "Dad and I have had a lot of time to talk."

"That's what I wanted to hear." A muffled exchange interrupted Rob before he returned to the line. "There's a young lady here who says she knows you; tells me she wants to say 'hi.'"

"Lisa!" Karen squealed into the phone with ear-splitting disregard of the receiver's amplifiers. "Mrs. Patterson sent some leftover turkey home with us, and we're going to save you some, but I'm going to give Chuck just a bite tonight, if that's okay."

"Chuck will really like that," Lisa assured her. "Does he act like he misses me?"

"He sleeps on my bed now, but I think he thinks about you a lot. *I* sure miss you."

"I miss you, too," Lisa said with a laugh. This conversation was beginning to sound as if she been exiled to Siberia for fifty years. "I'll see you at the airport on Sunday night, okay?"

"Okay. Here's Daddy, again. Bye, Lisa." Muted noises sounded from the receiver as it changed hands once more.

"I don't want to keep you all evening, so I'll just say goodbye now." Lisa heard Rob swallow noisily on the other end of the line.

"Goodbye, Rob, and thanks for calling." Something warned her not to hang up yet.

"I love you, Lisa."

"I love you, too, Rob," she replied without thinking. His parting words were still echoing in her ears as she let the receiver drop onto the phone cradle. He loved her; he had finally uttered those simple yet infinitely important words. And what amazed her even more, she had said them, too. *I love you, too, Rob.* No matter how powerful her attraction for him, how intensely felt her passion, she had never translated those driving emotions into words. Not until today. And now that they had declared their love for each other, she sensed their relationship had entered a phase for which she had not yet prepared herself.

"Time for more pumpkin pie," Lucille announced in a singsong voice as she made her way from the kitchen to the den with the uplifted pie tin in hand. "I hope you have room for some."

"Just a sliver." Lisa smiled absently as she followed Lucille's rounded shoulders into the den, for her mind was now three hundred miles away.

IN THE WEEKS following Lisa's return to Charlotte, she and Rob found more than one occasion to declare their love for each other. Although Lisa had discreetly returned to her own apartment, just as they had planned, their little experiment had shown them ways of fitting time for each other into their hectic schedules. Lisa now felt free to drop by Rob's house after work, knowing that her presence was a welcome addition to the little family of two. Rob, for his part, had gotten over his conviction that every encounter between them had to be a well-orchestrated date, complete with restaurant reservations and theater tickets. Both of them had discovered they were happier with a hamburger and some good conversation in Rob's roomy kitchen, and the tender loving that usually followed left nothing for either to desire.

Still, there *were* only twenty-four hours in a day, a fact that Lisa bemoaned to Anne Torrence during their joint Christmas shopping excursion to Southpark Mall.

"I must have been crazy to think I could get an article written before the end of the year." Lisa lifted her shopping bag to one side as she and Anne threaded their way around a line of children waiting to see Santa Claus.

"You'll make up for lost time once school is out," Anne assured her breezily. "Besides, the Christmas season is supposed to be hectic, with everyone running up their credit cards and giving parties and all."

Lisa edged her way up to a counter and began to poke through an assortment of scarves. "You've certainly been swept up in a mad social whirl lately," she remarked, shaking out a colorful silk square.

"'Ever since you met Scott.' Go on and say it." Anne sniffed as she held up a scarf and studied its pattern. "Well, you won't get any apologies from me. I've finally met someone who likes to get out and do things, and I'm enjoying it to the hilt. As far as I'm concerned, we can go to the theater or to a party or out to dinner seven evenings a week, and it won't be too often. Remember, I'm making up for lost time."

"You deserve it," Lisa remarked. Swinging the shopping bag over her wrist, she pulled away from the scarf table just before a saleswoman swooped down on them. "Things do seem to be going extraordinarily well for both of us these days. Just last Saturday, I took Randolph back for another X ray. I almost cried for joy when I saw how healthy his joint looked."

"He had a good therapist," Anne commented as if she had known all along the hawk would recover. "You know," she went on. "From what you've told me, you and Rob have a very nice holiday planned." Her brick-red lips curved into the knowing smile she always adopted when discussing Lisa's love life.

"We're going to trim the tree tomorrow night. Which reminds me: I had his gift engraved, and I need to pick it up right now. I can't wait for you to see it." She shifted the shopping bag to her other hand and steered Anne past the mob congregated at the perfume counters.

"If you've had it engraved, I gather it isn't house slippers or a trash compactor." Anne's eyes glowed like emeralds when they angled up to the fine jewelry display. "I'll hand it to you, Lisa; you have a real knack for choosing appropriate gifts. Karen is going to love those ballet slippers, and I've every reason to trust you've hit another winner with Rob's present."

"I hope he likes it" was all Lisa said, but her eager expression reminded Anne of the kids waiting to see Santa.

"Oh, Lisa!" Anne exclaimed when the sales clerk opened a small leather box and presented the exquisite gold cuff links for their approval. "They're just gorgeous!"

"Do you think so?"

Anne shook her head. "First-class. You couldn't have done better."

Lisa smiled diffidently. "I wanted to surprise him. Of course, I suppose he'll guess jewelry when he sees the flat little package."

"Not necessarily." Anne nudged one of the links with her finger, but Lisa could see the gears were already grinding beneath the ruffled red hair. "I have an idea," she announced, beckoning her friend closer with a crooked finger.

AND A WONDERFUL IDEA, at that, Lisa thought the following evening when she set out for the Randolphs' home. Sliding across the Chevette's chilly vinyl seat, she stole a glance at the back seat and the gaily wrapped parcels stowed there. She couldn't resist giggling to herself at the sight of the huge box she had wheedled from a television shop. That big box Anne and she had packed the cuff links in should thwart any pre-Christmas guessing on Mr. Randolph's part, she congratulated herself.

"Merry Christmas!" Karen's cry hailed her as she pulled up to the Randolph's garage. The energetic six-year-old had obviously been on the lookout for the yellow Chevette, and now she was doing her best to unload the back seat all by herself.

"Why don't you carry these?" Lisa handed her two small packages.

"This one's for me!" Karen squealed, wrinkling her nose over the dangling name tag. "I've got you a won-der-ful gift, too, Lisa, but you can't open it until Christmas."

Lisa sniffed. "Well, just for that, you can't open yours before Christmas, either!"

"Need any help?" Dressed in a roomy alpaca cardigan, Rob came bounding down the steps to greet her.

"There's one big package left in the car, but don't you dare shake it!" Lisa warned him.

"Why not?" Rob asked innocently, pausing long enough to plant a kiss on the tip of her nose. When he saw the huge package in question, he whistled appreciatively. "What on earth is this, my very own yacht or what?'' He gave the bulky package a not-too-surreptitious jiggle.

"You'll find out soon enough," Lisa retorted.

"This one sure does smell good.'' Karen's pug nose bobbed over one of the foil-encased loaves.

With a laugh, Lisa seized the package in question. "You two are impossible, shaking and sniffing my packages. Next thing you'll be sticking everything under an X ray! Don't you like surprises?''

"Of course, we do, and while we're on the subject, you can just close your eyes—'' one of Rob's broad palms slipped obligingly over Lisa's eyes "—and follow me.'' She felt his arm encircle her waist, guiding her into the den. "No fair peeking until I say so!'' he warned her, and she could hear Karen hoot her approval. "One. Two. Three.'' Rob ceremoniously spun Lisa in a circle before uncovering her eyes.

Lisa blinked up into Rob's face and was promptly rewarded with another kiss. "Is that what you call a surprise?'' she teased before he pivoted her around again. "Oh, Rob! It's magnificent,'' she exclaimed at the sight of the seven-foot fir reigning over the den's window wall. "Where on earth did you find such a perfect tree?''

"It's a special order, you might say. An old college buddy of mine owns a Christmas tree farm in the northern part of the state, and I asked him to keep his eyes open for a nice fir.'' Rob rocked back on his heels, obviously proud of his accomplishment and the approval it had won.

"One of those fruitcakes goes to your friend,'' Lisa announced as she placed one of the foil loaves on the coffee table.

"Those are fruitcakes? Our Lisa actually made fruitcakes?'' Rob's incredulous blue eyes widened in astonishment.

"Just because I don't exactly love to cook doesn't mean I can't,'' Lisa replied a little testily. "Lucille gave me the

recipe when I was in Lynchburg. She swore they were easy
to make and delicious. I can vouch for the easy part.''

''I bet they taste good, too,'' Karen interposed gener-
ously.

''We can find out tonight,'' Lisa concluded with a fatal-
istic laugh. ''Speaking of food, how are things going in that
kitchen of yours?''

''Baked ham is sliced and waiting; there's dark rye from
the bakery and all the mustard-mayo business. Plus Karen
and Mrs. Elliott personally baked two batches of cookies for
us,'' Rob announced. Swinging his giggling daughter into
his arms, he led the way to the kitchen.

Lisa was astonished by the array of food arranged on the
counter. ''I can see I've found the right man. I guess I don't
have to contribute anything to our meal, do I?''

''The fruitcake,'' Rob reminded her. ''And you might
want to pour off some of that eggnog and adjust it for the
Big People.'' He winked over Karen's dark head.

While Lisa and Karen piled ham, cheese, lettuce and tomato slices onto paper plates emblazoned with a chortling
Santa Claus, Rob returned to the den. When they joined
him, he had stoked up a bonfire suitable for a tree trim-
ming. With Nat King Cole crooning on the stereo about
''chestnuts roasting'' and ''yuletide carols,'' the three of
them began to deck the towering fir. Between bites of ham
sandwich Lisa and Rob managed to untangle the mare's nest
of Christmas tree lights and weave them through the fir's
branches.

''Now the real fun begins,'' Lisa announced when they
had at last replaced all of the burned-out lights. With Kar-
en's eager assistance she opened a carton of the Randolphs'
ornaments. She fished a silver star out of the crumpled tissue and presented it to Rob. ''As the resident tall person,
you get to do the honors of crowning our tree.'' *Our tree;*
the words echoed in her mind. But it *was* theirs, just as much
as the love and good cheer they would share together on
Christmas morning. Her eyes glistened as she handed Karen

a miniature wooden rocking horse dangling from a silver string.

Humming along with the recorded carols, the three of them set about decorating the tree with Rob decking the highest branches, Karen the lowest, and Lisa, as Karen aptly put it, doing the middle. Occasionally, someone would call for an opinion on the position of a particular striking ornament, and they would all stop to stand back and survey their handiwork critically. Finally Rob upended the last carton, letting the scraps of empty packing material waft to the floor like snowflakes.

"Looks like that's it for the decorations," he announced, smiling ruefully as he surveyed the carton's interior.

"Now we get to put the presents underneath the tree!" Karen cried. Her face was flushed with excitement as she placed a package on the edge of the tree's red flannel skirt. Giving the rather clumsily tied bow a final pat, she smiled up at Lisa. "I wrapped it all by myself, Lisa."

"And it's going to be the first one I open on Christmas morning." Lisa stepped behind Karen, and, clasping her hands around the little girl's neck, hugged her close.

"It looks just like the Sugarplum Fairy's tree, doesn't it?" The child's crystal blue eyes were sparkling as gaily as the tree's twinkling lights.

"It certainly does, sweetheart." Lisa smiled a little wider when she felt the little hands close over her wrists.

Rob had been silent since they had completed their task. Now he rested a hand lightly on Karen's dark head. "I hate to be a party pooper, but I believe it's past a certain young lady's bedtime."

Karen twisted around to send Lisa an imploring look.

"Tomorrow is a school day," Lisa reminded her. "But I promise you that you can stay up as late as you like one night over the holidays."

Karen obviously deemed this a satisfactory compromise, for she planted a kiss on the cheek that Lisa offered and docilely followed Rob upstairs. Smiling to herself, Lisa seized the chance to fill two old-fashioned glasses with eggnog, adding a generous jigger of bourbon to each. When Rob joined her again in the den, she had lighted the mantel candles to complement the tree lights and was waiting for him on the sofa.

"She must have been sleepier than I thought," Lisa commented, patting the cushion next to her.

Rob eased down onto the sofa. "No, just more cooperative. Since you've been around, Karen has been a lot less fussy at bedtime. In fact, she's been a lot less fussy in general." He took a slow sip of eggnog before falling silent again.

Lisa leaned her head on his shoulder, digging her hand through the crook of his arm. She sighed, basking in the happy glow created by the warm fire, the lovely tree and Rob's comforting closeness. "Isn't this nice?"

"Uh-huh."

Lisa roused herself enough to survey the bronzed face just above her head; the tension that she saw there surprised and disturbed her. As she thought back over the evening, she realized that Rob had been unusually quiet for most of it. "Are you all right?"

"Sure. I'm fine," Rob muttered in a tone that indicated just the opposite.

"I didn't put *that* much bourbon in the drinks, Rob. Something is bothering you." Lisa squeezed his arm playfully, eliciting a squeeze from him that seemed more like a nervous pinch.

"I...I've been meaning to talk with you about something, Lisa." Rob looked down at the half-empty glass cradled in his hands. The velvety blue eyes darted to one side and caught Lisa's prompting nod. "It's about Christmas. I guess I should have said something before tonight but..."

"What is it, Rob?" Lisa still held his arm, but her voice carried a trace of impatience.

"Karen's grandparents insist that we come to Winston-Salem for Christmas," Rob blurted out in one breath. As Lisa continued to stare at him, uncomprehending, he went on, "We won't be spending Christmas here together as we had planned."

Lisa's mouth opened, but no sounds came out. Her hands that still clasped Rob's arm felt numb, as if the shock of his words had drained all the life out of them. "I see," she finally managed to say in a scarcely audible whisper.

"God, I'm sorry, Lisa. You know I was looking forward to this as much as you were. That's why I waited so long to bring it up." Rob's free hand ran furrows through his thick hair. "Please try to understand."

"I understand, Rob." The glowing embers in the grate blurred before Lisa's eyes. With mechanical slowness she released his arm and groped on the end table for her handbag. Suddenly the bright decorations that had appeared so enchanting a few minutes ago seemed garish; the pine boughs and lights and reindeer figures were now only clutter, oppressing her with their forced gaiety. Lisa stiffly pushed herself up from the sofa.

"Are you going home now?" Rob's voice was heavy with misery as he followed her into the dark hallway.

Lisa whirled around, her eyes snapping fire in the muted light. "What ever gave you that idea?" Her voice cracked into a short, bitter laugh. Seeing Rob cringe at her words only encouraged her to go on. "Or do you expect me to sit here for the rest of the evening to soothe your conscience? After all, you've only been leading me to believe we'd spend the holidays together for the past month. Nothing, really, just a trifle. Maybe you think I should go to bed with you now, just to make sure you know you can dump on me at the last minute and still be forgiven, just like that." She snapped her fingers angrily. "Sorry, Rob, but I'm not so desperate for a man that I'll put up with anything you care to dish out." She spun away from him, intent on making a break for the door, but he caught the strap of her shoulder bag.

"Lisa, I can explain." Rob lifted one hand lamely, as if to caress her face, before letting it fall.

"You already have!" Jerking the strap free from his grasp, she stormed out the door, leaving him alone in the hallway.

Chapter Eight

"I'm tired. Aren't we ever going to get there?" Karen fidgeted with the seat belt, her cherub's face screwed into an irritable frown.

"Just another hour, honey," Rob promised. He fought to keep any annoyance from creeping into his voice, but as the long drive to Winston-Salem dragged on, it was becoming more difficult. "Just think how glad Grandad and Grandma will be to see you."

Karen didn't reply, but scowled out the window at the passing scenery. "I just wish we'd hurry up and *get* there," she repeated.

So do I, thought Rob. He tightened, then loosened his grip on the steering wheel, trying to keep his senses alert enough to pilot them safely to Max and Amanda Cheatham's rambling country estate. It would have been bad enough, battling the heavy holiday traffic and a grumpy child for four hours, but on top of these normal irritations Rob had an additional burden preying on his mind. Ever since the night they had trimmed the tree, the thought that, this time, he had finished things for good with Lisa had plagued him, gnawing at his conscience like a hound worrying its quarry.

And Lisa had done nothing to assuage his misgivings. He had made a couple of attempts to phone her, but, as he had expected, the cheerless answering machine was the closest he

had come to making contact. She had pointedly not returned his calls. He could, of course, have driven to her
home, hammered on the door and demanded the chance to
make amends. But that wasn't his style.

No, you're too much of a coward for that, he thought
contemptuously, *too afraid of the reception you might receive.* Like many gentle people, Lisa was deceptively strong,
and Rob's growing fear that she didn't intend to give him
another chance grew as their separation lengthened. If only
he hadn't been so damned spineless, he might have avoided
this whole mess. He and Karen would be standing in a
charity soup line for their Christmas dinner if he mishan-
dled his legal cases the way he had this last incident with
Lisa. If only he had broken the news to her as soon as he had
succumbed to Amanda's nagging. If only he hadn't dropped
the unexpected revelation in her lap on the evening when she
had arrived, eyes sparkling and cheeks flushed, with her
presents for them and her fruitcakes.

Rob winced at the sight of her mammoth present for him,
hulking in the back seat like a specter dispatched by her to
haunt him. He had wanted to leave it at home but Karen had
insisted. In her six-year-old mind, every gift had to be
opened on Christmas morning. Rob suspected, too, that his
estrangement from Lisa had not escaped Karen's canny notice. He could hardly expect such a bright child to fall for the
pitiful excuses he offered every time she demanded to know
when Lisa was coming over again. Nor did he discount her
disappointment when she had learned that Lisa was not to
be included in their Christmas celebration after all.

"Why not?" she had demanded in a tone unnervingly
reminiscent of Lisa's. "Why can't she come with us?"

Why, indeed. And it was this prickly aspect of the whole
affair that rankled Rob most of all. He loved Lisa; even now
he was as certain of that fact as ever. But how could he ever
explain that love to Max and Amanda? How would they
perceive a new woman in his life? In Karen's life? Rob drew
a deep breath, partially in relief at the sight of the stone pil-

lars flanking the gate to the Cheathams' homestead, partially in despair. He doubted if they would ever accept anyone who threatened to take Sylvia's place, and if he wanted a permanent relationship with Lisa, he was going to have to steel himself to that reality. He shook his head, his eyes following the gravel drive winding up to the columned colonial mansion. Forget about a permanent relationship; he would be lucky if Lisa ever spoke to him again.

"Gran'dad!" Karen sprung the seat belt's catch and wrestled with the door handle. Her grouchy mood magically vanished as she clambered out of the car and into her grandfather's arms.

"Such a grown-up girl!" Max Cheatham withdrew the pipe clenched in his teeth and swung the little girl off her feet for a moment.

"I should say so!" his wife chimed in. "I declare you've shot up like a sprout since the last time we saw you, but then that was quite a while ago," she added, giving Rob that reproachfully genteel smile she reserved for him alone. "You look tired, Robert." Her finely arched gray brows knit as she regarded her son-in-law.

"It's a long drive."

"Nothing a good shot of Jack Daniels won't cure, I wager." Max pounded Rob's back as if he were trying to dislodge something caught in his son-in-law's throat. "C'mon in, my boy. We'll give the womenfolk a chance to fuss around in the kitchen while we down a couple in my study." He gave the smaller "woman" an appreciative wink.

Karen beamed with pride, but balked on the steps. "What about the presents? They're still in the car."

"Well, let's bring 'em inside, sweetie." Max hurried to do his grandaughter's bidding, his face wearing the same doting smile that Rob had seen him lavish on Sylvia so often. "My, my, this is certainly a big present. I bet it's for me!" Max chuckled, and, before Rob could intervene, he had wrestled Lisa's enormous gift out of the back seat.

"No, that's Daddy's." Karen was quick to correct her grandfather. "From Lisa," she added to banish any lingering misunderstanding.

"Oh" was all the elderly man said, but Rob thought the look he gave him revealed a hint of suspicion.

Quit worrying about your in-laws, Rob admonished himself that evening after he begged off a second drink and made his way upstairs to the guest room. And quit worrying about Lisa Porter. Fat chance of either, he thought as he finally tossed aside the John Irving paperback that he had been staring at for thirty minutes and angrily switched off the bedside lamp.

And, on that count, Rob was right. Even in the midst of the Christmas morning excitement, while he snapped pictures of Karen tearing into Santa's surprises that he had secretly hauled to the Cheathams' in the Mercedes's trunk, everything reminded him that he was with his in-laws and not with Lisa.

"What lovely ballet slippers!" Amanda cooed, watching her granddaughter pirouette through the piles of crumpled wrapping paper.

"They're from Lisa." Karen executed a wobbly plié before turning to Rob. "Daddy, you haven't opened your gift yet."

"No, I haven't." Rob's titter must have sounded as foolish as his lame comment. "Well, let's see what we have here." With a game smile, he scooted the ponderous box from beneath the tree.

As Rob unwrapped the big box only to discover yet another, smaller box, he was acutely aware of Amanda's incredulous gaze riveted on him. Each package opened only to reveal a consecutively smaller package until, at last, Rob reached a leather case bound with gold ribbon. He hadn't been up to his ears in wrapping paper since he was a child, he reflected, and he felt every bit the kid as he slipped open the case and saw the engraved cuff links nestled on a bed of maroon velvet.

"Why, Robert, they are just exquisite!" Amanda's drawl dripped over him like warm honey as she stomped her way through the wrapping paper for a better look at the links.

"Those are right handsome," her husband agreed. He took a couple of thoughtful puffs on his pipe, and Rob could tell he was doing an instant appraisal of the stunning fourteen-karat jewelry. "Whoever picked those out has taste, I've got to say that." he coughed, expelling a draft of bluish smoke.

"They're from Lisa. Just like my slippers," Karen volunteered, pointing a pink satin toe for her grandparents' inspection.

"Well, they're certainly very lovely." Amanda's faded blue eyes swept the cuff links and Rob's weakly smiling face in one glance. "Now, let's try to clear away some of this mess before the rest of the family gets here."

Rob wished he could clear away his mess as efficiently as Amanda crammed the discarded paper into a polyvinyl bag and consigned it to the trash can, but, as Christmas day progressed, he only felt himself miring deeper into depression. The harder he tried to keep up a game front and join in the merriment, the more he felt the dejected outsider. Not that anyone seemed to notice: by noon the house was overflowing with guests, and Rob guessed that even an accomplished hostess like Amanda had trouble keeping track of them. Cheathams whom he hadn't seen since his wedding day had surfaced, men full of back-slapping camaraderie and women with the practiced smiles that had been Sylvia's trademark.

"Hey, I heard about the Jewett case down in Charlotte!" a husky baritone boomed at Rob as he hunched over Amanda's mahogany sideboard and spooned brussels sprouts onto his plate. "Way to go, Rob!"

Rob looked up into a round, florid face and managed a flaccid smile, but his congratulator—one of Sylvia's numerous cousins—had already moved on to the cranberry sauce.

"Where are you going to eat, Daddy?" Laden plate in hand, Karen tugged at her father's sleeve.

Rob had never been more glad to see that rosy, angelic face. "Anywhere you want to, muffin." With Karen, he had a good chance of enjoying his dinner, especially since he wouldn't have to listen to a lot of inflated golf scores and exaggerated stock market coups. He willingly followed the shiny dark head into Max's library, away from the little tables that Amanda had arranged for her guests in the living and dining rooms.

"We'll have to tell Grandma what a nice meal she cooked for us." Seated at Max's massive oak desk, Rob made a stab at upbeat conversation.

Karen nudged a glazed baby carrot with her fork. "Yeah."

"You sure took some big helpings for a girl who's not hungry." Rob eyed Karen's untouched food.

"I'm hungry," Karen insisted in a small voice. Suddenly she looked up from her plate. "Daddy, are you mad at Lisa?"

A wedge of sweet potato lodged painfully in Rob's throat. "No, Karen. Of course not." He laughed nervously before taking a gulp from his wineglass. "Whatever made you think that?"

"I just wondered." Karen risked a bite of turkey before adding, "'Cause I sure wish she was with us right now."

"I do, too, sweetie." This is what it feels like to be a heel, Rob thought. Not only have I ruined Lisa's holiday and mine, but this innocent kid's, as well. He cleared his throat, still struggling with the recalcitrant sweet potato.

"Why didn't she come with us?" Karen was unwilling to let the subject drop.

Because your dad is a fool and a coward. Because he's too stupid to grab hold of the one chance at happiness he's ever had in his life. "I thought she'd be bored with all our relatives," he lied, letting his self-loathing sink to unplumbed depths.

Karen lifted an eyebrow. "Well, it's not as much fun without her."

"You can say that again." Rob swallowed hard, at last dislodging the lump of sweet potato in a contortion that threatened to rupture his esophagus.

"Here's where you've been hiding yourselves." The library door slid open, and Max Cheatham's voice reverberated through the room as if he were pronouncing a particularly stiff sentence from the bench. "Crowd's simmered down a bit out here, in case you're wondering."

"We were just getting ready to join the party again," Rob assured him, for once glad to have a buffer against Karen's remorselessly frank probing.

"Oh, you can stay put. Pour yourself a brandy. Take a nap." Max chuckled jovially. "I just wanted to see if my special little girl would like to take a look at ol' Golden Boy."

"I'd love to," cried Karen at the mention of the Cheathams' one remaining saddle horse. "It's okay, isn't it, Daddy?" Her cornflower-blue eyes anticipated Rob's familiar objections to anything vaguely equine.

Rob's consenting nod brought another squeal of delight from her. "Just don't plant your new shoes in anything smelly, okay?" He smiled at the way Karen grabbed Max's hand and dragged him down the hall.

At least, Lisa would have been proud of that, he thought, offering himself faint consolation. Where horses were concerned, she was firmly rooted in Karen's camp. Although she had tactfully avoided telling him how to raise his child, she had often pointed out that his fears were far greater than the actual risks involved. And she was right, of course. For a childless, single person, Lisa possessed some powerful insights where children were concerned. In Lisa, he had found a woman who was not only bright, beautiful and sexy, but also wise. And he had jeopardized their relationship with his silly equivocation.

With that troubling thought in his mind, Rob wandered out of the library and through the living room. As Max had pointed out, things had quieted down noticeably. People had clotted together into little clusters, talking over their coffee and dessert; a few diehards sat mesmerized in front of a televised football game. When Rob reached the kitchen he found Amanda alone, ladling coffee beans into an electric mill.

"Robert! Max was just looking for you." Amanda tapped the spoon against the rim of the mill.

"He found me." Rob rinsed his plate in the sink before sliding it into the open dishwasher.

"Don't bother with that," Amanda scolded him over the noisy whir of the mill. "Go out there and enjoy yourself!" Her free hand fluttered in an impatient shooing gesture.

"I didn't come back here to help clean up, Amanda. I came to talk." Rob latched his fingers over the counter's lip and searched for the right words. He had never felt very chummy with his mother-in-law, and even if he had, what he now needed to say would not have been easy. "I want to tell you about someone I've met, someone who's become very special to me and to Karen, as well."

"Lisa?" Amanda's finger was poised on the coffee mill's control button, but she waited for Rob's answer.

"Yes, Lisa. I know this may seem very sudden to you. You may find it hard to understand, but, well, I've reached the point where I think you need to know about this woman. Because of Karen." He searched Amanda's pale blue eyes, trying to see if anything he had said made sense.

A pained expression clouded Amanda's patrician face. "You're trying to tell me that you've fallen in love with this young woman, aren't you?"

Rob nodded, gaining courage in the face of opposition. He was framing a sentence to tell her, politely but firmly, that his life must go on, however dearly she cherished her daughter's memory, and that she and Max would have to see that Lisa was a positive force in their granddaughter's life.

The coffee mill buzzed abruptly and then fell silent as Amanda released the button in annoyance and folded her arms across her frilly apron. "Well, then I just don't understand why you didn't include her in our family gathering." The iron-gray brows rose in perplexity.

Rob blinked. He must have misunderstood her; the damned coffee mill must have interfered with his hearing. But Amanda went on, "If you don't mind my saying so, it's about time you've gotten yourself into circulation. Honestly, it's pitiful the way you've cut yourself off, hovering over that child as if she were a hothouse plant. You were worse than an old maid." She shook her head over what she clearly considered her most searing indictment. "And that hasn't been all that good for Karen, as I've pointed out to Max more than once. A girl needs a mother." She pressed the control button with renewed vigor.

"I did what I thought was best for Karen," Rob mumbled. He was too relieved at his mother-in-law's unexpected reaction to take offense at the verbal thrashing she was bent on giving him.

"I know, son." Amanda abandoned the coffee mill long enough to give Rob's hand a tentative pat. "We all make mistakes."

Do we ever, Rob thought. But now that the air was clear, his confidence was returning. Maybe it wasn't too late to patch things up with Lisa after all. If Amanda had reacted so positively to his news, anything was possible.

"Amanda," Rob began cautiously. "Talking with you today has really helped me to put some things in perspective."

"I'm glad to hear that, Robert." Amanda gave her son-in-law a smug look before turning to fill the coffee maker.

All the better if she believes she's responsible for setting me straight, Rob thought. He felt buoyed by the same sort of heady elation that often gripped him in the courtroom as he moved in for the kill. "And now I have a favor to ask of you, if I may."

Amanda swung around, measuring spoon in hand, and regarded him with motherly pride. "Why, of course, you may!"

LET THEM TICKET HIM. He was willing to pay a dozen speeding tickets, but nothing was going to stop him from getting back to Charlotte as quickly as possible. Rob's eye traveled to the speedometer, watching the red needle edge a little farther around its axis. It was already dark, but if he kept up the fast clip, the city—and Lisa's little duplex apartment—were only a half hour away.

Thank heaven that Karen's badgering had prompted him to talk with Amanda. He was still recovering from the shock of that conversation. All these years, he had expected Max and Amanda to scorn a new woman in his life as an un-wanted usurper of their daughter's place in Karen's mem-ory. The revelation that the Cheathams' concern for their granddaughter had been quite different prompted Rob to regard them in a different light now. And he would never be able to repay Amanda for agreeing to keep Karen through the weekend. Now if his luck would only hold out for the approaching encounter with Lisa.

He had never been more relieved to spot the green exit sign for his area of south Charlotte. He had squelched the impulse to drive directly to Lisa's apartment in favor of stopping by his house first to pick up his Christmas gift for her. During the miserable days following their quarrel, he had mulled over possible ways of presenting her with the elegant diamond-chip earrings he had so carefully chosen. Now he was grateful he had ruled out mailing them to her or leaving the small box on her doorstep. Lisa was prob-ably going to be a little resistant to an immediate reconcili-ation—and rightfully so; a gift from his heart would be a good way to demonstrate his sincerity.

Rob left the motor running while he sprinted into the house and grabbed one of the two gifts remaining under the tree. Jumping back into the car, he caught sight of himself in the rearview mirror. His dark shock of hair was more tousled than usual; his collar was rumpled over the neck of his sweater; gray circles rimmed the cobalt blue of his eyes. As he roared out of the driveway, a sobering thought occurred to him: although he had practiced law for over ten years, this was the first time he actually knew how a reprieved client must feel. Rob was a man blessed with a second chance, and he was determined to make the most of it.

A lump rose in his throat as he turned into the quiet Dilworth street and spotted the yellow Chevette parked squarely in the drive. She was home; the first hurdle had been cleared.

Lisa, I'm sorry. I know I've been a jerk, but I love you. The words traveled through his mind like subtitles in a foreign film as he envisioned her lithe body framed in the doorway, her lovely face turned up to him. Her expression would be a little aloof, perhaps even angry, but that was all right. He would insist that she hear his apology, let him explain why he had acted the way he had. Her large dark eyes would search his face and recognize his honesty. She would look down, hesitate, and then he would take her in his arms, tell her all she meant to him, smother her face in kisses, let his fingers plunder her hair, love her.

Rob pressed the buzzer next to the front door and waited. No light footsteps sounded in the hallway. He rang a second time, this time a little more urgently. The thought that Lisa might be taking a nap set off a fresh wave of guilt; his stupidity had spoiled her Christmas, and she had decided to sleep away the boring evening. The third time he poked the doorbell, the curtain masking the front window rippled slightly as Lisa's cat sprang onto the sill.

"Hey, Chuck, old boy." Although Rob was sure the cat couldn't hear him, he was now desperate for any contact, however feeble, with a member of the household.

The big yellow cat regarded him without blinking, but the little inverted V of his mouth had a decidedly unfriendly look to it. If cats have thoughts, Rob could easily imagine this one thinking "What the hell do *you* want?"

He hadn't prepared himself for this, for Lisa simply to barricade herself in and ignore him. If she had come to the door, girded for battle, at least he would have had a chance to explain. But what could he say to a wall of silence?

"Lisa?" Rob rapped the door smartly. "Lisa, I want to talk with you."

The curtained windows stared back at him like blind eyes. Head sunk in dejection, Rob turned and walked slowly down the stone steps.

Chapter Nine

"They're all alike." Anne Torrence's green cat-eyes darted angrily from the red traffic light to Lisa and back again. "Talk, talk, talk, but when the chips are down," she scraped the gears noisily and lurched into the intersection, "they're worth zilch!"

Lisa continued to look out the window at the elaborately decorated lawns, replete with Santa's sleighs and life-size crèche scenes. "I'm beginning to agree with you," she mumbled, more to placate Anne than to encourage conversation.

"Take Scott." Anne snapped the turn signal so viciously, Lisa expected the spindly lever to snap off the column.

"No, *you* take him." Lisa turned away from the window, chuckling.

Anne shook her head. "At least your sense of humor is returning. That's a positive sign."

"Look, did you think I'd accept your parents' invitation to have Christmas dinner with them and spend the day moping? I intend to enjoy myself today." She leaned over and pecked Anne's arm with one finger. "You should, too, kiddo."

"I will." Anne wrenched the wheel resolutely, and angled the car into the curb. "I'm just a bit peeved that Scott isn't coming over until this afternoon. He should simply tell his friends that he'll see them later, after he has dinner with my folks. Period. This split-shift business is ridiculous."

"You wanted someone more socially inclined than Larry. And at least he'll spend the afternoon with you." Lisa groaned as she pushed herself out of the low-slung bucket seat.

"Sorry, Lisa. I guess my complaining does sound selfish after the trick Randolph pulled on you." Anne slammed the door and joined Lisa on the lawn.

"Don't apologize," Lisa said, linking her arm through her friend's. "I'm better off without someone as wishy-washy as Rob. He needs to get his own act together before he tries to have a relationship." If she repeated that maxim often enough, maybe she would begin to believe it herself.

Mrs. Torrence was waiting in the open doorway, her arms outstretched in welcome. "Merry Christmas!" she cried, throwing her arms around her daughter. Every time Lisa saw the still-curvaceous woman with her lively green eyes and cropped russet hair, she felt as if she were looking twenty years into the future at Anne.

"It's a pleasure to see you again, Lisa," Mr. Torrence said quietly in a drawl that still carried the soft echoes of his Tidewater boyhood.

"I really appreciate your including me in your Christmas," Lisa said. She followed the Torrences into their wainscoted den with its expansive tiled fireplace and traditional Christmas tree.

"Hey, Lisa," a cheerful voice greeted her.

Lisa smiled at the young man who had leaped from an easy chair to proffer a large hand. Even if she had never met Elliott Torrence before, his flaming red hair and puckish, freckled face would have identified him unmistakably as Anne's twin brother.

Elliott gestured to the chair in front of the fireplace. "When Anne told me she was bringing a friend along today, I didn't want to be outdone. I guess Roger Mac-Murphy doesn't need my introduction, but here he is anyway. Bet you didn't know that Rog and I are old pals; we roomed together at the university for two years. Rog, this is Lisa Porter.''

As Elliott made his introduction, Lisa redirected her attention to its subject, the man who was now ambling across the room in her direction. She couldn't imagine why Elliott had said he needed no introduction; she was sure she had never seen him before in her life. And one thing was certain: no woman, not even one as preoccupied as she, would be likely to forget a man as gorgeous as the one holding out his hand to her right now.

He was tall, so tall that his black blow-cut hair barely seemed to clear the low ceiling. But Roger MacMurphy's height was not his only extraordinary feature; in fact, everything about him seemed to have been designed to shock the observer with its sheer perfection. Dark matinee-idol eyes were spaced in exactly the right proportion to his squared jaw and straight nose; his cheeks glowed with the sort of tan that always reminded Lisa of her years in Florida. The cursory glance that she gave the rest of him discovered a physique that looked as if it had stepped out of an ad for body-building machines.

"Hello, Lisa" rumbled from somewhere inside his cavernous chest, while the dark eyes narrowed to convey a less impersonal greeting of their own.

"Roger," Lisa replied timidly when his big hand enclosed her own in a prolonged clasp.

As Roger returned to his corner, Elliott took the opportunity to elbow her slyly behind his friend's back. "Some surprise, huh, finding Roger MacMurphy under the Christmas tree." Elliott's shoulders shook in amusement, but the joke was totally wasted on Lisa.

"I'm prepared for anything these days, Elliott," she said with a wry smile. *Even for a setup as crude as this one.*

"You haven't seen the kitchen since Mom had it remodeled, have you, Lisa?" Anne said pointedly. An insistent jerk of her fiery head signaled Lisa to follow her. When they were safely out of the living room crowd's earshot, she fastened both hands on her friend's arm. "I swear to God, I had no idea Elliott was bringing Roger along," she whispered.

"Did you tell him anything about Rob and me?"

"Are you kidding? I love my brother, but our relationship as adults is pretty much confined to touching base now and then. I'd never discuss anything like that with him. I *did* mention to Mom that you probably weren't going to be seeing Rob any more." Anne bit her lip and looked at the floor. Hearing Lisa's despairing moan, she hastily continued, "But, believe me, this isn't what you think it is. Roger is a nice fellow, and if you sort of ignore him—"

"He'll go away?" Lisa interrupted, shaking her head in exasperation. "Sorry, Anne, but you'll have to do better than that."

Anne tittered, but quickly sobered under Lisa's perturbed gaze. "I'll help you, Lisa. Don't worry; we'll get through this one."

"I'm sure we will; I just wonder what shape we'll be in afterward."

Despite her initial dismay at finding a spare male in the Torrences' living room, Lisa had to admit that circumstances conveniently limited her contact with Roger for the remainder of the morning. Anne skillfully monopolized her time, showing her around the newly renovated kitchen and adjoining solarium, and afterward Lisa quite naturally offered to help with the cooking. Roger made his way back to the kitchen once, on the pretext of getting some ice cubes, but by then she had already wrapped herself in an apron and was occupied with a pile of fresh green beans.

"You like to cook, huh?" Roger jiggled the ice in his old-fashioned glass and propped an elbow on the counter. When he smiled Lisa noticed that his teeth were as perfect as the rest of him.

"Sometimes." Lisa returned his smile. Poor thing, she thought in a moment's weakness, he couldn't help it if Elliott had pared him off with a woman as unreceptive as she.

"Let me give you a hand." With remarkable agility Roger rounded the counter and shouldered up to Lisa. "I interviewed Julia Child once," he assured her modestly. Lisa was wondering what bearing that distinction could possible have on his ability to trim a pound of green beans when Mrs. Torrence bustled in from the dining room to rescue her.

"Now, Roger, you just get back to the front room and leave the cooking to us. I declare, with a big fellow like you in here, we'll be falling all over ourselves." Mrs. Torrence took the bean pods from Roger's hand as if she were confiscating matches from a child. Responding to a motherly pat on his husky back, Roger obediently retreated, but not without giving Lisa a suggestive parting glance.

"Do you ever watch Roger's show on TV, Lisa?" Mrs. Torrence asked after the sound of his footsteps had disappeared.

"Roger has his own television program?" Lisa asked, at last making some sense out of Elliott's grandiose introduction.

"Why, of course, dear!" The attractive redhead regarded her as if she had failed to recognize Johnny Carson. "Right before the news on Saturday evening. He always has such interesting guests, big celebrities, you know." Mrs. Torrence looked very girlish when she wrinkled her nose. Her voice dropped to a conspiratorial level as she went on, "And he's such a dreamboat."

Lisa nodded weakly, watching one of her two allies desert to the opposing camp.

At least Anne was still on her side, she consoled herself as they gathered around the dinner table a half hour later. Thanks to her friend's engineering, Lisa found herself seated next to Elliott, but Roger—with skills learned in years of interviewing reluctant guests, Lisa imagined—managed to land directly across from her.

"El tells me you teach at the university here," he commented after Mr. Torrence had offered the blessing and dishes were being passed around.

"Yes, that's right."

"Well, tell me. What do you teach?" Roger spooned a heap of mashed potatoes onto his plate without taking his eyes off Lisa.

"Biology."

"Biology? That's really interesting. I mean, not many girls go in for that sort of thing, do they?" Roger paused, gravy boat in hand, and gave her an encouraging talk-show-host smile.

"Over half of the doctoral candidates in my class were women," Lisa remarked with heavy emphasis on the last word.

Roger fostered a suitably amazed expression and completely ignored her putdown. "Isn't that something? Do you think that could be the new trend? I mean, what made you decide to become a biologist? Did you read about Margaret Mead when you were a little girl?" His perfect mouth glided into a wider smile, the better to coax a response out of that little girl.

Lisa was wondering whether it was worth the effort to tell him that Margaret Mead was an anthropologist, not a biologist, when Roger sensed the dead end and immediately jumped to another topic. "When you're not in the lab, what do you do for fun?"

"I read. I play racquetball or tennis sometimes," she muttered grudgingly, hating herself for letting him coerce any information out of her.

"You're a tennis player! I should have guessed, though. A girl doesn't stay in your kind of shape by hunching over a microscope all the time." He leaned back in his chair slightly, the better to appraise the shape in question.

Lisa cringed, wishing that the centerpiece of red and white carnations were positioned a mere six inches farther down the table, just enough to screen her from Roger's relentless efforts to draw her onto common ground.

"I play a little tennis myself, now and then. You know, Bunky Williams was a guest on my show last year." Roger cleared his throat and waited for the tennis pro's name to take effect on Lisa.

"No, I didn't know that," Lisa coolly responded to his rhetorical question. *But then I've never watched your show,* she wanted to add, just in case he didn't realize how unimpressed she was.

Accustomed to keeping a conversation rolling, Roger never gave her a chance. "After that show Bunky kept hounding me to get out on the court with her." His shoulders rose in the helpless shrug of a man imprisoned by his own stardom. "I said, 'Bunky, you're going to be sorry.'" A sudden burst of laughter interrupted his narrative, hinting at the hilarious details that were yet to come.

Lisa shrank lower in her seat, mindful that, unlike the guests on Roger's show, she could count on no merciful commercial break to bail her out. She was trying to steel herself for another round of name-dropping when the doorbell rang, drawing everyone's attention to the new arrival. When Anne returned to the table a few minutes later, an urbane-looking man who would have been an excellent candidate for the new James Bond was on her arm. After introducing Scott Purcell to everyone, she thoughtfully deposited him next to Roger. Thanks to Scott's well-honed social skills, the two men were soon thrashing out the merits of the Superbowl prospects, leaving Lisa to enjoy the remainder of her dinner in peace.

She had promised herself that she was going to have a good time today, but that promise was proving more difficult to keep than she had imagined. And it was all Rob's fault. Damn him, why did he have to pull the rabbit out of the hat the very night they had put up the Christmas tree? If he had discussed his plans with her at any other time, she probably would not have reacted so angrily. In retrospect, she could guess his reasons for not inviting her to accompany them to Winston. His in-laws would probably have been less than thrilled to meet a woman who threatened to occupy their daughter's place in his life and Karen's. But that was no excuse for his clumsy handling of the situation with her. Lisa was frowning over these thoughts as she excused herself from the table after dessert.

Locked in the welcome solitude of the Torrences' bathroom, she caught sight of her unsmiling face in the mirror. Did she really look older, or was it just her imagination? Lisa leaned across the vanity and inspected her usually sparkling eyes. Yes, those dark circles could not be attributed to smudged mascara; Rob Randolph had put them there with his infernal silliness.

"Forget him," she told the mirror image coldly. This was not the first time he had thrown her a curve, and it would surely not be the last if she weakened and made up with him.

Sighing, she pulled back from the mirror, as if resigning herself to what she saw reflected there. She loved Rob, and that love was not going to evaporate into thin air simply because they had quarreled. Worst of all, being around someone like Roger MacMurphy only reminded her of the qualities in Rob that had attracted her in the first place, the traits that had caused that attraction to ripen into love. She bit her lip, fighting the memory of Rob's caress, of his kiss, tender and passionate at the same time. How long would that memory rise to torment her before she could finally lay it to rest?

A timid knock at the door intruded on her musings. When Lisa opened the door Anne's freckled face popped into view.

"Lisa, Scott has been invited to a caroling party tonight. Lord, I'm beginning to think he knows everyone in Charlotte, but this does sound like a lot of fun. Would you like to come? We won't be gone long, so if you're not interested, you can stick around with Mom and Dad."

Lisa needed only a moment to weigh her options. Whether she joined Scott and Anne or decided to remain behind at the Torrences', Roger MacMurphy was certain to do the same. "If you don't mind, I think I'll pay my respects and head for home."

"I understand. You're welcome to take my car; Scott can run me home later." Anne gave Lisa's hand a sisterly squeeze.

"Thanks, Anne."

"You're going home now, too?" Roger MacMurphy sounded genuinely surprised when Lisa announced her intentions in the living room. "So am I, and I'd be glad to drop you off."

"That's really kind of you, Roger, but Anne has already offered me her car."

"C'mon. You live in Dilworth; that's right on my way."

Silently vowing to root out and punish the person who had leaked the location of her apartment to Roger, Lisa smiled resolutely. "That really isn't necessary." *Where are you, Anne? This is your cue to help me.*

But Anne only shrugged. "If he wants to give you a lift . . ." With a dark look Lisa warned her to go no further, but a sinking feeling told her the decision had already been made for her.

"Okay, Roger," she agreed. *We'll drive straight to my place; you'll let me out, and we'll never see each other again,* she silently reassured herself.

Lisa felt practiced hands settling her coat around her shoulders. "It certainly was a terrific meal, Mrs. Torrence," she heard Roger say as they moved toward the door.

Her face still frozen in a weak smile, Lisa thanked the Torrences and followed Roger down the flagstone walk. "What do you think of this baby?" he asked when they reached the curb. He tossed his key ring into the air before stooping to open the door of a racy black Porsche with the unequivocal license plate of "Rog-Mac."

"It's beautiful," she said, folding her coat over her legs as she scooted into the low-slung sports car.

"Like you." In a feat that defied all spatial laws, Roger had somehow fitted his muscular trunk into the cockpitlike driver's seat. He cut narrowed eyes in her direction before twisting the ignition key.

The engine revved, and Lisa stiffened in her seat. This was the worst she could have imagined—well, almost the worst: the two of them confined in a small car with Roger paying her idiotic compliments. Please, *please*, she begged the Fates that controlled her life, let him talk about Julia Child or Bunky Williams or himself, just don't let him get romantic. How he could entertain even remotely fond thoughts of her baffled her; she had acted like a monosyllabic dolt every time he had cornered her into a conversation. But then this was Roger, she reminded herself.

As soon as they reached the main thoroughfare, however, Roger's preoccupation with Lisa took an immediate second place to the piloting of his flashy sports car. Gears ground, tires squealed, the engine roared as they cut through the sparse Christmas evening traffic as if they were headed for a hospital emergency room. Once Roger turned to see how she was taking the wild ride, his jaw jutting in macho triumph.

"Watch out!" Lisa ordered, pointing toward the rear end of a city bus that had suddenly loomed up in front of them.

By the time they turned off Queens Road, she was wondering if her rubbery knees would carry her into the house. "There are kids in this neighborhood, so you'd better slow down," she told him tersely.

He gave her a slick grin, but slowed to a sedate pace. Another three blocks, and she would be home, Lisa consoled herself. At home, alone with her cat, insulated by her answering machine. She wisely began to rehearse the frosty but polite speech with which she would bid Roger goodbye before alighting from his car. She did not owe him a drink and an hour of chitchat in return for a ride home, she told herself sternly, squelching the well-mannered impulses that would only encourage his persistence.

"Mine is the red brick bungalow on the left," she told him.

Roger obligingly wheeled into the driveway, right behind the blue Mercedes sedan parked there.

Lisa's throat went dry; waves of heat, then cold washed through her as she recognized the car gleaming in the Porsche's headlight beam. She closed her eyes and let her head drop forward, clenching her teeth and hoping that by some miracle when she looked up, the Mercedes would have vanished. *I just don't believe it.* It was bad enough that she had to plot a strategy for tactfully dismissing this celluloid name-dropper whom she hardly knew; now, on top of that, she was facing a confrontation with Rob.

"Thanks so much, Roger. Drive safely, and have a merry Christmas." With that farewell address, Lisa hoped to leap out of the car and walk purposefully to her door, but the Porsche's space-age door handle foiled her plan. While her hand floundered against the door in search of the elusive handle, Roger seized his chance to bound from behind the wheel and rush to help her.

"Thanks," she repeated as the door snapped magically open and those unnervingly strong hands pulled her from her seat. "Well, have a merry one, what's left of it, and a happy New Year." Lisa tried to sound jaunty, but the knowledge that not one, but two potentially trying men stood between her and the tranquil security of her home drained the mirth from her voice. It had been a long day and promised to be an even longer night.

"Hey, you know, Lisa, I don't know much about you or anything, but I'd like to get together with you sometime. Whaddaya say?" Roger smiled—winningly, even Lisa had to admit—as he dug his hands into the pockets of his blazer.

If only he had tried a cocky, self-assured approach, it would have been easy to dispatch him with a scathing "no." But Roger's boyishly disarming attitude was much harder to deal with, making her feel cold and unkind. "I'm sorry, Roger, but I don't think so." Lisa bit her lip and, in spite of her resolve, avoided his eyes.

Roger dug the toe of his Gucci loafers into the gravel underfoot. When he cut his eyes up at her, they were full of resignation but free of spite. "I guess there's someone else then," he said, pouncing on the only reason he could imagine for any woman to pass up a guy as good-looking as he.

No sooner were the fateful words out of his mouth than a deliberate crunch of gravel signaled Someone Else's approach on the drive. As Rob stepped into the walkway lamp's beam, Lisa saw that his shadowed face was unsmiling, his mouth set in an unpleasant line.

"Rob, I didn't expect to find you here," Lisa said in an unnaturally even tone. They might as well go on and get this over with.

"I can see that." Rob stopped beside the Mercedes and propped a hip against the hood. His eyes swept Roger with a look of undisguised contempt.

Roger's mouth fell open; he looked from Lisa's taut face to that of this hostile specter who had materialized out of nowhere and then back to Lisa. Skilled as he considered himself in dealing with all kinds of people, something told him that this situation was rapidly getting beyond his control. He closed his mouth as his mental computations began to add up. "Well, nice meeting you, Lisa." He pulled a hand out of his pocket and half extended it, but thought better of it at the last minute. Without further ado Roger MacMurphy climbed into his Porsche and shot out of the drive, leaving Lisa to deal with her Someone Else alone.

"I thought you were in Winston-Salem." Lisa broke the silence left in the wake of the Porsche's powerful engine.

"I can see that." Rob folded his arms across his chest, as if he were prepared to spend the rest of the night leaning against his car.

"Can't you say anything besides 'I can see that'?" Lisa snapped, letting her temper surface.

"Yeah, plenty, but I don't think you want to hear any of it."

"Try me."

The lamplight set Rob's silhouette off in stark relief as he looked away. Lisa could see the strung sinews of his neck flex as he battled his emotions. "I could tell you that I drove back here to see you today," he said tightly. "Somehow I had kidded myself into thinking you'd be spending Christmas alone." Shaking his head, he looked down at the white graveled drive. He laughed without smiling, a short, cynical laugh. "You don't waste any time finding replacements, do you?"

Now it was Lisa's turn to stare, openmouthed. "You mean Roger? Me and Roger? Why, that's the most ridiculous thing I've ever heard!"

"I'll agree with you there; it is pretty ridiculous." His eyes locked with hers in a cold ice-blue gaze.

"Rob, be serious! Do you honestly think that I would be attracted to a guy like Roger?" Lisa broke off, for his hostile look said that he did indeed. He had to be insanely jealous to give such an incongruous match a moment's credence, but as she searched that rigidly set face, jealousy was what she saw, jealousy and an abundance of hurt pride. "Look, we've got to talk this out like adults."

"I tried that two weeks ago, but you weren't interested."

"Damn it, Rob! Quit trying to put me down with dumb one-liners! I'd like to know how you'd have felt if I'd pulled a trick like that on you." Lisa's hands balled into small fists, and she took a couple of steps toward him.

"I can tell you how it feels, Lisa." Rob pushed himself away from the car, rising to the bait. "You play hurt after we have a little misunderstanding, so I run back here like a fool, all the way from Winston, to find you with some phony glamour boy you've dragged out of a tanning booth.

"You can't talk to me like that!" Lisa jabbed his lapel with her finger. "After all the plans we made for Christmas, you dumped on me, Robert Randolph. If that's what you call a little misunderstanding, then we're not using the same vocabulary. And if you expect me to hang around the house until it's convenient for you to work me into your life again, you're wrong!" She paused for breath, sucking in the frosty night air in sharp gulps.

"So you admit it!" Rob's fist slammed his palm triumphantly. "You *were* out with that guy!"

"Save your hotshot attorney's tactics for the courtroom, Rob. They won't work with me. Whom I see is my business and no one else's." Lisa's voice had been rising steadily with each new onslaught; her last remark was delivered in a shout.

"Fine. I couldn't care less." Rob's hoarse voice matched hers, decibel for decibel. Anger had splotched his tanned face with red, and when he grabbed the door handle of the Mercedes, he looked as if he wanted to rip the door from its frame. Stepping around the open door, he faced Lisa again.

Lisa cleared her throat and took a deep breath. She was still furious, but not too furious to see what they were both doing. "Look, I think we're both too upset to discuss anything tonight, okay?"

"What's that supposed to mean? That we kiss and make up next week?" Rob's voice dripped sarcasm as he sank behind the wheel of the Mercedes.

"No, it doesn't! You're so sure you're right, you can't see how pigheaded you're being." Lisa's hand rapped the door of the Mercedes. "So go ahead and think what you like. You'd rather feel sorry for yourself than admit you're wrong."

"I admit I was wrong—about you," Rob sneered.

Lisa slammed the door of the big sedan so hard the whole car seemed to shake. "I never want to see you again!"

As the car's powerful motor blazed to life, Rob stomped the accelerator. Bits of gravel spewed from beneath the wheels as he jerked the gears into reverse. The car swerved under his agitated steering, narrowly missing one of the brick planters at the end of the drive. With clenched fists,

Lisa watched him pull out; the car cut short as it turned, uprooting one of the border azaleas at the same time.

Lisa ran to the end of the drive and watched the red taillights drawing away from her. Something caught the heel of her pump, and looking down, she recognized the azalea that had fallen victim to Rob's angry departure. Without thinking she picked up the mangled plant and hurled it after the speeding car. "And don't ever come back!" she spat through clenched teeth. Then she turned on her heel and stomped up the drive to the dark house.

Chapter Ten

"Rob! Rob Randolph!"

Stooped over the water fountain, Rob took a last gulp before letting the icy jet die. He straightened himself and scanned the throng filling the corridor of the courthouse, trying to pick out the person who had called his name so enthusiastically. A friendly clap on his shoulder spun him around.

"Where have you been hiding yourself? We haven't seen much of you at the Queen City Grill lately." A chiding grin animated the polished ebony face of Lew Perry, one of the city's finest public defenders.

"I'm eating legal briefs for lunch these days." Rob laughed and hefted the attaché case at his side.

"That's one way to get rid of them, but they make a lousy diet. Seriously, I know what you're talking about. You've heard I'm on the Rayburn case? There's one that'll make an old man of me before it's over."

"From what I've heard, you've done a very good job of stacking the odds in your favor with Rayburn."

Lew dug his fingers into the muscular column of his neck. "I think I have. But, hey, I didn't flag you down to talk shop. How about a drink before we head homeward?" He shifted a folded trench coat from one arm to the other and gave Rob's arm an encouraging poke.

"Sounds like a terrific idea to me."

They chose a bar not far from the courthouse, a new place, resplendent with dark paneling and Tiffany glass, that was just beginning to catch on with the legal crowd. As they edged their way through the throng milling around an hors d'oeuvre buffet, Rob realized that he had not been around this many people in a long time. His sense of isolation increased after they had squeezed up to the bar and ordered martinis. True to his earlier assertion, Lew adamantly refused to discuss work, and as his conversation moved from a family Christmas celebration to his oldest son's math award to the Florida room he and his wife were adding to their house, Rob only felt more acutely the emotional poverty of his own life.

"How's your little girl doing?" Lew jiggled his glass, skillfully maneuvering the green olive within reach.

"Karen's fine. She's taking ballet lessons now. No toe shoes, they tell me, until she's twelve, but she already acts like a little Margot Fonteyn." Rob smiled into his glass. Much as he liked Lew, proud as he was of Karen and her girlish aspirations, that smile felt strangely forced.

"And you? How are you doing?" Elbow propped on the bar, Lew cocked his head to one side and regarded his companion with intense liquid brown eyes.

"All right."

"You don't look all right," Lew said carefully.

Rob swallowed and pulled himself up from the bar. His face ached from the contrary smile he insisted on holding there. "What makes you say that? You know what it's like to burn the candle at both ends."

Lew nodded, but he was obviously not convinced. "Maybe so, but you seem depressed, as if something were eating at you. You've hardly said more than two words since we've been here. I'd almost believe you do nothing but hole up in your office and prepare cases." He chuckled, more to put Rob at ease than to express amusement.

And if you believe that, you're right. "I'm just tired; that's all."

But that was not all, and Rob was too honest with himself to deny it. Almost a month had passed since the ugly scene with Lisa, and he was still agonizing over his loss. It was his fault, he told himself with merciless frequency. If he hadn't been so self-righteous, he would have talked things out with her. In retrospect, he now saw how preposterous his accusation had been; Lisa would no more run into the arms of someone like that character in the Porsche than he would. In fact, he knew that Lisa would be slow to run into any man's arms. But when he had raced back to Charlotte, he had expected to find her waiting for him, ready to listen to him and forgive him as she had before. When the expected scenario had not materialized, his pride had been hurt, and he had lashed out with the weapon nearest at hand.

He cringed at the memory of himself that night, sullen and nasty and full of abraded feelings. His behavior had been worse than that of a clumsy teenager bumbling through his first heartbreak. But if what he had said had been juvenile and unthinking, it had hurt Lisa, nonetheless. Words could have a finality; he had seen judges pass sentence often enough to appreciate that. And Rob, in his anger, had passed sentence on their relationship, condemning it to death.

Rob felt like a sad old man as he pressed the electric eye control and watched his garage door slowly descend later that evening. He would be a sad old man someday. Karen would be gone, with a family and career of her own; he would be left alone in his big, expensive, cheerless house, alone with nothing but his pride to keep him company.

"I've left the chicken in the oven, Mr. Randolph, and there's some rice on the back burner." Mrs. Elliott was busy bundling herself into her heavy coat as she greeted Rob in the foyer. "My, my," she said, watching him shake particles of frozen rain from his Burberry. "I don't know when we're going to get some sunshine again.

"I don't either." Rob's reply was more heartfelt than the stocky housekeeper could imagine. "Have a good evening, Mrs. Elliott," he said, holding the front door for her.

"Same to you, Mr. Randolph." She waved from the walk before bustling toward her daughter's waiting car.

The best evening Rob could hope for was one when he fell asleep early, and those evenings were infrequent. Most nights, he crawled into bed, numb with fatigue, only to lie awake with Lisa's face floating above him in the dark to torment him.

"Daddy, I didn't know you were home yet," Karen called from the top of the stairs before skipping down to give him a big hug.

"How's my angel?" Rob swung the compact little body back and forth in his arms.

"I've been practicing my ballet." Karen extended one short leg to demonstrate.

"Your homework is done, I hope?" Releasing her, Rob ruffled her hair affectionately.

"Uh-huh. You know I always do my homework before I dance. That was our deal, remember?"

"I know" was all Rob said. Every time he tried to play big, mature adult with his daughter, he was reminded of how orderly her life was in comparison to his own. When something was off kilter in Karen's little universe, she spoke up about it. She had not learned the self-deception and artificial smiles that masked so much pain in the adult world. As he placed the casserole of roasted chicken on a trivet, he prayed silently that she never would.

"Want to watch TV?" Karen asked when they were loading the dishwasher after dinner.

"Sure. Let's see what's on." Rob wiped his hands on a terry towel and tried to sound enthusiastic. He had sworn he wouldn't let his private misery over losing Lisa seep through to Karen, but he often wondered just how much he could successfully conceal from this very perceptive six-year-old.

A damp chill hung over the Randolphs' spacious den; outside the freezing rain had turned into sleet that pecked delicately against the window wall. While Karen fiddled with the television set, Rob knelt at the grate and tried to fan a blaze from the damp logs. At last a few stingy flames responded to his coaxing. Stretching his hands over the fire, he was reminded of the many nights that he and Lisa had sat in front of this fireplace, arms and legs intertwined in snug intimacy on the big sofa. There was no point in thinking about that now.

"Can you see okay, Daddy?" Karen swiveled the TV set on its base, one hand poised on her hip in a very grown-up fashion.

"Just fine." Kicking his shoes off, Rob sank onto the sofa and swung his feet onto a conveniently placed hassock. Folding his arms across his chest, he watched Bill Cosby lope onto the screen, followed by one of his sit-com kids. Lisa and he had never watched much television, except for an occasional movie. Sometimes they had played Scrabble with Karen; they had listened to music a lot, but mostly they had talked, talked about everything under the sun, their respective childhoods, their work, their dreams, their love.

Karen bounced on the cushion and giggled uproariously. "But see, he doesn't *know* that she really bought it for *him*!" Still chuckling, she pointed a finger at the screen. "And then when he finds out..." She glanced over her shoulder to see if Rob were following her commentary on the program.

Arm lapped over the sofa back, Rob stared uncomprehending at the screen.

"See, Daddy?"

Rob blinked, the wide, exaggerated blink he had used on his tenth-grade English teacher when she found him dozing during her eight-o'clock class. "Yeah," he said smiling brightly.

But Karen was not as easily fooled as Mrs. Bullock had been. "No, you don't. You haven't been watching at all."

Her accusing blue eyes pinioned him to the corner of the sofa. "If you're not going to watch with me, I'm going upstairs to dance." Seizing the remote control, Karen abruptly silenced the TV.

"I'm sorry, honey, but I just have a lot on my mind," Rob apologized. Things had gotten worse than he had thought if he couldn't even watch television with reasonable competence.

"You always have a lot on your mind. We don't ever have fun anymore because you're always *thinking*." Karen paused in the doorway; her cherub's mouth was pulled down into a disparaging frown. "When Lisa was here, we did neat things all the time," she hurled over her shoulder before dashing up the stairs.

Yes, we did. How could he have torn down a relationship as satisfying as theirs in a few short minutes? How could he have condemned himself to such lonely misery with a few careless words? That Karen was suffering from the loss as well as he only intensified his regret. He would have to talk with Karen; that was certain. But not tonight.

Rob pushed himself up from the sofa and plodded to the study. A cursory inspection of the bookcase cabinet turned up a full bottle of Remy Martin; one thing, at least, had gone right today. Clutching the brandy bottle and a snifter, he shuffled to his desk and poured himself a shot. The smooth, liquid slid down his throat, leaving a warm trail behind it. Rob tipped the bottle again and dispatched the second glass as quickly as the first.

Lisa. Lisa with hair like ripe wheat, hair that caught the brilliance of firelight in its wave as it rippled across her bare back. Lisa with the limpid brown eyes that could burn with such passion. Rob slumped deeper into the leather chair and closed his eyes. He could feel her precise, small hands as they smoothed the plane of his chest, rounding the curve of his shoulders to descend the slope of his back. He could smell her skin, sweet with warmth, as she stretched herself along him, molding her much smaller body to his.

"Lisa." Rob's lips formed her name before he emptied his third glass. His hand groped the desk through a brandy haze and found the telephone. Clumsily he punched out the seven digits and waited.

"Hello. This is Lisa Porter. I'm sorry that I'm unable to speak with you right now, but if you'll leave a message, I'll return your call as soon as possible." Beep.

Cool, crisp and impersonal, she had stated the rules of the game. Rob listened to the machine's sterile hiss for a few minutes before dropping the receiver. He had no message to leave.

"THAT LITTLE GIRL will be mighty pleased to hear her bird is doing so well." In spite of the pile-lined gloves he wore, Sam Wheaton chafed his hands energetically. His eyes continued to follow the movements of the caged red-tailed hawk they were watching through the two-way mirror, but Lisa had the distinct impression that she was being observed as much as Randolph.

"I'm sure she will," she responded without looking at Sam.

Sam waited a few minutes, watching Randolph flap his impressive wings in preparation for another glide. "You know, I think it would be a good idea if you brought her out here someday for a look at him, as long as you stayed back here out of his sight."

"We'll see. Now I've got to check on that new barn owl." Lisa flipped her collar up protectively around her face and marched out of the observation room. She could hear Sam following her on the leafy path, but contrariness prodded her to ignore him. He had been entirely too interested in her contact with the Randolphs in the past month; although Sam had not said as much, she felt certain that he suspected all was not well between Rob and her. That there was now nothing between Rob and her, she had tactfully kept to herself.

"Why don't you bring her out this weekend?" Sam had followed her into the trailer and was watching her shuffle through the under-counter refrigerator. Like a bulldog clamped onto a pants leg, he was not about to give up without a fight.

Lisa glared at him over the refrigerator door. "Look Sam, I don't see that much of the Randolphs anymore." She carefully avoided referring to Rob specifically. "For all I know they've completely forgotten this hawk." She placed two vials of antibiotic on the counter and slammed the refrigerator door with unnecessary violence.

"Pshaw! The way that fellow was calling here all the time? They haven't forgotten Randolph." Sam edged closer to the counter; his calloused fingers idly toyed with one of the medicine vials. "You know what I think?"

Lisa jabbed a hypodermic needle into one of the vials without answering. She knew Sam was determined to tell her what he thought, whether she wanted him to or not.

"I think you're mad at Rob Randolph for some reason."

Lisa tried to look stern. "Rob and I dated for a while, but we didn't really have much in common. It's as simple as that."

"Too bad," Sam commented as Lisa plucked the vial from his fingers and began filling a second syringe. "He seemed like such a nice young man."

"Come help me with this owl," Lisa said, stomping down the trailer's corridor.

He had seemed like a nice young man to her, too, Lisa thought later that evening when she was curled up on her couch, trying to make some sense out of the scribbling on her calendar. In fact, Rob was, undeniably, a nice young man; in the innermost sanctum of her mind she had never quit believing that. But that fact did not alter the circumstances that had led to their painful separation. Their lifestyles were too different—no matter how hard she tried to pretend that they were not—to permit them the kind of relationship that she needed, wanted, deserved.

Not a day had passed since their fateful encounter on the driveway when she had not considered calling him up to say she was sorry, opening her arms to invite him back. But Lisa knew that if she allowed Rob back into her life, she would only be setting herself up for a repeat of the disappointment and frustration that had led to this last argument. Rob was responsible for another life in addition to his own; for Karen's sake he would always be tied to his in-laws in Winston-Salem.

Then, too, Lisa had begun to suspect that Rob was unsure about getting seriously involved in a relationship. Perhaps the loss of his wife had scarred him so deeply, he feared ever surrendering his heart to a woman again. She could only speculate, but the creeping suspicion that Rob may have subconsciously wanted to sabotage the relationship sealed her decision not to contact him. And—she always added for good measure—after the spiteful things she had said to Rob, he would probably reject any suggestion of trying again, even if she was reckless enough to suggest it.

If only she had not fallen in love with him, she could put him aside as slickly as she had Jerry McCloskey and get on with her life. But long after her mind had accepted the rational arguments for letting him go, her heart clung tenaciously to his memory. With Rob she had felt loved and cherished and understood; with him she had believed, for a short time, that a man and a woman actually could unite in heart and mind as completely as they linked in the act of physical love. She had been wrong on that count, and that was what hurt the most.

Lisa clapped the pocket calendar shut. Thank God, the rest of the winter was crammed full of activities. The Wildlife Rehabilitation Center's education program was in its peak season, and Lisa was scheduled to conduct two presentations a week in elementary schools around Charlotte. She was looking forward to the work; young children always made an appreciative audience for the birds she displayed. And with scarcely a moment free, she would have less time to think about Rob.

But the specter of his darkly handsome face was hovering in her mind the entire morning as she loaded the center's van with two caged exhibition birds and the other materials she would need for her first show-and-tell. Whoever said it was impossible to do two things at once had never nursed a broken heart, Lisa thought grimly as she piloted the van carefully onto the school parking lot.

Jenna Hall, Lisa's contact at the school, greeted her on the lot and offered to carry her handouts. "The children are very pleased to have you visit us today," the petite young teacher explained, proudly pointing out the construction-paper hawks and owls decorating a bulletin board they passed. "As I mentioned on the phone, we decided to combine the first, second and third grades for your talk today."

"I've prepared my presentation for that age group." Lisa smiled as the teacher held open a classroom door for her.

"Children, I'd like to introduce Dr. Lisa Porter from the Piedmont Wildlife Rehabilitation Center. She's going to talk to us today about wild birds and how the center helps these birds when they're sick or injured."

The low buzz of childish voices was interrupted by much foot shuffling and rearranging of desks followed by a resounding chorus. "Hello, Dr. Porter!"

Lisa greeted the group and quickly arranged her enlarged photographs of various birds along the blackboard's chalk tray. Turning back to the little assembly, she smiled at a freckle-faced girl in the front row. "I know you're all excited to meet my two friends that I've brought along with me today." Giggles rippled through the crowd as Lisa nodded toward the two cages she had placed on the teacher's desk. "But, first, let's play a game. Who knows what kind of bird this is?" She pointed to a photograph of a great horned owl.

A forest of hands shot up instantly. Lisa's eyes traveled the room, looking for a likely candidate to answer her question. It wasn't until a chubby boy with white blond hair had leaped from his seat to respond that she noticed the two large blue eyes staring holes through her from the back of the room.

"That's right," Lisa managed to gulp out. Her voice sounded as if it came from a warped record, but spotting Karen Randolph among these children had taken her totally by surprise.

How the hell could she have known this was Karen's school, she thought furiously. Lisa turned toward the board again and pretended to contemplate the photographs there. "What about this fine fellow?" She held up a close-up shot of a golden eagle, trying not to cringe behind the picture.

More hands implored to be called on, but Karen remained stoically unmoving in her seat. As Lisa continued her presentation she avoided letting her eyes stray to that corner of the room, but she was constantly aware of the steady accusing gaze riveted on her, following her every move.

Damn Rob, she thought while she was removing William the owl from his cage. No telling what sort of story he had given his daughter to quiet her curiosity about Lisa's sudden disappearance. A pang of guilt stung her at the thought that she had offered the child no explanation whatsoever. No wonder the little girl was hurt; she and Lisa had grown very close in the short time they had been around each other. Karen had understandably enjoyed having a mother figure to confide in, and they had shared some times that had been very special for both of them.

"May I present William!" Lisa's theatrical introduction sounded a little flat today, but the children did not seem to notice. They were too enchanted by the little screech owl perched on Lisa's hand. As Lisa launched her narrative of William's life at the center, the owl twisted his feathered head and fixed her with his unswervingly direct stare. Did she imagine it, or was there a trace of reproach in those enormous yellow orbs? William had been her companion the first time she had crossed paths with Karen Randolph, she reminded herself as she returned the little bird to his cage.

After displaying William's sidekick, an American kestrel that had come to the center after being raised in captivity, Lisa concluded her talk with a question-and-answer session. Karen Randolph posed no questions, but then she knew a lot about birds already, Lisa told herself. Any questions forming beneath that smooth dark pageboy would have nothing to do with injured raptors. Lisa hoped that she did not look too relieved when the hour finally came to an end and the children thundered their farewell thank-yous. She had early made the cowardly decision to have her back turned when the group trooped out the door; when she at last looked up from the photographs she was stuffing into a portfolio, she was alone with Jenna Hall.

"Thank you very much, Dr. Porter. It's always a pleasure to have a speaker who can teach *me* something." The diminutive teacher seemed genuinely pleased. "Can you manage all of this? I'm afraid I have playground duty right now." She eyed the bulky portfolio and the two cages doubtfully.

"No problem at all," Lisa assured her with a laugh. "I'll have everything out of here in a jiffy."

She had dumped the remaining handouts and the photographs in the back of the van and was returning to pick up the birds when a small figure stepped out of an open doorway in the deserted school corridor. Karen did not speak, but her pleading eyes stopped Lisa as firmly in her tracks as a scream.

"Karen?" Lisa said haltingly.

The little girl did not answer but continued to stare.

Lisa felt her hands go cold; a cruel knot twisted her stomach's complicated machinery into a leaden ball. She had prepared herself for anything but this. Let Rob confront her, and she knew what she would say. But Karen, sweet, innocent Karen, how on earth could she explain to her the messy complex tangle of stupid adult emotions?

Following instinct more than any rational urge, Lisa
dropped to her knees. Her lips were trembling as she extended her arms and then opened them wide. Now her eyes
were pleading with Karen. The child hesitated for a moment, as if uncertain whether to trust this adult who had already violated her trust once. Then she broke into a run and
flung herself into Lisa's waiting arms.

"Oh, baby, I've missed you," Lisa found herself blub-
bering through the hot tears that smeared her mascara and
made her nose run.

"I missed you, too, Lisa."

Lisa smoothed the thick, silky hair back from Karen's
brow; shame overcame her as she saw the fat tears welling
over the rims of the china-blue eyes. "C'mon," she choked.
Enfolding a small damp hand in her own, she led Karen into
an empty classroom and pushed the door closed behind
them.

"Won't you ever come see us again?" Karen sniffed
noisily and rubbed an eye with her free hand. "You never
even got to open my Christmas gift."

The damning question. Lisa drew a shaky breath and
tried to organize her muddled thoughts. "Honey," she began, sinking onto one of the tiny desk chairs. "I was wrong
not to talk with you for so long." She pulled Karen onto her
lap and was comforted by the little arms that immediately
clasped around her waist. "It was a dumb thing to do, and
I'm sorry." Getting that much out was a major undertak-
ing, but she was feeling better already. Now came the hard
part. "You know, Karen, big people sometimes care a great
deal for each other, but certain things happen, and they find
that, much as they care for each other, they just can't solve
all their problems together." She stroked the dark head
snuggled against her shoulder and hoped her reasoning did
not sound too convoluted. "Your father and I are two people like that."

Karen squirmed against Lisa's shoulder and looked up
into her face. Lisa was gratified to see that she had stopped

crying, even though her face still wore an unnaturally grave expression.

"Do you miss Daddy?"

Lisa's throat began to swell as a wave of undammed emotion rushed up through it. She felt as if all the pent-up pain of the past month had now localized in her aching face, stinging her eyes, tugging at her twitching mouth, destroying her composure. "Yes, I do, very, very much." The admission was wrenched from her in a rending sob. She let her face drop against Karen's head as the tears began to flow in earnest.

"I think he misses you, too," Karen whispered into the curtain of Lisa's dark blond hair. She fished a Kleenex out of her pocket and gently blotted Lisa's face.

A bell blasted down at the other end of the hall, signaling the end of recess. Lisa was suddenly reminded of the two birds she had left unattended in the empty classroom. Straightening herself, she gave Karen's chubby leg an affectionate pat. "Karen, I'm so glad we saw each other again today, and I wish we could spend more time together right now, but I've got to take William and Skeets home, and you've got to get back to class." She smiled, an easier feat than she had expected.

Karen nodded tractably and slipped to her feet. Lisa held her breath, dreading the child's demand to know when they would see each other again. She had betrayed Karen once; she could not afford to repeat her mistake, but she had no idea what she would say if Karen insisted on another meeting. But the little girl apparently sensed her uncertainty; when they reached the corridor, she only chirped a shy "bye." With one last look over her shoulder, she scurried around the corner to rejoin her classmates.

Lisa stood numbly in the corridor, staring at the spot where Karen had stood. She was emotionally drained from their encounter, although grateful that fate had conspired to give her a chance to say what needed to be said. A second series of bells sounded, reminding her once again of the stranded birds waiting on her. Lisa dashed back to the classroom and was relieved to find the room empty and the two cages where she had left them.

"It's time to get you fellows home," she muttered to the two birds, but she was really talking to herself. It was going to take some time to recover from the interview with Karen; although she had reassured the child, the ticklish subject of maintaining contact with her remained unsolved. Lisa acutely felt the need for solitude and for time to think.

The halls were again empty when she headed for the parking lot; she preferred to slip out of the school without anyone's spotting the red-eyed woman tottering along between two bird cages. Fortunately the bell had conveniently cleared the playground of kids, allowing her to make her way unnoticed to the parking lot. Usually she enjoyed fielding questions and showing off the birds she loved so much, but her public relations skills had sunk to an all-time low this afternoon. The sooner she got away from this school, the better.

She had secured both of the cages in the back of the van and was about to climb into the driver's seat when a voice froze her where she stood with the key jammed in the van's lock. "Lisa." The voice was unmistakable, and it was not Karen's high-pitched chirp.

Her brain signaled her body to turn around and face Rob, but she was motionless, unable to move a muscle. She could feel his presence as he drew nearer; in a moment he would be close enough to touch her, and it was this fear that finally propelled her around. The last time they had seen each other, his face had been partially obscured in shadow; what she had seen of it had been dark with rage and injured pride. But Rob was smiling now, a gentle, tentative smile, and there was no rancor in the rugged, tanned lines of his face.

"Rob, how did you know...?"

The smile widened as he interrupted her tremulous question. "Karen told me someone from the Wildlife Center was coming to school. I crossed my fingers and hoped it would be you."

Lisa looked down at the hand he held out to her with its two middle fingers tightly intertwined for good luck. Her own hand jerked reflexively, wanting to take his, but she held back. Countless times she had pondered the right tone to strike should she and Rob ever happen to run into each other again; she would be cool but civil, distant enough to let him know he had forfeited the place he once held in her life, polite enough not to rub it in. An equally countless number of times she had regretted her role in that silly tableau on Christmas night, wished secretly for an opportunity to tell him how sorry she was. But now that he was standing here in front of her, the speeches that she had rehearsed to the point of exhaustion all deserted her. All she could do was stand there with a blank expression on her face.

Fortunately Rob's presence of mind had taken no such flight. "I promise not to take up too much of your time, but there are a few things I really want to say to you." His marine-blue eyes added a silent plea of their own.

Lisa's eyes darted from Rob to the school building to the van. Of all the scenarios she had considered for a possible encounter with him, this was one that had never entered her mind. "Okay," she said uneasily. "But let's at least climb into the van."

Lisa scooted across the frayed vinyl seat, letting Rob wedge himself behind the wheel. The untidy piles of manila folders, the smell of feathers and pine straw reminded her that she was on her turf, but they did little to make her feel at home. With her back to the door Lisa positioned herself as far from Rob as the cramped cab would allow, crossing her legs on the seat between them. She was conscious of every breath she drew as she waited for him to begin.

"I've been doing a lot of thinking since the last time I saw you, Lisa," Rob began, and Lisa thought she detected him shudder at the mention of that fateful last meeting.

"Thinking about how I've led my life so far, about the hands I've won and those I've lost. And I guess if I've learned anything in my career, it's that you can't change something once it's happened. Like it or not, we're doomed to live with our past." He was staring out the window, not looking at Lisa; his knuckles pale as his hands tightened around the steering wheel. "I always remind myself of that unpleasant fact when I set out to represent a client, and I'm trying to accept it today while I'm talking with you. Lisa, I can't change the way I acted at Christmas; I can't take back any of the idiotic things I said. All I can do is say I was wrong. I guess the immature kid hiding under the attorney's pinstripes just got out of hand that evening." A lopsided smile briefly relieved the tense lines of his face as he shifted to look directly at her. "I'm sorry, Lisa. That's all I can say. Will you forgive me?"

Will you forgive me? Lisa glanced nervously around the cab for help, but she knew there was no prewritten show-and-tell guideline to get her through this one. Knotting her hands into a self-conscious ball, she let her voice drop to a near whisper. "Only if you'll forgive me, too."

"Forgive you for what?" Rob's voice rose from its contrite level, and he leaned forward as if to touch her.

Lisa held him at bay with an upheld hand. "I share the blame for our misunderstanding, Rob, and you know that as well as I. At first, I enjoyed feeling indignant and hurt over what had happened; I told myself you had no right to pry into my life or to make demands on me after running off to Winston at Christmas. I suppose I hoped to ease the pain by repeating those things to myself, but I was wrong. Rob, can you forgive me?"

The smile that eased his face was like the sun breaking through winter clouds. "You know what I think?" He took her hands, gently unweaving their tight clasp, and cupped them in his own.

Lisa shook her head, venturing a shy smile.

"I think we forgave each other a long time ago. We just didn't get around to saying it until today. Remember the other time we had a misunderstanding? You didn't waste time patching up the lines of communication. I'll never forget how wonderful I felt when I opened the door that evening and found you standing there on my front steps. That was big of you, Lisa; and because you had the courage to take that step, our relationship grew. Well, this time, it was my turn to be a grown-up and take the first step. I'm only sorry that it took me a month to find the guts to do it. You know, I like to stack the odds in my favor, and I figured you'd hesitate to kick me in the seat in the middle of an elementary school parking lot." He laughed, a boyish, self-deprecating laugh, and Lisa joined in.

"You were right."

"I love you, Lisa."

"And I love you."

A sheaf of manila folders slid to the floor as the space between them disappeared. Arms wrapped around each other, they welded their mouths in a kiss that blotted out everything but the joy of being together again.

Chapter Eleven

"I'm sorry we had to postpone our get-together, Cindi, but when you stopped me in the hall last week, I had completely forgotten about that meeting I was scheduled to chair." Lisa dumped an armload of books onto her desk and swung the swivel chair around. She looked decidedly unprofessorial as she collapsed onto the chair and began rolling up the sleeves of her striped silk blouse.

"That's okay, Dr. Porter," the slim girl assured her. Tactfully moving the pile of papers occupying the only other chair in the office, she seated herself opposite Lisa and smoothed the crisp pleats of her wool skirt.

"Let's see. You wanted to take Anatomy 101 next term, right?" Lisa's hands began to flip through the files in front of her; at the same time her mind shuffled through its equally bulging records of the eight biology majors whom she regularly advised.

The girl nodded helpfully. "I thought it would be a good idea since I'm planning to apply for medical school next year."

"I don't see any problem here." Lisa's eyes glided over the photocopy of Cindi Jordan's transcript that fairly bristled with A's; looking up into the girl's serious young face, she wondered if Cindi had been born wearing a Shetland sweater set and a crisply starched blouse. Feeling rather untidy and disorganized herself, she slid the transcript back into the folder. "I'll look forward to having you in my class, Cindi."

"Thank you, Dr. Porter." Cindi smiled gratefully. As she hurried out of the office, Lisa caught a glimpse of her color-coordinated knee socks.

Consoling herself that a few months in medical school would have Cindi Jordan looking as harried as she, Lisa grabbed the nearest pile of ungraded labs. When the phone jingled a few minutes later, she scowled at the blinking button. Never count on getting any work done if there's a phone within earshot, she thought with an annoyance that carried over into her voice as she answered. "Yes, hello?"

"Ouch!" Rob laughed into the receiver. "Don't tell me, let me guess. A giant mutant bacterium has taken over the lab, and your students are all being held hostage."

"I should be so lucky!" Lisa giggled, cradling the phone beneath her chin as she tried to corral the labs with a thick rubber band. "How's your day going?"

"Better than yours, if that labored breathing I hear is any indicator.

Rob's chipper voice was infectious; already Lisa could feel some of her tension draining away. "You're going to have to learn not to be misled by my flair for the histrionic. I swear, I've had a perfectly normal, hectic, crazy, ulcer-inducing day, but I'm holding my own. As always."

"Well, I called to tell you to conserve some energy for tonight because I have a big surprise planned, just for the two of us."

"Sounds good already. Can I have a hint?"

"Yes, a big one, as a matter of fact. You are to leave work in time to go home, pack enough clothes for the weekend and be ready for me to pick you up at seven-thirty."

"Huh? You mean, we're going off for the weekend? But I'd planned to prepare my midterm exam on Saturday, and..."

"I won't take any excuses, Porter. This is your last free weekend from the Wildlife Center for the rest of the month, and we're going to take advantage of it. I've already bought plane tickets; Karen is spending the weekend with one of her little friends from ballet class; I've even phoned Anne, and she's agreed to feed Chuck. I don't want to hear any nonsense about an exam. Okay?''

"Should I bring something dressy?" Lisa asked meekly.

"Just as long as it's sexy."

That she had even considered holing up with a pile of papers when Rob was offering her a romantic weekend seemed sheer insanity by the time Lisa pulled on her coat at the end of the day. With a wicked smile she shoved the remaining labs into a drawer and snapped off the light. A whole weekend, just for the two of them; the thought alone put spring into her step as she braved the sharp wind sweeping the parking lot.

Of course, Rob and she saw each other almost every day; since their reconciliation, they had been careful to make time for each other, even if it only meant a family meal at Rob's house or working on their respective homework together in front of the cheery stone fireplace. In fact, they often spent the entire weekend together. But judging from the way Rob had talked on the phone that afternoon, Lisa guessed that he had something special planned this time, something out of the ordinary.

When she reached her apartment a heady rush of anticipation had already chased away her usual five-o'clock fatigue. By the time the doorbell rang at seven-thirty, her blue nylon bag and its companion carry-on piece stood waiting in the hallway.

Rob's face was flushed from the cold when Lisa opened the door. "I'm glad to see you haven't unearthed any compelling reasons to stay in Charlotte in the past three hours." He eyed the two bags over her shoulder as he pulled her close enough to deposit a kiss on her forehead.

"You may think I'm a contrary woman, Mr. Randolph—" Lisa let her fingers trip along the sloping rim of his collar "—but I'm actually quite compliant." Standing on tiptoe, she just managed to graze his ear with her lips.

"If you keep this up, we're going to miss our plane for sure," Rob reminded her, but he showed no eagerness to release her from his embrace. He nuzzled her cheek with the tip of his nose before leaving a little trail of kisses along the curve of her jaw.

Lisa drew a deep breath and pushed gently against his sturdy shoulders. "What time did you say our flight takes off?"

"Eight-thirty-five. Nine. Ten. Who cares?" Rob murmured carelessly. He seemed far more interested in the silky skin of her throat that his mouth was now exploring with considerable exuberance.

"Rob!" Lisa laughed as she at last succeeded in freeing herself. "After the way you lectured me on the phone this afternoon, I won't have us missing this plane just because we were—"

Rob's straight dark brows rose devilishly as she broke off, but he dutifully gathered up the bags and carried them out to the car.

"Good Lord!" Lisa exclaimed when he opened the trunk of the Mercedes. "I thought this was just a getaway weekend. Why on earth did you bring these humongous bags?" She gingerly flicked the leather handle of an outsize suiter that dwarfed her two modest bags.

"You'll be glad I brought that stuff before the weekend is over," Rob admonished her, giving her wrist a playful hands-off tap.

Lisa cut a sideways look at him, but she obediently withdrew her hand. "If you say so. I guess I'm going to have to accept that fact that you're not handing out very much advance information about this weekend." She settled herself in the car with a resigned sigh.

"That's the spirit." Rob gave her a good-natured chuck under the chin before shifting the big sedan into reverse. His boyishly mischievous smile said that he was enjoying himself immensely, not the least because Lisa insisted on trying to wheedle their destination out of him. Her wildly improbable guesses elicited howls of laughter from him, but when they reached the airport he gleefully informed her that she had not even come close.

"Fairbanks, Alaska?" she asked as they scurried across the windy parking lot.

"Nope."

"Anchorage, Alaska!" Lisa snapped her fingers triumphantly, but she was finding it increasingly difficult to hold a straight face.

"Wrong again." He shook his head as he walked purposefully up to the Piedmont check-in counter. As he withdrew two airline ticket folders from inside his jacket, Lisa's hand neatly intercepted his.

She quickly perused the tickets before exclaiming, "Charleston! Oh, Rob, how marvelous!"

"I thought you'd be pleased, although I was beginning to have my doubts a few minutes ago. All your talk about Alaska has given me a chill." He shivered, shifting the collar of his wool overcoat up around his ears.

"I was teasing," Lisa chided as her fingers rolled his collar back to its normal position. She grinned as she pocketed the boarding pass he handed her.

The flight to Charleston lasted less than an hour, but, as far as Lisa was concerned, it could have gone on indefinitely. Rob had booked them into first class, and to their delight they found themselves sharing the spacious cabin with only two other passengers. Snuggled next to the man she loved, Lisa looked out the window at the brightly lighted city drawing away from them below. Her hand curled around his wrist as her thumb gently ruffled the fine hair beneath his cuff. How infrequently did they have the luxury of being alone together, just the two of them! Secure in their plane, high above all the traffic and courtrooms and biology laboratories below, Lisa savored the intimacy of the moment. Rob had been wise to plan this weekend for them, very wise.

"Alaska it's not," Lisa remarked when they passed through the automatic doors of the Charleston airport. The humid salt breeze that swept the brightly lighted taxi stand seemed almost summery in comparison to the icy gusts they had left behind in Charlotte.

And Alaska it certainly wasn't. As their cabby cut through the narrow streets leading to Charleston's famous Battery, Lisa was impressed by the tropical ambience of the city. In addition to the familiar pines and magnolias of the central Piedmont, lush palms and drooping cypresses added their unique charm to the pastel row houses they surrounded.

"I almost feel as if I've been spirited off to a Caribbean island," she commented as they cruised along the Battery. Feeling Rob's hand loop around her shoulder, she added, "Spirited off to an island hideaway by a handsome pirate."

Privately, Lisa doubted if any pirate would have shown the exquisite taste in choosing his lair that Rob's choice of hotels demonstrated. He had made reservations for them in a lovely guest house directly overlooking the harbor. According to a plaque discreetly posted next to the reception desk, the house had been built in 1834, and the present owners had taken pains to preserve as much of the original handwork as possible.

"Your suite is furnished with authentic period antiques," the proprietress, an attractive woman in her mid-forties, told them proudly as she personally led them upstairs. "We only have six rooms, but the small size of our operation allows us to offer our guests something we feel is very special."

"I can see what you mean," Lisa murmured. Following their hostess into the beautifully decorated room, she felt as if she had stepped back into the early nineteenth century. Her eye traveled appreciatively from the classic rosewood dressing table to the snowy white embroidered counterpane

covering the four-poster to the inviting fire that crackled in
the brick fireplace.

"If we could just have a bucket of ice sent up, I believe
we'll have everything in order." Rob's smile had never been
more charming as he accepted the fancy brass key from the
proprietress. Closing the door behind him, he turned to
Lisa. "I don't know about you, but I'm going to exchange
these work clothes for something more appropriate."

"Good idea," Lisa agreed. "I'll, uh, just change into
something more comfortable." With a self-conscious wave
over her shoulder, she slipped into the adjacent dressing
room that linked the bedroom with the ultramodern bath.

Lisa unzipped her bag and began to dig through the outfits she had chosen for the weekend. The hem of a lavender
crepe de chine cocktail dress immediately caught her eye, but
she just as quickly dismissed it as too dressy. This occasion
called for something more casual. A satiny length of black
lingerie fabric appeared between the folded garments. Pulling the flimsy negligee out of the bag, she held it up to her
in front of the vanity mirror.

"No way!" she told the seductive image swaying before
her. The negligee was a little too comfortable for right now.
Returning to the open bag, Lisa smiled as her fingers
touched something soft and velvety. Without further hesitation she undressed and slipped the midnight-blue hostess
gown over her head.

Like most of the more frivolous items in her wardrobe,
the gown had been a gift from her mother. Lisa had often
shaken her head over the slinky evening dresses and elaborate party outfits lurking beneath the tissue in her mother's
latest "care package"; her casual life-style included few oc-
casions to wear such dressy clothes, but tonight seemed the
perfect excuse for the velvet hostess gown. She took the time
to run a brush through her loose hair that shone like burnished gold against the deep blue fabric. With a last tug at
the daring neckline that stopped well below the beginning of
her cleavage, Lisa returned to the bedroom.

Rob was standing in front of the fire with his back to her. At the sound of the door's opening, he turned, but not before she had the chance to admire the sculpted outline of his shoulders beneath the black sweater he wore. The soft cashmere molded itself over every well-defined muscle of his torso before falling into a loose fold around his trim waist. Lisa swallowed, but her throat was too dry for it to do her much good. She was vaguely aware that the lights had been dimmed in her absence and that a silver ice bucket containing a magnum of champagne had magically appeared on the dresser, but all of these details merely formed a soft-focus background to the tall, maddeningly handsome man who was walking across the room to her.

"You've never looked more beautiful." Rob reached out and let his hand lightly trace the glistening wave of hair falling across her shoulder. His touch was scarcely perceptible, as if he feared a more forceful gesture would disturb the lovely vision.

Lisa answered him with a smile. Everything she wanted to say, she said with her eyes as they drank in the ruggedly hewed planes of his face—the oblique cheekbones, starkly delineated beneath the sun-darkened skin, the firm jaw with its persistent dark shadow, the masterful angle of the high-bridged nose. And his eyes, those hypnotic eyes that shone like the Mediterranean beneath a summer sky, but with a depth as infinite as the ocean itself.

Rob's hand had completed its appraisal of her hair, coming to rest against her cheek. As his finger began to descend the slope of her jaw with tantalizing slowness she turned, burying her mouth in his palm. She kissed his palm before working her lips along each finger to the tip. Fascinating as this task proved to be, she was not so distracted as to ignore Rob's free hand that was now teasing the skin exposed beneath her neck. Practiced in their timing, the fingers savored the satiny texture of her skin before daring an excursion into the invitingly low-cut bodice. Ecstatic shivers tingled up Lisa's spine as Rob's hand slowly separated

the warm velvet from the ripe curve of her breast. The kiss
she was about to impart on his little finger dissolved into a
low moan as his hand slipped beneath her breast, cupping
its supple curve while his thumb teased the nipple into a hard
point. She let her head roll against his chest, pulling the
hand she still held against her.

"Oh, Rob," she murmured. The cool air fanned her fe-
ver-heated body as the velvet gown slipped first from her
shoulders, then her back, then her flushed breasts. Rob
stooped to penetrate the fall of hair obscuring her breasts;
his mouth followed the path his hands had pursued earlier,
firing the flames of passion that smoldered within her.

Responding to their own instincts, Lisa's hands began
exploring the solid, muscular body they held in their grasp.
A thin film of sweat covered his skin beneath the clinging
cashmere, allowing her hands to glide easily over the rock-
hard pectorals and into the thick dark hair blanketing his
chest. As she began to roll the fine knit away from his taut
stomach, Rob grabbed the hem and pulled the sweater over
his head in a single motion. Resisting his own urge to finish
the job he had begun, he stood with his hands resting at his
sides while Lisa first unclasped the Cardin belt, then unfas-
tened the hook securing the snug European-cut slacks. Only
when she began to ease the slacks down his trim hips did he
intervene. Soon his slacks had joined the sweater on the
polished floor, followed quickly by the discarded hostess
gown.

The cool surface of the snowy linens stung her hot skin as
Lisa let Rob lower her back against the bed. Although she
had always enjoyed their lovemaking, she had never before
felt such a raging desire for Rob as the one that now quickened her breath and goaded her hands into pulling him
closer. The rosy warmth suffusing Rob's skin, the azure
glow of his eyes said that he, too, was experiencing new
heights of excitement, but he drew back slightly, stilling her
greedy hands inside his own.

Resting one knee on the edge of the bed, he began to massage her legs. His fingers plied her feet, dancing capriciously across the sensitive instep; then they formed a ring around her ankle, squeezing their way up the curving calf until they reached the thighs. Slowly and rhythmically his hands edged their way toward her torso, pulling back just before they grazed the strong hair masking the heart of her desire.

She felt as if every fiber within her were being stretched to its limit by the almost painful tension that his skilled fingers had wrought. Finally she could bear it no longer. Pulling herself half upright, Lisa locked her hands behind Rob's neck and lowered him onto her febrile body.

The hard evidence of his own arousal grazed her stomach as he moaned softly, "My love! Oh, my love!" Abandoning herself to his touch, she let her body squirm sinuously beneath him, following the pressure of his solid, masculine bulk, leading him as they at last united and began to throb against each other. "I need you," he cried once more, this time through teeth clenched in passion. And she needed him, ached for him, craved him in a way that only their joined ecstasy could satisfy.

Riding the crest of the powerful wave that their lovemaking had stirred, Lisa could no longer distinguish between their tensed limbs that intertwined into one; the love they were sharing had overstepped the physical laws that normally separate one person from another, uniting them into a single loving consciousness. When the wave peaked Lisa felt her head fall back, her mouth open in a soundless shudder as the heavenly sweetness engulfed her. She was still swaying in its wake as Rob's sweating body tensed, then released itself to the same tremor that had just passed through her. She could feel his chest rise and fall in perfect rhythm with her own breathing as he collapsed next to her on the bed.

They lay there in silence for some time, enjoying the closeness and the mellow warmth pervading the room.

When Rob at last spoke his voice was hushed. "I couldn't love you more, Lisa." His hand gently lifted the damp strands of hair crisscrossing her brow. "And I've never *never* been happier than I have since I met you."

Lisa rolled onto her side to face him. "I love you, too, Rob." She wanted to say more, wanted to tell him that she had never loved before, that she hadn't even known what love was until she met him, but the words remained lodged, unspoken, in her heart. As if looking into herself, she closed her eyes, and when she opened them again, a little tear trickled down her cheek.

Rob smiled and tenderly kissed the tear away. His eyes caressed her, assuring her that he understood all of the love expressed in that tiny salty bead.

"You amaze me. I mean, you couldn't have chosen a better place for our weekend," Lisa murmured dreamily, digging a nest for her head in the crook of his arm.

"I'm glad you're enjoying yourself. Which reminds me, could I interest you in a glass of champagne?"

"So I didn't imagine the bottle in the ice bucket! I'd love a glass." Lisa propped her head on her elbow and watched Rob climb out of bed. "I didn't know you could order champagne in these little bed-and-breakfast places."

"You can't." Rob stopped long enough to pull on his slacks. "I brought our bottle along on the plane. And the two glasses, carefully wrapped in plastic bubbles, of course." He held up a glass and tapped its rim.

"I'm beginning to see why you brought such huge bags." Sitting on the edge of the bed, Lisa stooped to retrieve the hostess gown. She shook her hair out as her head emerged through the plunging neckline and then joined Rob at the dresser.

Handing her a glass of sparkling platinum liquid, he lifted his own in a toast. "To love."

"To our love." When the crystal rims met they produced a clear, ringing sound.

Rob took a sip before looping his arm around Lisa. "Are you ready for another surprise?" He led her slowly toward the bed.

"Another?" she gasped, but she let him gently seat her on the bed. When his fingers stroked her eyelids, she obediently closed her eyes tight. Tantalizing sounds of suitcase locks snapping open and paper rustling teased her ears, but Lisa valiantly resisted the urge to peek until she felt something light but strangely bulky drop onto her lap.

"Now you can look."

She opened her eyes to find a box large enough to hold a small television resting on her knees and Rob regarding her with boyish delight. "What on earth is this?"

"Your Christmas present." Lisa's face fell at the memory of that miserable holiday, but Rob's voice reflected only cheerful anticipation as he went on, "Don't think Karen's bald eagle poster is the only gift you're getting from us. And since you didn't get to open mine when you should have, I thought I'd better find a pretty special occasion to give it to you. Go on, open it up," he urged as she continued to gape at the huge box.

She carefully untied the red satin ribbon encircling the box and loosened the metallic green paper. Bold letters on the cardboard carton indicated that it contained a twelve-inch Sony portable television, complete with earphones, but the box was much too light, even for a tiny TV. Casting a suspicious eye at Rob, Lisa dug into the carton and discovered another one with the label of a G.E. toaster oven. "What's going on here?" she demanded, but by the time she had plowed her way through three more boxes, each successively smaller in size, she had caught on. Rob had used the same ruse to disguise her gift as Anne and she had with his cuff links. When she at last reached a small cordovan leather case, she knew she need look no further.

"Oh, Rob! They're simply gorgeous," Lisa exclaimed. In keeping with his general good taste, she would have expected Rob to choose an attractive, unusual gift, but the stunning

diamond-chip earrings sparkling against the gray satin lin-
ing exceeded her wildest imaginings. "I don't know how to
thank you."

"A kiss will do." Rob's lips were still smiling as they met
hers.

IT WAS AMAZING how much could be said with one kiss, Lisa
was to marvel more than once during their weekend in
Charleston. But then kisses were so versatile: Rob's lingering kiss on the back of her neck just before he relinquished
her hand as she headed for her morning shower; her impe-
tuous kiss over the Continental breakfast they had served in
their room, this one flavored with strong coffee and playful
intimacy; the quick kisses they managed to exchange, some
mere pecks, while they strolled along the Battery and poked
through the various attractive shops. Their kisses were not
only a very enjoyable way to keep saying "I love you"
without wearing out the words, but also the perfect expression of fine subtleties that are the mortar of any solid relationship.

Who else but Rob would have shared her delight at discovering a primitive carved owl in a folk crafts shop? Who
else would have insisted on buying it for her on the spot?
And who else would have wanted to ramble aimlessly along
the old harbor with her for more than an hour, comment-
ing on the gulls and the boats and the other tourists, but
mostly just enjoying being together?

That was the aspect of their relationship that made it
special to her, Lisa decided; the pleasure they took in each
other's company did not depend on flowers and candles and
soft music. It had taken the trip to romantic Charleston to
clarify that truth in her mind, but she now realized that the
lovely guest house, the champagne, the diamond earrings,
all would have meant nothing to her with any man other
than Rob.

Rob, too, seemed especially pleased to be able to concentrate on their relationship without the usual mundane in-

terferences. "We're both so willing to let our work tyrannize us. Doesn't it feel great to be out of everyone's reach?" he asked that afternoon while they were examining menus in a seafood restaurant. He looked out the window that afforded them an unobstructed view of the harbor and heaved the contented sigh of a man who, for the moment, is in the exact place he wants to be.

"I'll say!" Lisa agreed without hesitation. When her eyes reached the bottom of the appetizer column, she paused for a second, looking carefully over the edge of the menu at Rob. "Karen does know how to get in touch with us if need be, doesn't she?"

"Karen, but only Karen." Rob laughed, but he was touched by the note of genuine concern in Lisa's voice when she had asked about his little girl. No, he hadn't imagined it; in the past months she had become almost as protective as he where Karen was concerned. "I'd be really surprised to hear from her, though. She's spending the weekend with Stephanie from her ballet class, and judging from what she told me, there's going to be some serious dancing."

"I imagine Stephanie's family will never want to hear another bar of *Swan Lake* as long as they live." Lisa chuckled as she smoothed a dollop of herbed butter onto a chunk of French bread.

Rob rolled his eyes. "I know I never do." He hummed the familiar theme of the ballet in a perfect imitation of Karen's squeaky, off-kilter record player.

Lisa giggled, only sobering slightly when the waiter arrived with their order. "She's really serious about dancing, isn't she? We laugh about it, but almost every time I come over to your house that miserably warped record is grinding away with those little toes thumping in rhythm."

"Those little toes have just about worn out the slippers you gave her for Christmas," Rob confessed.

"Good. That solves the problem of what to get her for her birthday."

Rob looked pleased, whether with her choice of gifts or the Oysters Casino the waiter had just delivered, Lisa was hard pressed to tell. His voice was faintly wistful when he said, "She's got it in her head to become a professional dancer. I guess she's told you already about her plans to take the New York dance world by storm when she's old enough."

Lisa nodded. Karen's dream of one day becoming a famous ballerina was a favorite topic of their "girl talk" sessions. "Before she starts packing her bags, she'll have to talk with my mother. I'm sure she could offer a fledgling performer some pointers on cold-water flats and casting calls," she commented dryly.

Rob chuckled, but quickly reverted to his serious tone. "I really want the best for that kid. Hell, I guess any parent says that." He shook his head at the bewildering complexities of raising the young. "But I find it really hard to strike the right balance between guiding her and letting her follow her own inclinations."

"She is only six," Lisa reminded him gently.

"Seven, in less than two weeks."

"All right, seven," Lisa conceded, barely stifling a laugh. Poor Rob, there was something so endearingly innocent about his concern for Karen, the hard-as-nails criminal lawyer agonizing over his first grader's fanciful dreams. "That still gives you both eleven years to consider a lot of options, and then she'll be in college for another four. A lot can happen in fifteen years. Who knows? She may suddenly decide she wants to go to law school." She narrowed her eyes over the wineglass covering her grin.

"God forbid that! I'd much prefer she become a bird lady." Rob's face loosened into a self-deprecating smile. He reached across the table and covered Lisa's hand, giving it a little shake. "Thanks, though. I can always depend on you to put things in perspective. You can't pull all of the strings where your children are concerned, no matter how much you want to make perfect lives for them."

"We can't make perfect lives for anyone we love, Rob," she corrected him gently. "Not our children's lives, our parents', no one's. You know, for a long time, I cherished the notion that Mom and Dad would, by some miracle, patch up their marriage and live happily ever after. They haven't, but they both seem happy, in their own way. I suppose I still keep hoping that Mom will find someone she can love, someone who loves her, but that just doesn't seem to be in the stars." Lisa shrugged, pausing as her philosophical argument suddenly took a very personal turn. "For all my big talk, I guess I'm just an old mother hen at heart," she added, smiling down at the two hands linked across the table.

Rob lifted her hand and pulled it to his lips. "If that's so, then that old mother hen is one I love very much."

"I NEED YOUR EXPERT ADVICE, Rob. Which dress should I wear tonight?" Lisa poked her head in front of the dressing room mirror, where Rob stood twisting his tie into a knot. She held up two dresses for his inspection.

Tie askew, Rob studied the lavender crepe de chine shirt dress and the glittering black cocktail gown. "Since you insist on shrouding your plans for tonight in secrecy, I haven't the faintest idea what would be appropriate," Lisa prompted. "Choose!" She shook the hangers for emphasis.

Rob fiddled with his tie. "I'll have to see them on you before I can decide." Ignoring Lisa's groan, he nodded toward the black dress. "Try that one on first."

Lisa withdrew into the bedroom. He was sweet enough to deserve humoring some of the time, she thought, as she tossed her robe onto the bed and pulled the cocktail dress over her head. The filmy fabric felt deliciously luxurious against her bare skin, and she was already leaning in favor of this dress by the time she had tugged the close-fitting hem down to her knees. Then she caught a glimpse of herself in the dresser mirror. The clingy black fabric hugged every curve of her body as closely as her own skin.

Lisa shook her head in the mirror; she did look good in the dress, that much her critical eye would allow, but, accustomed as she was to tailored suits and businesslike dresses, she couldn't imagine herself stalking into a crowded restaurant in a dress that looked as if it had been painted onto her. We'll leave this number to Joan Collins, she thought and was about to wriggle out of the dress when a voice stopped her.

"Fantastic!" was Rob's enthusiastic verdict.

"You haven't seen the other one yet." Lisa fretted with the uncooperative zipper.

"Forget the other one!" He took a step forward, then halted and cocked his head for a better appraisal.

Lisa wheeled around to face the mirror. "I'm not so sure," she began, but two arms slithering around her waist made her forget whatever it was she had intended to say.

Rob's hands skimmed over the smooth fabric, tracing the tempting curve of her hip, then retracing their route back to her waist. "If you really like this dress so much, I'll wear it," Lisa said meekly, but she was more interested in the exquisite blue eyes beckoning to her than in any trivial garment.

"I like what's inside the dress." Having clarified this point, Rob began to work the zipper down her back. The sticky metal teeth responded more cooperatively to his eager tugs than they had to Lisa's; when the dress fell to her ankles, she stepped lightly over it. Their fingers interlaced, their eyes locked, as they led each other to the bed.

With their bodies pressed together, they joined in the ageless ritual, celebrating the difference in man and woman, seeking the oneness that their love demanded. Reveling in the pleasure that Rob bestowed on her with such care, Lisa realized how much of her own enjoyment stemmed from her ability to delight him. Theirs was truly a union of equals, she decided as they finally lay satisfied in each other's arms, with each of them giving and receiving in a harmonious balance. This was what love should be; this *was* love, and anything else was just a paltry imitation. Rob gave her so much happiness, she thought. And, most importantly, he gave her himself to love as completely as he loved her.

"We should get dressed and go to dinner" Rob's lips formed the words against her cheek, but he showed no inclination to follow his own advice.

Lisa finally took the lead. Swinging her legs over the side of the bed, she dug her feet through the velvety rug in search of her slippers. Without further consultation with Rob, she slipped on the lavender silk and returned the black dress to the closet.

"Not bad," he commented as he helped her into her coat. "A little sedate, perhaps."

"We are going to a public restaurant," Lisa reminded him with mock severity. "Besides, the black thing has already served its purpose," she couldn't resist adding, winning a delighted howl of laughter from Rob.

But when they were seated in the elegant restaurant that Rob had selected for their special dinner in Charleston, Lisa realized with a sobering shock that the weekend was rapidly drawing to an end. Their flight to Charlotte departed at three the next afternoon; after Sunday breakfast they would have time for little more than an abbreviated walk along the Battery or some hasty sightseeing. But she would treasure priceless memories from this weekend.

A guarded look at the darkly handsome man studying his menu across from her told her that Rob, too, would not quickly forget their very special, very intimate time together. If only it could last, Lisa thought, catching herself before she added "forever." But every day isn't Christmas, a bitter fact that big boys and girls sometimes had trouble understanding, too. Straightening herself in her chair, she focused her attention on the waiter, who was presenting a bottle of wine for Rob's approval. She was not going to allow a pensive mood to dim the last night of their wonderful weekend.

But as the meal progressed, Rob seemed less jocular than he had earlier in the day. He kept up his share of the conversation, cracked a few jokes and laughed unfailingly at hers, but Lisa knew him too well to mistake the serious expression hovering on his face every time the laughter subsided. Rob was preoccupied, with what unspoken concerns, she couldn't guess. Perhaps he, too, was feeling sad that their delightful getaway was almost over, perhaps he was fretting over Karen's future again; whatever it was, she decided not to probe. If Rob needed to talk something over with her, he would find a way to bring it up, sooner or later.

He found a way after the plates had been cleared and they were waiting for their dessert. "It's funny, isn't it, the turns life takes sometimes." Leaning back in his chair, he smiled at her, the sort of deliberately ingenuous smile that juries always loved.

"Yes, it is." Lisa had been surreptitiously digging through her bag under the table, trying to turn up a tube of lipstick, but at the first sign that Rob wanted to talk, she folded both hands on the table and gave him her unblinking attention.

Rob seemed a little discomfited by the rapt listener seated across from him. He gazed out the window for a few seconds before resuming where he had left off. "Take you and me, for instance," he began, cutting his eyes to catch Lisa's reaction. She nodded reassuringly, encouraging him to go on. "All these years we've worked so hard to achieve what we wanted. I've got my law practice; you have your position at the university. I think it's safe to say we're successful in our chosen professions, don't you?"

Lisa nodded again. Rob continued to stare at her, as if she had forgotten her lines. When her puzzled "yes?" didn't seem to satisfy him, she repeated herself with conviction. "Yes!" Perhaps she had not listened as carefully as she usually did, perhaps two glasses of wine were too much for her, but she failed to see the connecting thread running through Rob's rambling about life and work and success.

"When you're successful in one area of your life, you tend to think you've got it all sewn up. But if you believe that, then you're calling the verdict while the jury is still out." His finger pecked the immaculate tablecloth to underscore this pithy, if slightly out-of-place axiom.

"You should know" was Lisa's perplexed comment. "Rob," she began in a low voice, leaning across the table as she spoke, "I hate to say this, but I'm having a hard time following what you're saying."

Rob heaved a deep sigh and let both hands drop onto the table. "What I'm saying, Lisa, is that . . ."

Whatever he was saying never got said, for, at that moment, their waiter piloted a serving cart alongside their table, parking it with a flourish that captured their immediate attention. "Madame. Monsieur." He bowed smoothly before giving the cherries simmering in the chafing dish an adroit stir. Lisa and Rob watched like two kids at a carnival sideshow while the waiter sloshed a generous amount of cognac over the steaming concoction with the deceptive gestures of a magician. They both drew back, and Lisa gasped audibly as he ignited the mixture. Flames soared from the silver chafing dish and licked the air before receding into a fiery blue halo blanketing the cherries. Unfazed by the whole process, the waiter ladled the flambéed fruit over bowls of ice cream, which he then placed in front of his stunned audience.

Lisa took a cautious spoonful of the dessert and tried to remember where Rob had left off before the waiter's pyrotechnics had interrupted him. "This is delicious, isn't it?" she commented, trying to resume normal conversation.

From the way Rob was gaping at her she wondered if her eyebrows had been singed away by the blaze, but he caught himself and smiled quickly. "Delicious, really delicious."

Maybe he's going through a midlife crisis. The thought occurred to her after they had left the restaurant and were strolling, arm in arm, along one of the cobblestone side streets. Successful men in their mid-thirties often felt dissatisfied and restless; she had skimmed through a magazine article on this contemporary problem the last time she had had her hair trimmed. Wishing that she had perused the piece more carefully, she squeezed the muscular arm curved through her own. "Ever wish you'd chosen another career besides law?" she asked, trying to sound as supportive and positive as possible.

"Never," Rob answered without hesitation.

Lisa frowned, watching all of her do-it-yourself analysis crumble in her mind. So much for Rob's midlife crisis. Perhaps he was worrying about Karen again, she mused. As they sauntered past a restored storefront that had been converted into a bar, the thought that a drink might help him open up occurred to her. "I'm in the mood for a nightcap, aren't you?" she suggested.

Rob inspected the fanciful art deco lettering arching across the fern-bedecked window before answering. When his "sure" sounded a little less enthusiastic than she had hoped, Lisa gave his arm another coercive squeeze. "We don't have to stay late. I'd just like to relax and talk a bit," she promised with heavy emphasis on the last-mentioned activity.

A glamorous platinum blonde dressed in a tuxedo met them at the door and guided them down a perilously steep flight of steps to the jazz cellar. When they had been seated at a small round table not far from the stage and had ordered Brandy Alexanders, Lisa pulled her chair closer to Rob's. "You know, Karen may really have some talent for ballet," she remarked, pulling his hand over into her lap.

Rob squinted awkwardly, but it was hard to tell if he were thinking or just trying to make the most of the limited illumination. "She very well may."

"I remember people trying to dissuade me from going to graduate school. Mom was awfully worried about the academic job market, kept telling me how hard it would be to find a job. And look at me now." Lisa laughed, cutting her eyes up at Rob to see if her lighthearted approach to career decisions was having the desired affect. He smiled back at her, but made no comment. Lisa was thinking that she fortunately had not wanted to become a psychologist, a profession for which tonight's experience showed her woefully ungifted, when Rob suddenly threw one arm across the back of his chair, twisting around to face her.

"Lisa, you remember what I was talking about over dinner, about material success not being enough?"

"Yes." Here it came, at last.

"Well, since I met you, you've helped me see how true that is. More than anything, you've given me the courage to admit that I don't have all the answers right here in the palm of my hand." He held up a palm for her inspection. Lisa looked at it self-consciously before catching herself, but he didn't seem to notice as he went on. "Before I met you..." Piercing electrical feedback from one of the stage speakers obliterated his words.

Lisa leaned closer, but the combo's drummer had now scooted behind his instruments and was getting warmed up for the first set. Between the earsplitting drum rolls she caught something Rob said about depending on her so much; in the glow of the table's single candle, she could see that his gaze was direct and earnest. As she strained to hear him, she glanced nervously at the stage where a buxom woman in a red sequined jump suit was blowing and pecking at the microphone.

Lisa jumped in her seat as the singer launched into a lusty rendition of "New York, New York." Looking back at Rob, she found him slumped back in his chair with the resigned expression of one condemned to suffer through a school play. She wished now that she had paid more attention to the performance times before she had dragged them into this place; whatever was preying on Rob's mind would definitely have to wait until after the show. Folding Rob's hands inside hers, she decided to let the sultry torch singer dis-

tract her in the meantime, but when the set finally ended her
hand shot up instantly to signal their waitress for the check.

"I'm sorry the band interrupted our conversation," she
apologized as they emerged from the smoky cellar into the
refreshing salt air of the deserted street.

"I enjoyed the show. Didn't you?" He gave her shoulder
a playful jostle.

"I would have enjoyed it more if we'd had a chance to
finish talking first," Lisa countered. Now that they were
back on the right track, she was determined he should have
his say. But Rob remained stoically silent.

On the corner the traffic signal winked to red; although
few cars were in sight, Lisa halted, pulling at Rob's hand
until he turned to face her. "Look. What's bugging you? Is
it Karen's future?" she asked simply. Her fingers played
inside his hands that held them while she waited for an answer.

"Damn it, Lisa! Why do you keep bringing Karen into
this?" he snapped.

"But I thought . . ." Lisa began, but Rob cut her short.

"I want to talk about us, Lisa, *us*! And you keep sidetracking me with all of this nonsense about our careers and
Karen's ballet and God knows what else."

"*I* keep sidetracking us?" Lisa dropped Rob's hand
abruptly and propped both fists on her hips. "How can you
say that when you're the one who's been talking riddles all
evening? What is this supposed to be, a game of Clue?" She
would have gone on, if Rob had not clamped both hands on
her shoulders. Although he said nothing, his decisive grasp
was enough to silence her for the moment.

Rob looked down the vacant street for a long minute before releasing Lisa gently. Thrusting his hands into his
pockets, he shrugged as if to adjust his coat before clearing
his throat with some difficulty. "What I've been trying to
tell you all evening, Lisa, is that I—" he punctuated his delivery with a deep breath "—I love you very much. And I

want to be sure you realize just how deep and boundless my love for you is.''

"Oh, Rob," Lisa began. No matter how often he reminded her of his love, the words never failed to spark a flutter of the warmest emotions, even in the wake of a near argument. The brightly lighted street receded into a soft focus through the film of moisture veiling her eyes as she continued, "You find a thousand little ways to remind me constantly of your love. How could I not know? You need never worry about that." She reached for his wrist, lifting a hand from its refuge in one of the deep coat pockets. When she clasped the hand, the fingers unfolded, revealing the small square object it had concealed.

Rob pressed the leather jewelry case, no larger than the one that had contained the diamond earrings, into her palm. "Go on. Open it."

Lisa's mouth dropped in disbelief, but closed just as quickly as Rob nodded and smiled. The bright street behind them, the proud old city of Charleston, the entire world seemed very far away as she snapped the lid back and saw a sparkling diamond flanked by sapphires. She had to be dreaming, and Rob's voice in the background, that was surely a dream, as well. "I love you more than I ever thought possible, Lisa. I want to marry you." *I love you, and I want to marry you.* All of his false starts and beating around the bush had been leading up to those simple yet enormously powerful phrases.

Lisa looked up into Rob's face. He was smiling tenderly, and his eyes shone as luminously as the stunning sapphires adorning the diamond ring. This was no dream, but a flesh-and-blood man, warm and passionate and full of hopes and yearning. "Will you marry me, Lisa?"

"Yes. Oh, Rob, yes!" Throwing her arms open, she let him sweep her into his embrace.

Chapter Twelve

Lisa ran her finger over the cake server, carefully scraping up the last dollop of strawberry butter-cream frosting. She had just popped the gooey remains of Karen's birthday cake into her mouth when an unseen observer admonished her from the kitchen door.

"You'd better be careful, or you'll get as fat as I am!" Babs Wingate wagged her head at Lisa; when she stepped around the swinging door, her tailored slacks revealed a svelte figure that was anything but fat. "Not that you haven't earned a treat today. Let me tell you, I wouldn't even *think* of inviting twenty seven-year-olds to an indoor birthday party. Rob really lucked out when you offered to orchestrate things."

"It was fun. Fun and exhausting." Lisa laughed between licks from the cake server. "But you're only seven years old once."

"Don't remind me!" Babs leaned on the counter for support. "Well, I'm going to try to tear Stephanie away so you can get a chance to put your feet up and rest."

Wiping her hands on a shredded pink napkin, Lisa followed Babs out into the den. Planning Karen's birthday party had been quite a production; she and Rob had fretted over every detail, from the dainty ballerina perched atop the strawberry cake to the pastel tablecloth and party favors. But the results had been a howling success, Lisa congratu-

lated herself. She knew she would long cherish the snap-
shots of Karen's ecstatic face as she opened the big white box
and discovered not only new lavender ballet slippers but a
matching tutu, as well. A smile warmed her face at the
memory.

Is this what it feels like to be a mother? Folding her arms,
Lisa leaned against the doorway and watched Babs dab
traces of ice cream from Stephanie's freckled cheeks. Just
thinking about the very important role she would soon assume was enough to activate a peculiar ticklish feeling
within her, exciting and not altogether predictable. Karen
and she had always gotten along so well, there was no reason to think they would not in the future. And Rob was
confident that she had a special talent for dealing with children; he had said so on more than one occasion.

She felt certain Karen would be pleased to learn of their
engagement. Although almost two weeks had passed since
their weekend in Charleston, Rob and Lisa had postponed
sharing the happy news with the little girl. "We don't want
to steal the thunder from her birthday," Rob had said. Lisa
had agreed, and they had decided to reveal their plans on the
coming Sunday, after a cozy family dinner. It was important to introduce children to this sort of major change in a
tactful and reassuring way, they had reminded each other a
dozen times during the past week. But Lisa was beginning
to suspect all this tact and reassurance was designed pri-
marily for the benefit of two well-meaning but inept adults.

"Bye, Stephanie." Karen waded through the crumpled
wrapping paper and discarded streamers to wave to her de-
parting guest. She watched from the window wall while the
Volvo station wagon pulled out of the drive. Satisfied that
her last guest was safely on her way home, she turned and
pranced across the room in her new slippers. "They're all
gone," she told Lisa, adopting a very grown-up tone.

"They sure are, but I bet they're going to remember the
good time they had at your party for a long time." Lisa

gently booted a pale blue balloon that had drifted into her path.

"You know what Mrs. Wingate told me? She said that even the mommies enjoyed my party." Karen smiled proudly, relishing what she obviously considered the supreme compliment.

"I imagine mothers always take pleasure in seeing their children have a wonderful time." Lisa nudged the balloon again and watched it slowly bounce beneath the coffee table. An unexpected quiver had suddenly rippled through her stomach, and she suspected it had nothing to do with too much ice cream and cake.

Karen nodded wisely; a pensive expression had suddenly sobered her little face. "Did you have a good time today?" she asked in a voice so timid that Lisa realized she was asking much more.

Lisa squatted on her heels, the better to see eye to eye with the diminutive ballerina. Wrapping the small, ice-cream-sticky hand in her own, she swallowed hard. "Of course I did, sweetheart. I guess I'm just like all the others, I like to see you have a wonderful time, too."

"Last call for lemonade." Pitcher in one hand, an overflowing trash bag in the other, Rob ambled into the den, but Karen was looking so intently into Lisa's eyes that she did not even hear his offer.

"That makes me glad, Lisa, 'cause the other kids have their mothers, and I have you, isn't that right?" The clear blue eyes, at once innocent and knowing, were seeking reassurance.

Lisa glanced up at Rob for support. When she raised her eyebrows in a silent question, he immediately understood and gave her an encouraging nod.

"Karen, your dad and I have been wanting to share something very special with you." To Lisa's amazement, it was her own voice speaking, low and clear and charged with emotion.

The lemonade pitcher rattled as Rob's unsteady hands deposited it on the coffee table, but when he joined them on the floor, he was smiling. Draping a hand over Lisa's shoulder, he spoke gently. "You know, muffin, when you really love someone, you want to share everything with that person. Remember how you always want to show me a new dance step you've just learned or the nature notebook you worked so hard on? I treasure all of those things because they're important to you, and I want to be as much a part of your life as I can."

Karen's head bobbed in understanding. "I like showing Lisa stuff, too," she reminded him. Her damp fingers wriggled against Lisa's palm, wrapping themselves around the larger fingers and giving them a squeeze.

"And I love you for that. Very much." The words came out before Lisa had a chance to think; she caught herself as her voice began to break. Rob and she had spent so much time discussing exactly how they would approach Karen with their important news; they had even consulted a few parenting manuals—the modern sort that dealt with issues like divorce and stepparents. They had rehearsed their presentation in well-modulated, rational voices. But she had not prepared herself for the tidal wave of emotion that this small, serious face with its direct blue eyes elicited in her. "Your father and I are going to be married, Karen. Because we love each other."

"That means we'll be a real family, sweetheart." There was no trace of the brash attorney in Rob's tremulous voice as he echoed Lisa's thoughts.

"And you'll have both of us to love you. Always." Lisa's brimming eyes had reached their limit; the hot tears were now overflowing, streaking her cheeks with crooked rivulets. She smiled, a little shakily, but she did not feel the least bit foolish.

Like a delicate tea rose opening into full bloom, Karen's face blossomed into a radiant smile. Suddenly releasing Lisa's hand, she pirouetted on her new satin slippers before throwing her arms around the two adults' necks. Looking first at Lisa and then at Rob, she heaved a contented sigh. "And we'll be the most wonderful family in the whole wide world."

"I BET YOU NEVER GET TIRED of looking at it." Anne stuffed a balled sheet of newspaper into the box of china she was packing and sat back on her heels. Wiping the inky smudges from her hands, she lifted Lisa's unresisting hand for the umpteenth time. "This has to be the most gorgeous engagement ring I've ever seen."

"Is there room for a quiche dish in that box?" Without retracting her hand from Anne's admiring grasp, Lisa leaned for a better look into the open carton.

"Quiche, shmeesh!" Anne dropped her friend's hand in disgust. "How can you be so practical? I swear, for the past month, you've done nothing but make lists and tape them on refrigerator doors. You act more like a tough old quartermaster in the marines than a blushing bride-to-be. I guess it's pretty rough, being sentenced to marry a hunk like Rob Randolph." She shook her head ruefully. "If I were looking forward to spending the rest of my life with such a sweet, thoughtful man, I'd probably be dragging around with a long face, too."

"Okay, Anne, you've made your point." Lisa gave her a tolerant grin as she folded the sports section around the quiche dish. "But before you get too hard on me, let's remember that the wedding is only two months away and I do have to coordinate most of the plans myself. On top of packing up my stuff for the move at the beginning of June. On top of getting through the end of the school year in reasonable shape. On top of pulling my share at the center."

"Right, and, as always, you have everything under control." Anne held up fingers, grubby with newsprint, and began to tick off Lisa's accomplishments. "Your idea to pack up all the nonessentials early will make the move itself child's play. As far as the wedding is concerned, the invitations are out, the caterer is booked and your mother is taking care of your dress. And don't forget that your dear friend and maid of honor—'' her hand fluttered dramatically to her chest "—will be there to see you through to the very last.''

''Maybe that's what I'm afraid of.'' Lisa laughed, ducking just in time to dodge the paper wad aimed at her head. ''But while we're on the subject of wedding plans, I think you may have overlooked a very critical detail. You haven't even mentioned whom you're bringing with you.''

''I haven't decided yet, but, for heaven's sake, don't start worrying about that.'' Anne's blunt tone announced that, for now, the subject was closed to discussion. ''Your wedding is going to be perfect, so quit stewing.''

But as she and Anne continued to sort and pack the contents of the china hutch, Lisa could not deny the truth lurking beneath her redheaded neighbor's ribbing. In the month since Rob and she had announced their wedding plans, she had worried almost constantly. Perhaps she was expecting superhuman efficiency from herself; perhaps the nervous excitement accompanying any major change in life was getting the best of her. Whatever the reason, she had to admit that, as her wedding day drew closer, the myriad attendant details looked less like fun and more like plain, hard work.

What had started out as a simple family affair to be held in the garden behind the Randolphs' house had turned into a major event. After taking inventory, both of them had counted enough friends to raise a small army; family members alone represented a formidable contingent. Rob's parents and his brother were flying in from Chicago; the Cheathams, too, would be coming down from Winston-Salem for the occasion. With Lisa's father and Lucille booked into one hotel and Sarah Porter into another, the wedding party had begun to take on the character of a summit meeting.

Just relax and try to concentrate on the ceremony and what it means to you, Lisa repeated to herself several times each day; afterward, you and Rob can fly off to Bermuda for a nice, private honeymoon, with no one to distract you from each other. But even that blissful vision had begun to dull of late.

What is wrong with me? Lisa thought after Anne had bounced back to her apartment. Pushing the door closed behind her, she surveyed the little kitchen that had been the scene of so many gulped cups of coffee and tasteless frozen dinners during the past four years. Like the rest of the apartment, it had fallen victim to her and Anne's industrious hands; stripped of all but the barest necessities, the kitchen had never looked cleaner or more characterless since the day she had moved in.

Chuck seemed to agree. The stocky yellow cat had sprung silently onto the empty counter and was inspecting the startlingly barren surface with his inquisitive pink nose.

"We had some good times here, old boy, didn't we?" Lisa leaned her elbows on the counter and submitted her own nose to a loving sniff from Chuck. At the same time, the memory of moving into this apartment flashed through her mind. In her mind's eye, they looked much younger then, she and her tiny fluff ball of a kitten. She remembered how proud she had felt, at last reaping the rewards of so many years' grueling work; her brand-new university position looked promising, and she finally had a little nest she could call her own.

You're nostalgic, Lisa Porter. She straightened herself as this sobering thought gained coherency, following in the path of those four-year-old memories. But how could she feel even one moment's regret at exchanging her often lonely single life in this usually cluttered apartment for a shared life with the man she loved?

She had spent enough time with Rob in the past months to realize that she was happier with him than she had ever imagined possible; everything he said and did showed that he shared those sentiments, as well. Karen, for her part, was nothing short of ecstatic at the prospect of their little family's union. So why this maudlin lapse over parting with her apartment? Just because she was getting married didn't mean she was losing her identity. She would merge her life with Rob's with the harmonious give-and-take she had learned over the past months; she would follow her natural instincts and learn to be the good mother that Karen deserved. And she would still be the same person, with the same profession and the same friends; she would just be happier. Wouldn't she? A tiny voice tacked on its doubt.

Angry with herself and the tangled psychological morass that the empty kitchen had dredged up, Lisa flicked off the light and headed for the living room where a formidable pile of school work awaited her. As she dropped onto the sagging end of the sectional, where she always curled up to correct papers, she told herself that the hectic pace of the past few weeks was responsible for her attack of doubt, and nothing more serious than that. If she just put her shoulder to the plow and forged through her crowded schedule, she would find her anxieties vanishing with each completed task. She hoped.

A STEADY TORRENT POURED from the gutter, submerging the flagstone walk in a flood of leaves and sediment and gray rain water. Rob watched the channels that formed between the smooth rocks before looking back to the driveway. Nervously shoving back the sleeve of his faded blue work shirt, he checked his watch for the fifth time in as many minutes. A quarter till seven and still no sign of Lisa. He stared at the rain-slick drive, as if he were trying to will the little yellow Chevette to materialize. But the space remained stubbornly bare. Then he sighed, letting the curtain fall back into place.

Where on earth was she? Even with a show-and-tell to do in Salisbury this afternoon, she should have arrived an hour ago. Rob had already called the Wildlife Center three times, but no one there had heard from her since she had loaded up two owls and a kestrel and headed for her appointment at the elementary school. She hadn't stopped off at her apart-

ment, at least not since Anne Torrence had arrived home at
five-thirty. At seven o'clock he was going to call the state
police, Rob told himself grimly.

A siren rose and fell in the den, echoing the unnerving
thoughts his latest decision evoked. "Cut that thing off,
Karen!" Rob muttered irritably on his way to the kitchen.

"It's only the news, Daddy," Karen retorted, but she adjusted the volume in an effort to compromise.

Only the news, Rob thought, as he paused in the den
doorway. Revolving blue lights flashed from the television
screen before the camera panned across a highway overpass
to a tractor-trailor rig lying jackknifed on its side. He felt his
blood turn to ice as the cameraman zoomed in on the trail
of mangled cars that the rig had left in its wake. His hands
were trembling as he shot across the room and turned the
sound up to its former earsplitting level. "...the accident
that occurred between Rock Hill and Charlotte," the com-
mentator was saying. Rob took a deep breath; at least this
accident was well out of range of Lisa's travels.

He was trudging dejectedly to the kitchen when the sound
of a car door's slamming sent him tearing back through the
den. Flinging open the door, he was relieved to find Lisa
running up the walk. Despite the brisk downpour, she had
not bothered with an umbrella; her hair was plastered to her
head in dripping strands, and as she cleared the steps two at
a time, Rob saw that her feet were bare.

"What kept you so long? I've been worried out of my
head." Rob greeted her, stepping aside only enough to allow her into the foyer.

Not bothering to answer, Lisa peeled off her soaked
raincoat and let it drop to the floor. Her soggy shoes sprin-
kled the inlaid tile with droplets as they unceremoniously
joined the coat.

"Are you all right?" he ventured, watching her shake
herself like a wet sheep dog.

"I'm fine, Rob," Lisa said in a voice that sounded anything but fine. "I just need to get out of these wet clothes."

Leaving a trail of little puddles, she headed up the stairs with Rob close behind her. He watched from the bedroom door as she dug a pair of his sweats out of the dresser and began to shed the rest of her wet garments.

"When you weren't here by six, all I could think was that you'd been involved in an accident or something. And every time I called Sam at the center, he hadn't heard anything from you, either. When Anne hadn't seen you at the house, I really began to worry."

Lisa cinched the drawstring of the sweat pants snugly around her waist. "I stopped in a rest area on the way back from Salisbury, and when I tried to crank up the van again, it wouldn't start. As luck would have it, the distributor cap was cracked." She frowned at the limp half-slip she had just hung on the doorknob. "I phoned a service station right away, but it took a while before someone could get to me."

"I wish you had called me, just to let me know you were okay." Rob wandered to the bed and dropped onto the edge, managing to look both annoyed and hurt at the same time.

"I didn't expect to be this late," she explained with a shrug.

"No, I guess not," Rob agreed, but he was still frowning as he pushed himself up from the bed.

The source of his disgruntled look was not lost on Lisa. "Look, Rob," she began in a tight voice. "Calling home every five minutes is something I associate with junior high, not with my adult life. If there's a problem I'll let you know, but otherwise you can just assume I'm doing my job. It isn't necessary to keep tabs on me." She glowered into the mirror, trying to wrestle the tangles from her hair with her fingers.

Rob hesitated in the doorway. He hadn't meant to anger her, but the cold look she gave him in the mirror told him to leave well enough alone for now. She had a hard, annoying day behind her, he told himself as he slouched down the stairs; at the moment his solicitous concern was just another irritation for her.

When Lisa appeared in the kitchen a few minutes later, she wore a set smile that utterly failed to mask her grouchy mood. As she began to slap corned beef and Swiss cheese between slices of bread, Rob gave her a wide berth. An unnatural quiet reigned in the kitchen, save for his spoon scraping the bottom of the pan as he stirred the soup and the interminable rainfall drumming against the eaves.

"Is it almost ready?" Karen broke the silence as she swung open the door.

"Uh-huh," Lisa mumbled, not looking up from the tomato she was slicing.

The little girl rested a chubby hand on the counter edge and squatted into a plié, humming the Sugarplum Fairy's theme under her breath. "Dah-dah-dah-DAH-dah-DAH." Rising awkwardly, she thrust a leg out behind her. "Dah-dah-DAH-dah-DAH-dah-DAH-DAH!" Her pointed toe edged a half-inch higher and clipped the plate Lisa was carrying, sending tomato slices and lettuce flying.

"Karen, please!" Lisa smacked the plate down on the counter. "Take those shoes off and go wash your hands for dinner. On the double!" She pointed uncompromisingly toward the door.

Karen's lower lip swelled noticeably, and she fixed her adversary with an insulted glare before huffing out of the kitchen.

"And see if you can quit humming that wretched tune for five minutes!" Lisa muttered under her breath as she stooped to retrieve a mashed lettuce leaf.

"What's wrong with you tonight?" Rob whispered harshly, stepping around her with the pot of soup.

"Nothing," Lisa rasped through clenched teeth. "But after the kind of day I've had, I'm not in the mood for a ballet recital. Or a barrage of questions." They glared at each other like two gamecocks, before Lisa brushed past into the dining room.

The meal they shared that night was as miserable as the monotonous rainfall outside. Rob could tell that, like him, everyone wanted to say "I'm sorry," but, like him, no one wanted to risk breaking the edgy silence. Instead, they all picked the brown bits out of Rob's tomato soup and dismantled Lisa's corned beef sandwiches that were much too thick. It was a relief when Karen finally excused herself, bringing to an end an excruciating thirty minutes.

I'm sorry I was such a pestering old fogey, Rob wanted to say as he and Lisa slammed the plates into the dishwasher racks. *It's only because I love you,* he wanted to add, at the same time he would throw his arms around the trim body hiding inside the droopy sweats. But instead, all he said was "You need to call your mother. I almost forget to tell you that she phoned earlier."

"I guess it's about the wedding dress she's picked out for me," Lisa said. With her dull tone of voice she might as well have been talking about a shroud.

Still bent over the sink, Rob watched her out of the corner of his eye. But if she wanted to say that she understood his apologetic thoughts, she was saving it for later. Without another word she turned and marched out of the kitchen.

THE STUDY WAS TERRIBLY CHILLY for the end of April, but perhaps it was just the dampness. Or, more likely, it was her ruffled state of mind, Lisa thought as she closed the door behind her and whirled Rob's leather chair around to the desk. Of course, she had been out of sorts after the van broke down, but that was no reason to snap Rob's head off. Or Karen's, for that matter. Why was she so irritable lately, and with the very people she loved most? It was almost as if she were trying to alienate them.

While she pondered that disturbing possibility Lisa dialed the Miami Beach number and waited for her mother to answer.

"Hello?" Sarah Porter's energetic tone contrasted starkly with Lisa's bone-tired state.

"Hi, Mom. It's me."

"Lisa, darling! I'm so glad you called me back promptly. We need to talk about your dress, dear."

"That's what I suspected, Mom." Lisa cupped her hand, but not soon enough to stifle a gaping yawn. "I hope there's no problem," she added, smiling in an effort to impart some cheer into her voice.

"Oh, no, no problems." A moment's puzzled silence intervened before her mother went on. "Is there something wrong, Lisa?"

If people kept asking her that often enough, she was going to start believing there were. "No, Mom, I'm just very tired." The sentence seemed to end in midair, and Lisa realized that there was much more that she wanted to say—especially to her mother—if she could only find the right words.

Sarah Porter had not parlayed the failing dress shop she had purchased for a pittance into a thriving enterprise by accident. With the same canniness that had served her so well in her business endeavors, she correctly interpreted her daughter's moody tone. "Sounds to me like you need to talk," she countered gently, the same way she had wheedled so many adolescent dilemmas out of Lisa fifteen years earlier. "Rob is fine, I hope?"

"Oh, yes, just fine. Karen, too. We're all just fine. I think we have the wedding plans well under control, and Anne is helping me pack already. It's just..." She paused. At that moment a thought so horrible, so inconceivable had formed in her mind that an involuntary shudder passed through her.

"What is it, dear?" Her mother's voice was soft and caring, and Lisa could almost feel the cool, delicate hand that had often smoothed her hair in earlier years.

"I'm scared," she blurted out without giving herself the chance to think twice. If she had thought about this troubling, restless feeling in those terms, she would never have dared to describe it so accurately. She would have ascribed the edge in her voice to fatigue, just as she always did when Rob or Anne prodded her. But sequestered in the safe solitude of the study with this woman who knew her so intimately the truth behind her moodiness had at last surfaced. "I love Rob so much, I want everything to be perfect for us. He's the only man I've ever wanted to marry, but the closer we come to merging our lives, the scarier the whole thing becomes. Marriage seems so . . . so risky, I sometimes think it would be better if we just continued to see each other." She interrupted her outburst with a weak laugh. "Once, I couldn't do anything but complain about not seeing him often enough, and now I'm frightened of what will happen when we're living under the same roof."

"Your fears are perfectly natural, Lisa," Sarah Porter said soothingly. "You've seen firsthand how painful it can be when two people's dreams shatter." Lisa winced at the torturous memories those words must represent for her mother, but as Sarah continued her voice was surprisingly calm. "But do you remember what I've always said?"

Lisa hesitated. She could remember quite a few things her mother had said about the precariousness of human emotions and the unreliable nature of male-female relationships, but something told her these maternal axioms were not those her mother had in mind right now. "Yes, but it's just that so much is happening to me all at once. I mean, I'm going to wake up one morning and find that I've become a little girl's mother overnight, just like that. Helping someone grow up is an enormous responsibility; what if I turn out not to be very good at it?"

"You've got to be willing to take risks, Lisa," her mother said deliberately, answering her own rhetorical question. "That's what I did when I bought the shop and see what happened? I could have gone broke, you know, but the important thing is, I didn't. And if I had sat tight and kept working for someone else all those years, well, I'd still be working for someone else without any of the successes I've enjoyed with my business. It's the same way with love and parenting."

No, it isn't. Love is different. Just look at you and Dad.
Her mother's counsel had unleashed a tumult of unsettling
thoughts. Stoicism and a grim determination to make the
best of the hand she had been dealt, those were the qualities that Sarah Porter had always relied on to get her
through; based on what she had witnessed while growing up,
Lisa would never have expected her mother to encourage
risk taking where matters of the heart were concerned. But
that was exactly what she seemed to be doing in this phone
conversation with her only child.

"The risks are great, but so are the rewards," Sarah
commented to Lisa's further astonishment.

"I guess you're right, Mom," Lisa agreed slowly, but, to
her surprise, she realized that talking with her mother had
eased much of her tension.

"You'll see that I'm right, but remember: if you ever need
to talk, you can always call me, okay?" She hesitated a
minute, letting her words soak in before moving on to the
next topic. "Now, about your dress. I'm afraid I'm not
going to be able to send it to you before the wedding."

"You're not! You mean I'm going to hop into a dress I've
never seen before on my wedding day?"

"Yes. I'm sorry, but it can't be helped. Just trust me."
Sarah Porter's voice was brisk and businesslike, as if she
were dealing with a demanding client rather than her own
daughter. "Have I ever failed you where clothes are concerned?" she added in a slightly more conciliatory tone.

"Mom, you've never failed me, period," Lisa assured
her, wishing that the electronic wizardry that made their
conversation possible also allowed for a little hug.

"I promise you; this dress is going to be worth waiting
for." Her voice conveyed the glow that surely colored her
still-pretty face. "And now I'll let you get back to Rob and
Karen. I love you, darling."

"I love you, too, Mom. Bye." Lisa waited for the sever-
ing click on the line before replacing the receiver. She continued to sit at Rob's polished desk for some time afterward,

pondering her mother's advice and the perspective it had thrown on her approaching marriage. There was no reason to doubt the sincerity of her mother's words, but, of all the people Lisa knew, she was the last person from whom she would expect to hear such gentle sentiments on love and marriage. Perhaps one does mellow with age, although, on second though, Sarah Porter was not old enough to have softened that much in her attitude toward relationships. Or was she? Whatever the case with her mother might be, Lisa knew that she had several emotional hurdles of her own to clear before she would be at peace with herself. Her mind might agree that one had to take risks, but what she felt in her heart was another matter altogether.

"HOW LATE DO YOU THINK you'll be at the center? I was hoping we could grab our rackets and play some tennis after lunch." Rob's voice, coming from the receiver, sounded as hopeful as the pale sun sifting through the clouds outside Lisa's window.

"I'll be finished in plenty of time for lunch and tennis. I only need to take care of—" she hesitated for a moment "—a few things."

"Great! I'll see you around noon then. I love you, darling."

"I love you, too." Lisa was smiling tenderly as she replaced the receiver. The mere thought of sharing simple pleasures with Rob—something as ordinary as a leisurely Saturday lunch with a game of tennis afterward—never failed to fill her with a sense of delicious anticipation. Anticipation and gratitude, she mused, for she was certain she would never take for granted her extraordinary fortune at having found a man as loving and lovable as Rob.

Perhaps if she concentrated on the reward awaiting her after her morning's chore, the tension surrounding the latter activity would lessen a bit. But as Lisa steered her Chevette over the bumpy drive leading to the Wildlife Center, the ticklish churning in her stomach showed no signs of subsid-

ing. Climbing out of the car, she shot a furtive glance at the
center's office and saw a light burning in a corner window.
That would be Pat Taylor, up before eight, even on a Saturday, and already buried in his studies. The thought that
she could always ask Pat to help her drifted across her mind
like a lifesaver bobbing on a turbulent sea, but Lisa quickly
rejected the idea. What she needed to do this morning, she
needed to do alone, and, for that reason, she had told no
one of her plan, not Pat, not Sam, not even Rob.

A new barred owl fluffed his plumage in a defensive
stance when Lisa entered the raptor trailer, but, save for his
nervous warning signal, the rows of cages remained quiet
while she picked up her gloves. Her hands felt clammy inside the thick gloves as she followed the crooked path leading to the flying cages.

Randolph spotted her almost immediately. His piercing
eyes followed her every move as she approached the large
pen that had been his home for the past two months. The
red-tailed hawk had graduated to his first outdoor cage
shortly after the first of the year, steadily progressing
through a series of larger cages culminating in this one, the
largest flying cage available at the center. Now there was
only one place left for Randolph to go: back to his home in
the forest.

Despite his acute defense instincts, Randolph did not seem
unduly wary of the bow trap that Lisa placed in the pen.
Retreating into the observation hut adjacent to the flying
cage, she watched through the two-way mirror, almost
holding her breath until the chunky hawk fluttered into the
humane trap that would hold him captive without injuring
him. She felt a strange constriction in her throat as she returned to the cage and lifted him from the trap.

Does he know, she wondered. Has that mysterious sen-
sitivity all wild creatures possess given him a clue to the
dramatic turn his life was about to take? Lisa wished she
knew, but, then, there were many things in life she wished
she understood better. Right now, she could only hope that

her training and experience with birds would stand her in good stead.

"He'll soon be ready to fly on his own," she had told Karen a month ago when the two of them had watched the big hawk through the observation mirror. The little girl had nodded knowingly, not taking her eyes off the handsome bird as he settled onto a high perch.

And, by all indications, Randolph seemed to have recovered full use of his wing; in fact, his convalescence had been the sort that wildlife rehabilitaters fantasize about, in spite of the complications affecting his joint. Why, then, did she look forward to the day of his release with such trepidation? True, she always worried about her patients, but when the time came for them to return to their natural homes, she was never unwilling to let one of them go. Randolph was a special case, of course; his arrival had coincided with Rob's entry into her life. The events that had followed that fortuitous meeting still seemed incredible to her.

They had reached the edge of the small clearing that served as the center's flying field, and she paused for a last inspection of the hawk she had nursed back to health. He was so vibrant and strong, it would be cruel to deny him his freedom any longer. But what if his wing were not as strong as she thought? What would prevent Randolph from flying into the sights of another gun someday? Who would protect him, once he was out in a big, open world, fraught with hidden dangers?

The risks are great, but so are the rewards. Her mother's words echoed in her mind, bolstering her courage enough for her to loosen her grip slightly on Randolph's pinioned legs. "This is it, fellow. For you and for me," she whispered, but her hand was trembling as it smoothed the hawk's wing and felt the warm, feathered power surge beneath it.

As Lisa lifted the hand that held Randolph, at the same time she released her hold on him, but he needed no cue from her to spread his impressive wings and lift himself into the air. In spite of the months he had spent in captivity, in spite of the affectionate name she had given him, Randolph had never stopped being a wild bird, and now that he was free of human restraints, that inescapable fact was more apparent than ever.

Through eyes blurred with tears, Lisa watched him beat his wings until they carried him above the tops of the tall pines; the strong, graceful strokes of those wings, the impulsive, joyous cry he let out as he reached the air currents proclaimed the sweeping urge of free flight: he was free now, free to live his life as nature had ordained, free to take the chances that came with a life in the wilderness. This realization sent tears coursing down her cheeks. She could no more have kept that proud creature safely imprisoned in a cage than she could restrain her own heart from the uncharted course it had chosen in love. Randolph's release poignantly demonstrated the wisdom of her mother's advice. Risk was an inherent part of living, for her as well as for Randolph, and shunning those risks would reduce her existence to the joyless level of a healthy wild bird that is never allowed to spread its wings.

"Goodbye, Randolph. I'll never forget you," she murmured softly, just before his fading outline was swallowed up by the towering trees.

Chapter Thirteen

"Bellissima!" The tall, slender man gave the lacy veil a final pat before stepping back to admire the work of his skillful hands. *"Si! Bellissima!"* he repeated. A satisfied smile eased the critical frown that had hovered on his face for most of the morning.

"It couldn't be more beautiful, Massimo," Lisa assured him. Turning in front of the floor-length mirror, she could scarcely take her eyes off the captivating vision it held long enough to thank the handsome, dark-haired man. Knowing her mother's taste as she did, she had never doubted her ability to select a suitable wedding dress, but this stunning ivory silk-and-lace confection exceeded her most extravagant expectations.

"What did I tell you?" Sarah Porter reminded her with more than a hint of proprietary pride in her voice. "You were so anxious to have a peek at your wedding dress before we flew in for the big event, but if I had told you that Massimo was personally designing a gown just for you, it would have spoiled the surprise."

"When I learned that you wouldn't arrive until the night before the wedding, I was a little nervous," Lisa confessed.

"But everything, it is quite perfect, no?" Massimo interposed in charmingly accented English. "A lovely gown for a lovely bride," he concluded, although his dreamy gray eyes seemed decidedly more fascinated by the bride's mother than by the bride modeling his creation.

A jaunty rap preceded the appearance of Rob's face in the half-opened doorway. "She's the loveliest bride in the entire world," he confirmed.

The bridal gown's flowing skirt rustled as Lisa rushed across the room. She had just lifted her veil in preparation for a kiss when Anne Torrence stuck her tousled red head around Rob's shoulder.

"Oh, no, you don't!" she cried a split second before the couple's lips connected. "Save that for after the ceremony! Besides, haven't you ever heard that it's bad luck for the groom to see the bride in her wedding dress before they get to the altar?"

"I'm not superstitious, Anne," Lisa said with a laugh. Anne had constantly assured her that the big wedding would be a snap to pull off, but to judge from her harried expression and ruffled hair, her opinion had changed slightly this morning.

"Well, whether you're superstitious or not, the whole world is waiting out there for the main event while you guys dillydally around offstage." Flipping Lisa's veil back over her face, she plucked at the lace with nervous fingers. "So let's cut out the smooching and get on with the show," she commanded with the despotic inflexibility of an old-time movie mogul.

In flagrant violation of Anne's orders, Rob's lips formed a silent kiss in the air, a kiss that his bride returned from behind her veil. Let Anne tease them all she liked; Lisa was certain of one thing: Rob and she were destined for each other, and it would take more than an old wives' tale to shake that conviction. The look in Rob's eyes conveyed his perfect agreement in that matter.

"Anne? Are you up here?" Nervousness had heightened Pete Rossi's midwestern twang. "Everyone downstairs is ready to begin. Except the bridal couple."

"That's what I've been trying to tell them," Anne complained as she poked her head into the hallway and waved to her escort.

"I have an idea." Rob's blue eyes were sparkling with mischief as he draped one arm around Lisa's shoulders and led her into the hall. "Why don't you just herd everyone up here, and we'll hold the ceremony in the guest room."

Anne hooted her disgust at this suggestion, and she even took a playful swat at the big hand clasping Lisa's shoulder. "Okay, just an idea," Rob agreed. With a parting wink at Lisa, he let Anne and Pete lead him away.

Lisa waited at the top of the stairs, her gaze following Rob and her friends as they hurried downstairs. She couldn't help but smile at the sight of Anne's fiery red head juxtaposed beside Pete's squared shoulder. It was the same smile that had come to her lips when Anne had announced that Pete would be attending the wedding with her.

"Just because we agreed to see other people doesn't mean we can't still see each other," she had explained a little testily. Stretching her logic for Lisa's benefit, she had gone on. "Look, I can trust him not to show up in hiking boots, he won't try to remodel the bathroom after the ceremony, and he won't have a half dozen other invitations for the same day."

And you're both probably relieved at the chance to get together again, Lisa thought. Alone in the hallway, she smoothed her already perfectly arranged skirt and waited for her father.

"Lisa?" The chirped greeting bore no resemblance to Paul Porter's diffident drawl, and when Lisa spun around she found Karen lingering in her bedroom door.

"I thought you'd be downstairs with the party," Lisa exclaimed. "Grandma will be turning the house upside down looking for you."

Karen shifted from one patent-slippered foot to the other. "I know," she admitted in a voice that was little more than a peep. "But I wanted to see you in your dress."

"Do you like it?" Lisa turned slowly for Karen's benefit.

Karen nodded, but her large blue eyes seemed more cap-tivated by Lisa's glowing face than by the fairy-tale bridal gown. "Are you excited?" she asked in a breathless whis-per she often employed for their "girl talk."

"Very." Disregarding Massimo's painstaking handi-work, Lisa crouched to look Karen in the eye. "And do you know why, darling?"

Karen shook her head, letting her small hand gently graze Lisa's lace-encrusted sleeve.

"Because I'm twice as lucky as most brides. I'm going to marry the man whom I love with all my heart, and at the same time I'm going to be getting another very precious gift: a very special, very dear daughter, in fact, the most won-derful daughter in the whole wide world." She had bor-rowed Karen's favorite phrase, but anything less would have seemed inappropriate. Opening her arms wide, she em-braced the little girl.

They broke their warm hug when Paul Porter's hesitant drawl prompted Lisa from the corridor downstairs. "Are you about ready, baby?"

"C'mon. You need to find Grandma," Lisa reminded Karen. She smoothed the child's pale yellow dotted swiss dress before taking her hand and leading her down the stairs.

She found her father waiting for her, lingering at the banister. As they watched Karen scamper happily away, a bashful smile spread across his dignified face. When he took her hand it felt warm and comforting, curled protectively around her own.

As they walked slowly toward the French doors, Lisa heard Anne's nervous giggle rise and fall from the kitchen; then a strange, anticipatory silence fell over the house. They paused in the doorway leading to the backyard. While they waited for the four-piece band to begin playing, Lisa scanned the crowd. She picked out her willowy mother eas-ily, standing right at the edge of the rock walkway with

Massimo at her side. Through the veil's crusty lace, Lisa stole a look at her father. For so many years she had longed to see those two people whom she loved so dearly reunited. That wish had been denied her, but she felt strangely satisfied that her love had at least brought them onto common ground for this one day.

Fatherly pride filled Paul Porter's handsome face with emotion when he stepped forward, gently leading his daughter. As they began their measured walk to the arbor, Lisa looked down at the big hand resting on her arm. She was reminded of the wise and unobtrusive way in which he had always offered her his guidance. She realized now that nothing could have been more fitting than for him to share with her this ceremony, the beginning of her married life.

Rob's parents—with a beaming Karen in tow—had taken their places in the path's curve. Lisa had just spotted Amanda Cheatham's pink linen suit when the first strains of the wedding march redirected her attention to the rose arbor at the end of the walk. She managed to nod in recognition of Lucille's furtive wink from the crowd just before she and her father turned toward the arbor. There could have been two hundred guests; there could have been none; as Lisa walked toward the trellis with its blanket of white roses, she was conscious of only one other person in the world.

Rob was waiting for her with his brother at his side. Through the delicate filter of her veil, his tanned face looked very solemn; once his eyes—direct and serious in their gaze—connected with hers, they did not falter. Lisa was aware of the minister's resonant voice reciting the wedding ceremony, just as he had during their rehearsal. She was aware of Rob's voice, low-pitched and husky with emotion, as he repeated his vows. When her turn came, the terrifying thought that speech would fail her at the last moment darted through her mind, but was just as quickly stilled when she heard her own trembling voice promise to love and cherish Rob for the rest of her life. She was vaguely conscious of a stifled gasp behind her, evidence that her iron-willed maid of honor had broken down at the eleventh hour, but when she lifted the flimsy veil that separated Rob from her, everything but his adoring face faded into the background. When their lips met they made their own vows, promising a lifetime of loving and sharing. Lisa and Rob were still joined in a kiss when the first chords of the recessional signaled them to begin their walk together down the garden path.

"Oh, darling, I'm so happy for you," Sarah Porter stammered when she intercepted the bridal couple at the end of the walk. Lisa turned and saw that her mother, like all mothers of the bride, was crying. As Lisa's mouth pulled into a shaky smile, she realized that she, like all brides, was crying, too.

She had a right to laugh and cry and do all those other things that went along with being deliriously happy, she reflected after she and Rob had reluctantly parted hands and stood together to receive their guests' congratulations. You didn't have a wedding for the sake of the gardenia sprays or the outlandish cake that towered like a biblical ziggurat under its inch of vanilla icing or the jumble of fondue pots and bath towels and warming trays that covered the gift table in the dining room; you have a wedding to feel these serious, giddy, uncontrollable emotions that are an undeniable part of falling in love for good.

"Does your right hand have calluses, too?" Rob whispered into her ear with a chuckle when the band had struck up in earnest and they were at last reunited in each other's arms for their first dance as man and wife.

"This turned out to be a bigger wedding than either of us had imagined," Lisa agreed. "But then it's a pretty big occasion, isn't it?"

"I should say." Rob pulled her cheek against the fine wool of his tuxedo as their bodies swayed in time with the sentimental Bacharach tune. "Your mother certainly seems to be enjoying herself," he commented while they worked themselves through a rhythmic turn of the dance step.

Lisa lifted her head slightly for a better look. "Yes, she does" was all she said, but her eyes continued to follow the graying woman with the figure of a Vogue model and her very sophisticated, very European partner.

"Are you thinking what I'm thinking?" Rob's smile bore more than a hint of mischief.

"That she and Massimo are not strictly business all of the time? Uh-huh. It looks to me as if ours isn't the only romance that's blossomed this year." She chuckled, nestling her face once more against his lapel. "It's about time," she murmured.

But when the band finally took a break thirty minutes later, a disturbing thought had intruded on her initially pleased reaction to her mother's unexpected love interest. She herself had found the suave Italian designer a very personable, charming man; how Paul Porter would feel about a new man in his ex-wife's life might be another story altogether. Of course, her parents had been divorced for almost twenty years; her father had remarried, and, rationally speaking, he certainly had no right to object if her mother chose to date. But the emotional jolt of seeing the still-attractive woman hanging on the arm of another man still might arouse painful feelings for him. Lisa wanted both of them to be happy today, and the thought that her father might be struggling with some unresolved emotions right now prompted her to seek him out once she had left the dance area.

"Have you seen Dad?" she asked Lucille, who was fussing over a freshly decked tray of canapés.

The little woman frowned over the dainty finger foods. "I think he was sitting on the patio steps the last time I saw him," she muttered, but Lisa could see that her mind was totally occupied with lox and cream cheese. From the moment they met, she and Amanda Cheatham had formed a solid alliance; both women were having a wonderful time hounding the caterers and generally making a nuisance of themselves in the kitchen. With a pat of thanks on Lucille's plump arm, Lisa headed for the azalea-shrouded patio.

She pulled up short as she rounded the corner and came face-to-face with her parents. "I was just looking for you," she stammered, but to her relief both of them were smiling.

"And we were just preparing to look for you!" Sarah Porter tipped her salt-and-pepper head back and laughed, but her slim hands remained firmly linked to her ex-husband's elbow. She gave his arm a gentle shake as she continued. "I hope you'll excuse us for sneaking away from the crowd for a few minutes, but we wanted to talk over some old times, didn't we?" She cast a fond look at the man standing beside her.

"We're entitled to a little reminiscing," Paul Porter insisted in the closest facsimile of a gruff voice that he could muster. "After all, it's our little girl's big day, isn't it?" He settled his broad hand over the small one clamped around his arm.

"Sure. Of course. I mean, great," Lisa mumbled. She took a step backward, a silly grin still plastered across her face. Even when they had still been married, her parents had seldom looked this comfortable together, but here they were talking over the past and kidding each other as if they were the best of friends.

She was still coming to terms with her amazement when Arlene Patterson, the wife of Rob's law partner, swooped down on them in a pink chiffon cloud. "I've been dying to talk with your mother all day," she announced in a breathless whisper. "You know I write a social column for the paper, and ever since I realized that *the* Massimo Cinquetti was accompanying her—" she bit her frosted pink lip like a naughty child and eyed Sarah Porter longingly "—I've been trying to get up the courage..."

"If you'd like to meet Massimo, I'd be delighted to introduce you," Lisa's mother interposed, setting Arlene

Patterson off in a frenzy of hand clasping and eyelash fluttering.

Lisa cut a glance at her father to see how he was taking all of this attention that her mother's partner had excited, but his face wore an expression of quiet amusement, as if he were infinitely relieved that Massimo, and not he, was about to fall prey to this predatory pink butterfly.

A sharp whistle pierced the thick azaleas' screen; when Lisa wheeled around she found Rob slipping from behind the bushes. "It's about time for us to make our getaway, wife of mine."

Her father gave her a knowing wink. "Rob's right; you two don't want to break any traditions, now do you?"

Lisa looked down at the untanned spot on her wrist that her watch usually occupied. "I've really lost track of the time," she apologized. A glance at the beige linen suit that had replaced Rob's tuxedo told her that he was ready to depart.

Rob snaked an arm around her waist and led her gently toward the house. "I've enlisted Mike to keep an eye peeled for the limo, and good ol' Sergeant Torrence is going to hold the crowd at bay until we're safely loaded up and ready to pull out."

"I guess they're going to throw rice?" Lisa sounded doubtful. Suddenly she wanted nothing more than to get out of her extravagant dress and be alone with Rob in their honeymoon suite. The fact that the suite in question was miles away in Bermuda only made the thought more enticing.

Rob nodded reassuringly. "But all we have to do is wave out the window and tell the driver to hit the gas. You're packed and ready to go?" he repeated the question that he had posed at least a dozen times in the past twenty-four hours.

"I only need to change clothes." She lifted her embroidered silk skirt lightly.

"Limo's in the driveway," Mike, Rob's younger brother, hissed from the doorway as they entered the empty house.

Gathering her long skirt like Cinderella fleeing at the stroke of midnight, Lisa rushed up the stairs and ran into the master bedroom. She had succeeded in wiggling out of the elaborate dress and was adjusting the belt of her raw silk skirt when a small voice startled her from behind.

"I'm all packed to go to Chicago," Karen announced proudly, holding up her little Day-Glo schoolbag as proof. "Nana promised that we're going to visit the aquarium, and we'll fly kites on the lake, and—" her voice dropped to a reverent hush "—we're going to the ballet."

Lisa squatted beside the bed and motioned Karen to come closer. "I hope you have a good time with Granddad and Nana while we're away," she said. Although she knew Rob's parents were looking forward to having their granddaughter during the two-week honeymoon, she wondered if Karen would miss Rob and her after a few days.

The little girl quickly allayed her fears. "It's too bad you and Daddy won't get to go to the ballet. Maybe next time," she consoled Lisa as she wrapped chubby arms around her neck.

"For sure next time!" Lisa agreed with a laugh. "And now I've got to get my things in order if I don't want to miss our plane. Why don't you run and give Daddy a goodbye kiss?" she suggested, sending Karen pelting off down the hall.

Hair dryer, suntan lotion, bathing suit. Lisa's fingers touched each object as she took a final inventory of her suitcase. She was just about to snap the locks into place when a timid hand tapped her on the back.

"Don't forget anything," Sarah Porter commented with uncharacteristic shyness.

"Maybe you'd better have a look. You have a lot more traveling experience than I do." Lisa laughed, giving her mother a fond hug as she pushed the suitcase lid back.

Sarah Porter began to tuck and fold and rearrange the items crammed into Lisa's suitcase. Her beautifully manicured hands seemed to flutter through the rolled blouses and lingerie; usually the epitome of confidence, she now seemed nervous and uncertain in her daughter's presence.

"I'm so happy, Mom. I know now that marrying Rob is the wisest thing I've ever done. Thank you so much for giving me your little pep talk when I needed it." Lisa instinctively grabbed her mother's busy hands and squeezed them warmly.

When her mother smiled it was like the self-conscious grin of a prom queen hiding her braces. "That's what mothers are for. And now I'm going to ask you to do me a favor and listen like a good daughter while I tell you something I've been carrying around inside me for a while." She sank onto the bed, pulling Lisa with her. "Dear, I know how you felt when Paul and Lucille decided to marry. You were only twenty then, and it was hard for you to accept your father's decision."

"I was thinking of you, Mom," Lisa interrupted. "I guess I always hoped that you two would find a way to be happy together."

Sarah shook her head. "Your father has found a way to be happy with Lucille. Just as—" she took a deep breath as if trying to draw courage from the air "—just as I have found happiness with Massimo. Lisa, we're planning to marry in August, and if you think you can stand going through another big wedding so soon, I want you to be there."

"Oh, Mom, that's marvelous!" Joy quickly superseded Lisa's amazement, and she threw both arms around her mother's neck.

"I hoped you would say that," her mother said quietly. "But now we need to get you launched on your honeymoon." She patted her daughter's back, urging her to her feet.

Lisa later reflected that if they had chosen to elope, their departure would not have been any more madcap. Rob and his brother had no sooner dumped the bags into the limo's trunk than the horde of guests swarmed around the side of the house with Anne in the lead. By then, both bride and groom were safely ensconced in the back seat. As she had expected, a shower of rice pelted the black limousine. As she had feared, someone had succeeded in tying a pair of old shoes to the bumper. As she had hoped, the faces of all of her favorite people—from her parents' and Karen's to those of Sam Wheaton and Anne Torrence—were visible through the rear widow as the limo pulled out of the drive.

Lisa and Rob waved to the guests thronging the front lawn before rolling up the windows. "Have a good honeymoon!" she heard Anne squawk as the limo turned into the street, but by then they were both wrapped in each other's arms with their mouths joined in a sweet, lingering kiss. For Rob and Lisa, the honeymoon had already begun.

Harlequin American Romance

COMING NEXT MONTH

#193 PLAYING FOR TIME by Barbara Bretton

Strange comings and goings, odd disappearances—Joanna's New York apartment building sizzled with intrigue. At the heart of it was Ryder O'Neal. She tried to maintain a safe distance from the elusive, mysterious man, but Joanna wasn't safe—from Ryder or from the adventure of a lifetime.

#194 ICE CRYSTALS by Pamela Browning

Monica Tye's entire life was focused on overseeing the training of her daughter, Stacie, as a championship skater, leaving her no time to sample the pleasures of Aspen. Duffy Copenhaver couldn't see the sense of it. Duffy had his own prescription for happiness—it included lots of love— but would the Tyes slow down enough to sample it?

#195 NO STRANGER by Stella Cameron

Nick Dorset dreamed of being in Abby's neighboring apartment. He longed to sit beside her, talk to her, hold her. But when she took off her bulky coat, Nick knew he would have to care for her, too. Abby Winston was pregnant.

#196 AN UNEXPECTED MAN by Jacqueline Diamond

When busy obstetrician Dr. Anne Eldridge hired handsome Jason Brant to cook her meals and clean her Irvine, California, home, she didn't dream that he would meddle in her social life. But Jason took it upon himself to protect Anne from her dismal choice in men. Was there a method in his madness?

HARLEQUIN HISTORICAL

Explore love with Harlequin in the Middle Ages, the Renaissance, in the Regency, the Victorian and other eras.

Relive within these books the endless ages of romance, set against authentic historical backgrounds. Two new historical love stories published each month.

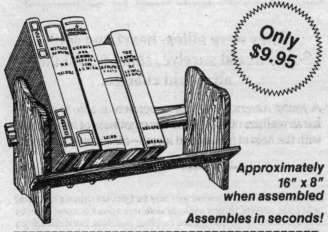

ELIZABETH QUINN

ALLIANCES

**They were allies, heart and soul.
Some would survive, some would die—
all would change.**

A young American war correspondent is able to face the
harsh realities of WWII and the emptiness of her own life
with the help of friends and lovers—alliances of the heart.

———————————————————

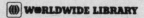

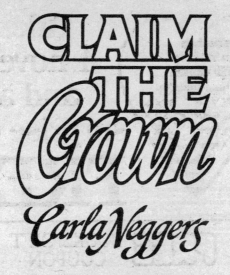

Take 4 novels and a surprise gift FREE